Erotica 107:

Boobs, Boobs, Boobs

22 Titillatingly Top-Heavy Tales

James Dawson

Contents

Introduction

This omnibus of humongous busts gathers all of my big-boobs-oriented men's magazine fiction that has not appeared in earlier Erotica Collections volumes or in my "Hooter Hunter" mini-trilogy.

Although I occasionally wrote serious (or at least semi-serious) fiction for the specialty genre of oversized-breasts-obsessed porn mags, a lot of my work there was as silly as it was sexy. My female characters' bazongas in those ridiculous romps were not merely bra-bustingly bouncy, they were bombastically Brobdingnagian.

Most of those tongue-in-cheek titanic-tits tales originally appeared in *Gent: Home of the D-Cups*, thanks to the fact that the editors there apparently had a sense of humor as gleefully sophomoric as my own.

As I have done previously, I once again must salute legendary artist Otis Sweat, whose fantastic illustrations for many of those *Gent* stories perfectly captured their cartoonish, over-the-top outrageousness. One of my favorites was his amazing rendition of the sensationally stacked surfer girl from "Hang Two," a story I like so much that I put it first in this collection's batting order.

(You can gaze upon that painting's sublime glory by going to http://www.sweaterotica.com/SDGallery/index.html—it's the sweet sixteenth thumbnail in the grid there—and you can see other examples of Sweat's wondrous work at SweatErotica.com.)

In clean-up position at the end of this book is a story I think is one of my best, the naughty and noirish "My Holster Is Hot." Although I always assumed it had been published, I realized when going through my files that this priapism-producing period piece actually never made it into print. Finally rectifying that cosmic crime against culture, "My Holster Is Hot" appears here for the first time anywhere.

Nestled in the expansive cleavage between those two big attention-getters are 20 other appreciations of the funbags-flaunting female form, along with some all-new introductions.

Hooray for boobies!

—James Dawson
EroticaCollections.com

5

Hang Two

I heard her before I saw her. I was concentrating on waxing my board, so I hadn't noticed her walking up behind me on the sand.

She daintily cleared her throat before saying, "Excuse me, do you think you could show me how to use one of those?"

She sounded so totally "val" that I almost didn't bother looking up. This undoubtedly was just another rich San Fernando Valley girl, slumming at the public beach and flirting with the wrong-side-of-the-tracks locals who couldn't use country club pools. I've been burned by those kind of stuck-up teases before. Just when you think you're riding the big wave to Intercourse Island with one of them, they put up a squall and wipe you out.

It would have been easy for me to blow this one off. I could have kept my eyes on my board and told her to go back to the mall where she belonged.

Then again, what the hell, I thought. Maybe I would get lucky this time. Hope springs eternal, you know?

I looked up. A single word appeared in my mind.

COWABUNGA!

Valley, schmalley. Suddenly, the only thing that mattered was that this babe had a pair of tits on her that made me want to hyperventilate. They were so huge they bulged from the top, sides and bottom of her white bikini top. That skimpy tit-sling barely covered her big nipples, which brazenly poked out against the thin fabric.

Her straight blonde hair was pushed behind her ears and hung below her narrow shoulders, her G-string bikini bottom highlighted the bulge of her pussy lips and her legs were as long and slender as a model's. When she breathed, her massive double-D tits bulged even bigger, swaying slightly from side to side with their wonderful weight.

The awkward silence as I stared in awe at her charms was broken by the rubbery squeak of my dick getting hard inside my tight wet suit.

"What was that sound?" the blonde asked.

"Nothing," I lied. "My name's Bobby, by the way."

"Hi, Bobby, I'm Kristen. Well?"

"Well what?"

She tilted her head to one side, which made her look even more adorable. "Well, can you teach me how to surf?"

"Oh, yeah, that. Sure, I'd be glad to. You don't have a wet suit, do you?"

"No. Do I have to wear one?"

If I had my way, she wouldn't even be wearing the bare-minimum bikini she already had on. And I salivated at the prospect of seeing that white bikini go transparent when it got wet.

Still, I didn't want to be a total prick. "No, you don't absolutely need to wear one, but the water is kind of cold today."

"Oh, that's okay," she smiled. "I'm from Norway, so I like swimming in cold water. It's so much more refreshing, especially on my big breasts." She emphasized that last statement by giving both of her gigantic jugs a hearty squeeze.

Maybe that total lack of self-consciousness is common in Northern Scandinavia, but in Southern California it was enough to make my nuts get tight. My dick abruptly grew another inch, making my rubber wet suit give out another long squeak.

"There's that sound again...oh!" Her eyes went wide. She was staring at my crotch. I looked at myself. My upright hard-on was clearly outlined in the otherwise smooth black rubber of my wet suit. My boner was so clearly defined that the ridge of my cockhead and some thick veins on my shaft were discernible. Worst of all, my rod was visibly throbbing with desire.

I quickly moved one end of my surfboard in front of my body. The blonde looked in my eyes and giggled.

"You don't have to hide it," she said, gently pushing the tip of the board aside. "I've already seen it, and I'm not offended. You're a man, I'm a woman. It's natural."

"Uh, well, whatever you say." I glanced around to make sure nobody else was at this end of the beach. By now my cock was pounding against my belly like the foot-pedal smacking the bass drum in the "Hawaii Five-O" theme.

She put one of her hands on mine. "Let's have our lesson, then maybe we'll take care of your...condition."

She started walking toward the water. The back of her bikini bottom was wedged out of sight in the deep cleft of her butt. The cheeks of her ass were rounder and firmer than her tits, barely jiggling at all as she crossed the sand.

I stumbled after her.

First, I stood in the water and held the board so she could practice getting on her knees from a lying-flat position, and then standing up while maintaining her balance. Sure enough, her bikini became completely transparent as soon as it got wet.

Her fantastic flapjack nipples were as big around as my palms. They were so pale pink that they were almost the same color as her alabaster tit-flesh, but raised and puffy.

When she assumed a wobbly stance on the board, I had a clear view between her legs. I could make out every curl of her neatly trimmed blonde bush. Even more exciting, I could see the crumpled lips of her cunt where they were wedged tightly against her pussy's slit by the snug bikini bottom.

I tried to keep my mind on the impromptu lesson.

"Once you've gotten your feet in place, keep them flat and don't move them any more than absolutely necessary," I instructed. "When you catch a wave, ride it by moving your arms and upper body. Keep one foot in front of the other, with your knees slightly bent."

"But aren't my toes supposed to be over the edge?" she asked, looking down at me where I stood in the water. "Isn't that what they call 'hanging ten' in surfing?"

"You've been watching too many old beach blanket bingo movies," I said, gazing up at my slick, busty goddess. "Hanging ten is strictly for experts. Even I have trouble doing it," I added, somewhat immodestly.

"Oh. Well, can I go out on your board and try to ride a wave in now?"

"Sure. I'll wait for you here."

As she paddled to where the waves were breaking, I looked behind myself at the beach. A crowd of guys had gathered. They must have seen Kristen standing on my board in the water. The sight of a body like hers was enough to attract every male from Redondo to Zuma.

Kristen turned in the water, looked back at me, and waved. I gave her a "thumbs up" to indicate she was out far enough. When she emerged from the water to climb onto the surfboard, a gasp went up from the crowd behind me. Even from this distance, Kristen's nipples and bush were plainly visible through her tissue-thin bikini. Her fabulous tits swayed enticingly from side to side.

Before she could place her feet correctly, a big wave came up from nowhere behind her, picking up the board and shoving it toward shore. Kristen tried to keep her balance, but her titanic tits made her way too top-heavy for that.

9

What happened next made the jaws of every guy on the beach drop open in awestruck amazement.

The front clasp of Kristen's bikini top popped open as she lost her footing, freeing her balloon-sized breasts. Her newly exposed nipples must have been at least three inches long. They obviously had stiffened up a lot from being immersed in the cold water on her paddle out.

We all watched in dumbstruck fascination as Kristen clumsily fell forward onto the surfboard. Her enormous breasts ended up straddling the board's pointed end. One titanic tit was on either side of the narrow fiberglass tip.

Some law of physics might explain what happened next, but I flunked that subject so I'll just describe what I saw. Kristen's tits acted like two fat and buoyant water skis, guiding the surfboard in a perfectly smooth trajectory to the shore. Her chin was lifted high and she was grinning like a maniac. She must have been doing 80 miles an hour.

"Hang two!" somebody yelled from the crowd. Pretty soon it became a chant. "Hang two! Hang two! Hang two!"

Kristen didn't even bother looking for her bikini top once she reached the beach. She just went out again and rode another wave with her beach-ball-sized tits...and then another...and then another. She got faster and better each time.

Then it was time for her to thank her teacher, even though the technique she had developed by accident meant that my instructions had been pretty useless.

My apartment wasn't much to look at, but it was within walking distance of the ocean, and that's all that mattered. Kristen was so thrilled over her first surfing experience she didn't even seem to care that my bed consisted of a mattress thrown on the floor.

She threw off the towel I had put around her shoulders to cover her bare breasts on the walk from the beach. "Bobby, you just can't believe how good it feels! The salt-water rushing over my big breasts...my stiff nipples acting like two rudders in the surf...it's just heavenly!"

She put her arms around my neck, pressing her swollen bosom-pillows against my chest. "And I owe it all to you, my sweet teacher."

Her nipples still were hard. She put her tongue in my mouth and squirmed against me, making little circles with those sweet, stiff tit-tips.

I cupped both cheeks of her ass and squeezed. I wormed one hand down inside the front of her bikini bottom. My middle finger traced the slit of her pussy, pushed her thick cunt-lips back and forth and then found the tight little mouth of her fuck-hole. I eased my finger up into that slippery love muscle. Kristen gave a long sigh and hunched her crotch toward my hand, obviously wanting more.

She slipped her thumbs in the waistband of my wet suit and skinned it down, finally baring my hard cock. As I stood there finger-fucking her cunt, she wrapped one of her small hands around the shaft of my erection. She wasn't shy about what she was doing. She squeezed my cock good and tight, jerking her fist up and down its length.

"Let me suck you, Bobby," she breathed. "I want to suck your cock now. Then I want you to fuck me."

I put my hands on her shoulders and guided her to her knees, so her face was level with my crotch. Opening her tiny mouth, she flicked out her tongue and licked all around my purple cockhead. She used the hand that wasn't clutching my cock to caress my balls, which were drawn up against the base of my rod.

I grabbed both of her swollen udders and kneaded them roughly while she blew me. Her nipples were fully erect and as pale pink as coral. The halos around them were as big around as sand dollars.

I pushed my cock toward her mouth, wanting to fuck her porcelain-pale face. Once my dickhead was between her lips, I kept pushing, seeing how much she could take. I was almost all the way in before she gagged a little and made me stop.

With my cock still in her mouth, she glanced up at me with an apologetic expression. Then she closed her eyes as if she were concentrating. She slowly moved her face toward my body again, taking more and more of my erection into her throat.

Soon she was all the way down. Her top lip was pressed close against my pubic hair, while her fuller bottom lip was wedged against my ball bag.

I let out a long, low groan. The head of my cock was down inside her warm throat. It was all I could do to keep from gushing my load then and there, but the best was still to come.

Kristen began bobbing back and forth on my meat. She started out with short strokes. Then she began pulling back to my cockhead, in order to plunge her mouth all the way back down my shaft in one smooth motion, over and over. Her lips were tighter around my tool than any pussy ever had been, and her tongue was swirling around my cock the whole time.

I couldn't help myself. I clutched her head close to my crotch and pumped my juice down her throat. She gave a big swallow following each jet of semen I spurted. The sensation of her throat muscles literally trying to swallow the end of my cock kept me hard even after I was drained dry.

"I want to fuck you now, Kristen. I want to fuck you from behind so I can feel those big tits of yours hanging away from your body. Get on your knees."

She batted her eyes at me and dutifully turned around. She got on all fours on the mattress. Her ass was tilted up at me. Her cheeks were spread wide so I could see everything she had.

Her pussy had thick, bulging lips surrounding her pink fuckhole, which glistened with creamy girl juice. Blowing me had clearly turned her on.

I grabbed my still-hard cock down at its base and pushed it into Kristen's beautiful cunt with one thrust. She bit down on my pillow as I plowed her from behind. With one of her hard ass cheeks in each hand, I pumped her hot pussy without mercy.

"Yeah, that's how I like it," she moaned. "Fuck me hard. Ride me long and hard with that big cock of yours." She wiggled her ass from side to side while I boned her from behind. Each time I pulled back, she greedily clutched at my cock with her well-toned cunt muscles, as if she couldn't bear for her hole to be empty for even a second.

I leaned forward to reach under her body and squeeze her huge, hanging teats. That really set her off. She started grinding her ass back against me, impaling her pussy with my hard dick.

I felt my second orgasm coming on like a tidal wave, rushing from my nuts and up my shaft and out the tip of my cock like a goddamned tsunami. When it was over, both of us were wiped out, in the best possible sense of the term.

It didn't take long for Kristen's new surfing technique to spread up and down the California coastline to other big-busted beach bunnies. In no time, hordes of other top-heavy surfer girls began whipping off their tops and using their tits to guide their boards.

The beach patrols haven't had much success at cracking down on the craze. It seems that once a top-heavy beauty gives tit-surfing a try, she's hooked for life. Like Kristen said, there's apparently something about the feeling of all that fast-moving water on a girl's nipples and knockers that keeps her coming back for more.

Also, any authority figures who try stopping a bare-breasted babe who has mastered that surfboarding skill always have a hell of a time making their way through the multitudes of funbag fans cheering her on.

Two months after her first history-making tit-surf, Kristen was out in the water with a dozen other busty babes for the unofficial first-ever "Hang Two" competition. Word had spread up and down Pacific Coast Highway about the contest. Close to 20,000 spectators had turned out for the completely unauthorized event.

On my signal, all 13 competitors stood up on their boards. Each of them was gloriously topless. Their bust sizes started at double-D and went up from there. Way up. Each set of those titanic tits stood out before their owners like pairs of taut pink beach balls adorned with extra-long nipples that acted as rudders. Only the biggest and the best were competing.

Far out in the distance, a massive wave was rolling toward that luscious line-up of balloon-busted beauties. When the wave broke, all of the girls flopped forward, just as Kristen had done that first day. Their huge tits straddled the front points of their boards and acted like the pontoons of seaplanes, guiding them to shore at speeds of up to 100 miles per hour.

The crowd chanted, "Hang two! Hang two! Hang two!"

Kristen was way out in front, preceded by her gloriously naked tits. The crotch of my rubber wet suit started to squeak with what was becoming a very familiar sound. As proud as I was of her for pulling off such a prize-winning performance, I couldn't wait to get her home and out of the sun for more of our own kind of fun, fun, fun.

The Trouble With Trina

It's damned hard being faithful to your wife when you wake up with another girl's pussy in your face. If you think it matters that you're a newlywed and the forbidden fruit happens to be your bride's best friend, you better take a quick look between your legs to make sure you're still a man.

It was Joyce's idea to bring Trina along on our honeymoon cruise around the Greek islands. That wasn't as stupid as it might sound. Joyce had been living with me for a year when we finally decided to tie the knot, so we already had done everything honeymooners do. It's not like we were dying to be alone at last for our first fuckfest or anything.

Joyce and Trina had been best friends since junior high. They even looked alike, with wavy blond hair, bright blue eyes, slender waists and long, perfect legs.

Both of them also happened to be very large-breasted. No, that doesn't do them justice. The truth is that they both had big, gorgeous, incredible sets of tits that were every man's dream.

On the overnight flight to Athens, I could tell that Joyce was feeling horny. She'd had a lot of champagne at the wedding reception, and alcohol always seems to make her more uninhibited. Plus it was her wedding night, after all, even if we were spending it on a 747.

She managed to wait until Trina appeared to be asleep before making her move. Then she wiggled around in her seat and leaned over my crotch.

With one of the airline's thin blankets covering her head, Joyce tugged down my zipper, pulled out my cock and started blowing me on the plane.

I closed my eyes as her tongue lapped up and down the shaft of my rigid dick. I hoped the other passengers wouldn't notice the slurping sounds she was making. When I opened my eyes to make sure no one was looking, I discovered that Trina wasn't asleep after all. She was staring right at me as Joyce's head bobbed up and down on my dick under the blanket.

Trina was wearing a button-up white sweater with a deep V-neck that showed a lot of cleavage, enough to make it obvious she wasn't wearing a bra underneath. Still looking in my eyes, she undid the sweater's top button and pulled down its neckline.

She let the globes of her big, heavy breasts hold the halves of her tight sweater apart. Her nipples were unnaturally big, spread over half the area of her huge jugs.

In all the time I'd known Trina, she never had made a pass at me, and I either had been too smart or too chicken ever to make one at her. I always told myself that I would be crazy to risk the good thing I had with Joyce by making a play for Trina, no matter how hot she was. That didn't mean I never had thought about what it would be like to be with her, though. Christ, I'm only human!

Why the fuck had Trina waited until my wedding night to come on to me? Was she just testing me, seeing if I would betray her best friend now that Joyce had made the ultimate commitment to me?

The passengers across the aisle from us were asleep. Between my legs, my darling bride Joyce was running the tip of her tongue around my cockhead. She still was under the blanket, so she couldn't see Trina's slutty display.

Trina gave me a dirty smile. "Like what you see?" she breathed, softly enough that Joyce wouldn't hear. She tugged at one of her pretty nipples, as if she just couldn't help herself.

I nodded and smiled back, hoping I wasn't walking into some kind of trap. I mouthed the word "nice."

Trina glanced down at the bobbing shape of Joyce's head under the blanket covering my crotch. "She's a lucky girl," Trina whispered. Then she began slowly massaging her naked breasts and squeezing her jutting nipples between her long fingers.

When Trina moved a hand down to rub her pussy through her khaki shorts, I couldn't help bucking my crotch up against Joyce's face. Joyce made a gagging sound under the blanket, but didn't take her mouth off my cock.

"Oh, Bobby, I just can't help myself," Trina breathed.

With that she slipped the hand she had been pressing against her cunt down inside her shorts. Her eyes were half-closed as she fingered herself.

What put me over the edge was when she pulled out that hand and placed her fingertips under my nose. I could smell her woman-scent, rich and sweet on fingers wet with her pussy juice.

I snaked out my tongue and licked them, tasting the flavor of her pussy. There was no holding back after that. She pushed those delicious fingers between my lips so I could keep tasting her cunt while I came in my new wife's mouth.

After I finished spurting my load, Trina quickly flipped the front halves of her sweater back up to cover her massive tits. She quickly pretended to be asleep again when Joyce emerged from under the blanket.

"Wow, that was some mouthful!" Joyce whispered, wiping her chin with the back of a hand. Her face was slightly flushed from being under the blanket so long, but she looked extremely satisfied with herself.

"You were fantastic, Joyce," I said, feeling incredibly dazed and confused.

After the jet landed, the three of us took an ancient taxi to the cruise ship. I kept telling myself that I didn't really have anything to feel guilty about. Technically, all I had done was watch Trina play with herself. And then I licked her fingers. Was that so bad?

Considering where those fingers had been, Joyce probably would think so.

Once we had explored the ship as a threesome, Joyce and I went back to our cabin for a little wedded bliss. By the time she pulled her tank top over her head and peeled off her shorts and panties, Trina was the furthest thing from my mind.

Joyce lay back on the bed. Her delicious tits were so large and heavy they spilled out over the sides of her chest. Her knees were pulled up and parted, so I had a good view of her trimmed blond bush and the neat lips of her pussy.

"I'm all yours, Bobby. Come and take me." She let her legs fall open a little farther.

I shucked my clothes and climbed onto the bed so I was straddling her face. She grabbed my cock and rubbed it all over her perfect skin, then she was sucking me again.

Seeing that sweetly innocent face blowing my cock always turned me on. Joyce had such a wholesome appearance that a stiff dick between her lips made her look irresistibly lewd.

I tweaked her big nipples so they stood up stiff and proud on her massive tits. Then I reached behind myself to rub her pussy mound, dipping two fingers into her wet fuckhole. She was so juicy I couldn't wait another second to put my cock inside her.

She wrapped her legs around my back. I was plowing in and out of her creamy slot when the door connecting our room with Trina's quietly opened. Joyce's eyes were closed, so she didn't notice. I buried

17

my face in Joyce's neck so she couldn't turn her face in that direction toward the doorway.

Trina was standing there naked, fingering her cunt. She was watching us fuck. She slowly mouthed the words, "I want you." Then she held her thick, glistening cuntlips apart and pointed between them, silently adding, "Right here."

I shook my head and went through a variety of facial expressions ranging from regret to pleading to exasperation, trying to get Trina to leave before Joyce could see her.

"God, your dick is so fucking big," Joyce moaned beneath me. "I love it when you fuck my little pussy, Bobby. Keep fucking me hard, real hard."

Trina gave me a mischievous grin, blew me a kiss and gently closed the connecting door.

Joyce's pussy was squeezing my cock like an oiled fist. Three strokes later, I came inside her like a fire hose while she groaned with her own shuddering orgasm.

The next morning, I woke up with the pussy-in-my-face predicament.

Joyce was showering in the cramped stainless steel bathroom of our cabin. I was sleeping on my back when I felt something move beside me on the mattress. I opened my eyes and thought I had to be dreaming. Not six inches from my mouth was a woman's bare crotch.

I knew right away it wasn't Joyce's. She always keeps her pubic hair trimmed way back, and her cuntlips are narrow and neat. The pussy above me had thicker, darker hair. Its lips protruded more, hanging sloppily from either side of its slit. This pussy looked vulgar and slutty and very, very sexy.

It was Trina's, of course. She had one foot on the floor and the other on a pillow, straddling my face. The tail of her long T-shirt was pulled up around her waist.

The cabin porthole was open behind her. The delicious aroma of Trina's musky cunt blended with the fresh saltwater scent of the Aegean Sea to form an intoxicating perfume.

"Go ahead and kiss it, Bobby," she whispered. "You know you want to." She bent her knee a little so her pussy was even closer to my mouth. All I had to do was stick out my tongue and I would be tasting her beautiful, exotic cunt.

This wouldn't be as one-step-removed and only moderately wrong as licking her woman juice from her fingers, the way I did on the plane.

This would be my mouth and tongue coming in direct contact with Trina's beautiful, musky, irresistible pussy.

The water in the bathroom shut off. Two seconds later, the door opened and Joyce emerged, naked and dripping.

Trina had moved to the porthole. The tail of her T-shirt had dropped to cover her bare ass, although just barely. I had pulled up my knees under the sheets, so my hard-on wouldn't be as obvious.

"Oh, hi, Trina," Joyce said, completely unconcerned about her own wet nakedness. She began rummaging through her suitcase. "Forgot my conditioner." She pulled a bottle from under some clothes and hurried back into the bathroom.

When the door closed and the shower came back on, I raised myself on one elbow, keeping myself covered below the waist. "Trina, what the hell is this all about?"

"Don't you think I'm attractive, Bobby?" She pulled her T-shirt completely over her head. She wasn't wearing anything underneath. Pushing out her bottom lip in an innocent pout, she crossed her arms under her fat tits, holding them up to show them off better.

"Hell yes. I think you're absolutely gorgeous. But..."

She giggled like a naughty schoolgirl. "Maybe next time, then." She draped her shirt over a bare shoulder and strolled through the connecting door that led back to her cabin. Her ass was as smooth and firm as pink marble.

I was still so hard when Joyce got out of the shower that I wasn't satisfied until I had fucked her twice. I felt like I should have been awarded a medal of honor for resisting Trina's temptations. Or maybe I deserved the dunce of the year award.

The ship's first stop was the island of Mykonos, known mainly for its whitewashed architecture and the deep blue water of its beaches. Trina, Joyce and I were walking up a narrow footpath when Joyce ducked into a pottery shop. Before I could follow her inside, Trina grabbed my arm and said, "Ow! I think I twisted my ankle. Help me, Bobby."

She rubbed her ankle while she leaned against me. After about half a minute, she said, "Must've only been a cramp. It feels okay now."

When we went inside the shop, Joyce was nowhere to be found. The proprietor told us in unexpectedly good English that she had left by a different doorway that faced another winding, cobblestone street.

Half an hour later, Trina and I still hadn't found my blushing bride. That wasn't surprising, since the streets were like mazes with endless branchings. We also had left our cell phones back home, so we wouldn't be tempted to use them in Greece and run up ridiculous roaming charges. I was starting to regret that decision.

We were almost at the summit of a steep hill. Trina said we should have a better view of the winding footpaths from this height.

We looked over the wide, whitewashed stone wall at the edge of the trail, surveying the winding pathways and the waterfront. An olive tree offered a little shade, but it was almost noon and the sun was bearing down.

"It's pretty warm up here, huh?" Trina wiped her glistening forehead with the back of an arm.

"I'll say."

"Would it be all right if I took off some of these hot clothes?" Before I could answer, she had hooked her thumbs in the elastic waistband of her satin running shorts and pushed them down. Naturally, she wasn't wearing panties.

Next off was her tank top. Sweat gleamed on the taut skin of her swollen breasts. She already had gotten enough sun that her tits were glowingly white below her tan line.

Except for her little white tennis shoes, Trina was completely naked. She leaned forward with her elbows on the stone wall. Her fat jugs hung and swayed from her chest, and her hard, round ass was sticking up in the air.

"There, I'm feeling cooler already," she purred. Still looking out to sea, she added, "Come on and fuck me now, Bobby. There's nobody around up here, just you and me. Shove your big cock in my pussy and fuck me good."

Well, there's only so much a guy can take. I took a step back and looked at the dark cleft between Trina's ass cheeks, her slut pussy with its thick lips and her swinging, oversized breasts. I shoved down my pants and put the tip of my boner against her wet slit, then I pushed in with one quick shove.

Her pussy was slippery with her juice and wonderfully tight. She groaned softly with each of my thrusts. I stood there on that chalky dirt path shamelessly screwing my new bride's best friend and feeling like a fucking king.

Then I felt a hand on my ass. I turned my head. It was Joyce's hand.

I was so shocked I froze, my dick buried hilt-deep in Trina's sopping cunt. Trina still was staring out over the blue Aegean, and apparently hadn't seen Joyce walk up behind us.

"Don't stop fucking me, Bobby," Trina moaned, not looking back. "Keep slamming that monster cock in and out of my hot cunt! God, I need it so fucking bad!"

Joyce was staring at me with an expression I couldn't read. She looked down at where Trina and I were joined, my slick cock in her best friend's spread cunt. Then she looked back in my eyes again.

"Go ahead, Bobby," Joyce said. "You like fucking her, don't you?"

"Well, yeah, but..."

"Then you should fuck her. You should do whatever you want on your honeymoon." She gave me a quick kiss and moved to stand beside the wall where Trina was resting her elbows. Trina didn't seem at all surprised to see her. In fact, Trina quickly untied Joyce's halter-top and started kissing my wife's large, hanging breasts.

Stunned but delighted, I resumed pumping in and out of Trina's pussy from behind, my cock harder than ever. Joyce was holding out her big tits for Trina to suck. Then she stepped out of her cut-off jeans and sat spread-legged on the low wall, her pussy in front of Trina's face.

Trina energetically began lapping my new wife's cunt. "Is he fucking you good, Trina?" Joyce asked, stroking her friend's hair.

"Mmmm, he's wonderful. But he really is crazy about you, Joyce. I was starting to think I never would get him to fuck me."

"How about you, Bobby? Do you think this is a nice wedding gift from a wife to her new husband?"

Joyce was rubbing her big, swollen tits while Trina ate her. It was obvious this wasn't the first time the two girls had made love to each other.

"Are you saying you wanted me to fuck Trina all along?"

Joyce smiled coyly. "I thought you should experience something new for your honeymoon, darling. Besides, Trina couldn't think of a thing to get us for a wedding present."

"And I looked everywhere, too," Trina said, her voice muffled against Joyce's pussy. At the same time, she reached between her legs to caress my balls.

"Everything's perfect," I said, pulling out my dick to shoot my load up the cleft of Trina's flawless ass. The sight of my cock gushing onto her best friend's back made Joyce tremble with her own climax.

When I shoved my meat back between Trina's legs, I reached around her waist to massage her clit. Then she was coming, too, milking my cock with the muscles of her cunt as she orgasmed.

"Just perfect," I added.

The steward didn't have to make the bed in Trina's cabin for the rest of the cruise. And when we got back home, Trina moved into our one-bedroom apartment with us. Who says three's a crowd?

I've learned since then that there are certain advantages to having a wife who shares everything with her best friend.

Especially if one of those things happens to be your cock.

The Milk Maid

This is the first of two stories in this collection that feature lactating lovelies and the kind of manly men who think that milk does a body good.

Whether imbibing a big-busted beauty's breast beverage is outrageously kinky (that stuff's meant for babies!) or the most natural thing in the world (when you suck a tit, that's what's supposed to come out) is a matter of individual taste. Personally, I think drinking what comes out of a cow's udders is a lot weirder than the idea of gulping down some warm boob juice from a nubile woman's nipple.

But maybe that's just moo. I mean me.

The Bavarian farmhouse in the forest clearing was postcard perfect, with a thatched roof and carved shutters. A brown cow grazed next to a stone well, while some chickens clucked nearby.

Unfortunately, not a single human was in sight. Just my luck. I was starting to wonder if I ever would find anyone who could give me directions back to civilization.

I reached in my pocket and randomly picked a coin from the jumble of change I had collected over the past two weeks. During that time, I'd been bumming around Europe on a "walking tour." That was a fancy way of saying that I was wandering from country to country like a wayward bum, spending as little money as possible in the process.

I hadn't been able to score with a single European girl since leaving America. I had made passes at busty Berliners, bosomy Belgians, big-breasted Brits and blouse-stretching Bulgarians. Each of them reacted as if she thought she was too good to talk to me, much less jump in the sack for a quick round of *schtuffen zee sausage*.

My dick was so hard from lack of female companionship that I could have used it as a walking stick. To top things off, yesterday I'd managed to get lost in the Black Forest. Maybe I should have left a trail of breadcrumbs behind me.

I didn't recognize the coin I pulled from my pocket. It had foreign writing on one side and a woman wearing a crown on the other. I noticed that Queen Whoever-She-Was had a damned nice set of cans.

My dick gave a little throb. You know you've gone too long without pussy when you start having erotic fantasies about pocket change.

I flipped the coin toward the well. I originally intended to wish for somebody to give me directions to the nearest airport, so I could get back home to the USA ASAP. But while the coin was in mid-air, I decided to up the ante.

"I wish that I would find a milky, fat-titted fraulein in that farmhouse who would fuck me to a frenzy," I said. The coin clinked against the inside of the well and plopped into the water far below.

What the hell, I thought. In for a pfennig, in for a pound.

"Guten tag!" a female voice called from behind me.

I almost was afraid to turn around.

I turned around anyway.

A twenty-ish blond carrying two silver milk pails was coming out of the farmhouse. Her huge tits were practically bulging out of the pleated bodice of her white blouse. Her apron-style blue skirt hugged the soft curves of her hips. Her waist-length hair hung in two thick braids tied with red ribbons. She was giving me a smile that belonged on a billboard.

The milk pails meant that whoever granted my wish had a sense of humor. What I had wanted was a lactating girl who could give breast milk when I sucked her tits, not a milk maid who got milk from a cow. But I wasn't about to complain. This big-busted beauty otherwise was damned close to perfect, even if she couldn't provide the chest cream.

"Guten tag," I answered, smiling. "Do you speak any English?"

She cocked her head to one side. *"Da,* a little," she said. "Are you from United States?" Her accent had a slight lisp. I thought I must have died and gone to heaven.

"Yeah. I got lost yesterday." I adjusted my backpack and stepped toward her. She smelled like strawberry soap, and her skin was so clear it glowed. "My name is Steve, by the way."

She put down her milk pails and gave a little curtsy that made her big double-D tits shake. From this close, I could tell that she wasn't wearing a bra. Her nipples made thick points against her cotton blouse. The material was thin enough that I could make out the saucer-sized circles of her deep pink nipple halos.

"I am Gretchen. I live alone here. Are you hungry?"

Something in the way she said it sent a tingle through my cock. There almost was a yearning in her voice. Maybe "alone" meant that she was lonely. I had the feeling we both might want the same thing.

24

I stared at her tits, resisting the urge to lick my lips. "Yes. Are you hungry, too?" I hoped she would understand my double meaning, even with the language barrier.

She threw back her shoulders, proudly pushing out her ample chest. She didn't mind a bit that I was staring. With that one gesture, she transformed herself from a wholesome farm girl to a seductive slut. *"Da,* hungry," she said. "Very hungry."

I reached for her tits, but froze in disbelief when my hands were just inches from her blouse. The cotton covering her nipples was getting wet. A spreading stain from each tit-tip was soaking through the material.

Gretchen was a milker after all, and she was so turned on that she was lactating before my eyes. Within seconds, enough milk had soaked through her blouse to gather in big, white droplets. They dripped from her bustline onto the tops of her shoes.

She lunged toward me, put her arms around my back, and shoved her tongue in my mouth. "Fuck me, Steve. Fuck me and drink please my milk! I am wanting sex now so much, so much!" She was practically weeping with desire.

I reached up and squeezed one of her fat udders. The whole front of her blouse was soaked with milk now. I yanked down the elastic neckline of the blouse to free both of her swollen mammaries. I leaned over, took one of her red nipples into my mouth, and started to suck.

A warm gusher of her sweet milk filled my mouth. I swallowed that creamy mother's milk in big gulps, loving every delicious ounce.

Gretchen clutched at my cock through my jeans. She soon had my zipper down and my dick out. She knocked over one of her silver milk pails as she dropped to her knees in the grass to blow me.

She made loud slurping noises as she bobbed back and forth on my rod. She knew just how to use her tongue, swirling it all around my cockhead and massaging the underside of my shaft. Her milky tits glistened in the bright sunlight. She was cupping my balls in one of her soft palms.

"Your cock tastes so good, so good," she moaned. "I want to suck your milk now. I want your cock milk."

She started tugging one of her nipples with the hand that wasn't massaging my ball sac. Soon her fingers were dripping with breast milk as she twisted and tugged at that heavy teat. Then she reached behind me, probing the crack of my ass with her milk-wet fingertips. When she found my sphincter, she shoved a milky finger deep inside my asshole.

I let out a long, low groan. Gretchen's mouth was sucking hard on my dick. She was squeezing my nuts with one hand and furiously fingering my asshole with the other. When she pushed down hard on my prostate, I filled her mouth with jet after jet of hot semen. She hungrily swallowed each big gusher from my straining cock.

She looked up at me and wiped a little dribble of come from the corner of her mouth. "Take me inside and fuck me now, Steve. Fill my pussy with your cock." She said those foreign words as if she knew they were forbidden and very, very dirty.

My dick hadn't wilted a bit after I shot my load. Just looking at that hot, milky bitch kept me rock hard. Her tits were so fat and sloppy they hung away from her chest like pink balloons. She left them hanging out over the neckline of her blouse while she led me to her bedroom.

As I undressed, she pulled off her blouse. Then she unbuttoned her apron skirt and let it drop to the floor. Her white cotton panties were embroidered with a needlepoint design that spelled out her name. But it was the design at the crotch that interested me. Her pussy cream had soaked through her panties there. I could smell the musky perfume of her cunt from across the room.

She looked down at herself. She seemed slightly embarrassed at the big stain that showed how much her pussy wanted my cock. She turned away from me and quickly pushed down her panties. As she bent over, I could see the deep crack of her ass, her dainty pink asshole and the glistening lips of her pussy from behind.

Before she could stand back up, I had crossed the room and shoved my hard dick into her well-lubricated cunt. She squealed with surprise. I followed her without slipping out of her pussy as she climbed up onto the bed on her hands and knees. Her huge tits slammed back and forth underneath her body as I pumped her slick, tight twat.

She was groaning so loudly we almost didn't hear the knock on her front door. A female voice was calling out, "Gretchen? Gretchen?"

Gretchen looked back at me from over her shoulder. "It is my neighbor Helga," she whispered. "She helps me with the milking every day."

I remembered the two silver milk pails Gretchen had been carrying. We had left them outside.

Gretchen bucked back against me, impaling herself with my cock, before continuing. "We could invite Helga in, if you want. I know she is a lonely girl, too. Lonely like me, you know?"

"Gretchen?" came Helga's voice again from outside.

My expression must have been enough to let Gretchen know what I wanted. She wriggled her ass back against my crotch and called out, "In here, Helga. In the bedroom."

Helga rushed in carrying both of the milk pails. Although she was brunette while Gretchen was blond, both girls were similarly well developed on top. Helga's tits rode higher on her chest, though, pointing up and out.

Helga dropped both of the pails in surprise when she saw the two of us naked on the bed. Gretchen was still on her hands and knees before me, her heavy tits swinging free. I was embedded in her cunt from behind, holding apart her hard ass cheeks with my hands.

"This is my new friend Steve, Helga," Gretchen whispered. She apparently was speaking English just for my benefit. "Would you like to join us? His big cock feels so good in my pussy."

Helga looked like she was in a trance as she stared at us. Almost unconsciously, she started unbuttoning the front of her peasant blouse and slipping off her skirt. She had little gumdrop nipples on her fat tits. Her pubic bush was as thick and dark as the forest surrounding the farmhouse, but the hanging lips of her pussy hung lewdly from that sweet thatch.

Those pussy lips already were shining with lubrication.

Helga stepped toward the bed. I pulled her close for a long kiss. She stared at my cock as it slid in and out of Gretchen's pussy. Gretchen's asshole winked with each of my thrusts, squeezing tightly shut each time I pushed into her cunt and relaxing each time I pulled back.

Helga acted as if she never had seen a fuck this close-up before. The two girls apparently hadn't shared any men in the past.

She started stroking Gretchen's smooth, hard ass. Hesitantly, she reached for my cock shaft. She encircled it with her fingers, forming a little collar around it as it plunged in and out of Gretchen's cunt. Then she brought those fingers to her mouth and licked them.

"Oh, it is so good, so good," Gretchen sighed. "He fucks good, Helga. Let him fuck you, too."

Helga turned and got on her hands and knees beside Gretchen. I slipped out of Gretchen's fuckhole and slipped into Helga's hot, hairy cunt. She was even tighter than Gretchen, and much wetter.

When I switched back to Gretchen again, Helga got off the mattress. She moved to Gretchen's end of the bed and lovingly began stroking Gretchen's face and shoulders. She leaned close and kissed her. I could tell it wasn't their first kiss.

"Do you want me to help with the milking today?" Helga asked. "I would love to help you."

Gretchen nodded.

Helga picked up the two milk pails and brought them to the bed as I kept fucking Gretchen from behind. All of a sudden, I caught on.

Gretchen hadn't been about to milk a cow when I first saw her. She was heading for Helga's house. Gretchen was the one who needed milking.

Gretchen rose up enough so the two silver pails could rest on the mattress under her hanging tits. Helga situated one pail under each of Gretchen's swollen udders, then took both of those huge breasts in her hands. Next she started squeezing Gretchen's tits, pulling downward on each thick nipple the same way a farmer would milk a cow.

Streams of mother's milk squirted from each of Gretchen's breasts into the silver pails, one after the other. Helga got into a regular rhythm: squeeze, relax, squeeze, relax. I matched the rhythm with my cock thrusts, plunging in and out of Gretchen's gripping cunt. The sound of Gretchen's thick jets of milk hitting the metal bottom of the two pails, one after the other, was so deliciously erotic that my cock started pounding.

I knew I had to have this beautiful milker under me in every way possible. Her pink asshole was flexing so invitingly that I couldn't pass up the opportunity to fuck it. Sliding my cock up her beautiful ass would be the final element that would make this the best sex session of my entire fucking life.

As Helga continued milking my lover's fat mammaries, I pulled out of Gretchen's cunt and positioned my cockhead at the rim of her little sphincter. I rubbed the purple helmet of my dick against that small hole, getting it wet with Gretchen's cunt juice.

Gretchen knew exactly what I wanted. She relaxed her anus, letting if flex open enough to show me the coral pinkness inside.

I slowly, gently pushed my cock inside that furrowed pink sheath. Gretchen gave a low cry of animal pleasure as I gently fucked her precious back-hole. She started French kissing Helga as Helga continued milking her jugs.

My nuts drew up tight against my shaft. I shot long jets of semen deep into Gretchen's bowels as she moaned with her own orgasm. She was bucking back against me so hard that she upset one of the milk pails, spilling her creamy milk all over the bedspread.

Thankfully, there was plenty left in the other pail.

Helga came close and kissed me, running her tongue all over my face. I closed my eyes just to enjoy the sheer, dirty pleasure of it all.

Later, the two girls filled my knapsack with food and my water bottles with plenty of Gretchen's milk. I started out in the direction they said would lead to a nearby town.

Then I did the smartest thing I ever had done. I looked back at the two of them to wave goodbye.

They both had tears running down their pretty faces.

"What the fuck am I doing?" I thought. Without a moment's hesitation, I was running back toward the farmhouse. If Gretchen would have me, I never would go wandering again.

And I would have cream of teat for breakfast every day for the rest of my life.

The Minotaur

The silent Minotaur stared back at Theresa from a shadowy corner of the stone labyrinth. Although he stood at least a dozen feet away, he looked so imposing that Theresa felt as if she could reach out and touch him without moving.

Theresa's big breasts heaved in her white safari-style blouse as she panted with nervous excitement. She wasn't wearing a bra. She knew that a bra would have been too civilized in this setting, so she had put her pleated shirt on over her bare skin this morning.

A drop of sweat rolled down the narrow space between her heavy tits, leaving an icy trail on her flesh. The coarse cotton of her blouse felt rough and scratchy against her big nipples each time she breathed.

She liked the feeling.

The Minotaur was naked, as Theresa had expected, except for wide metal bracelets that encircled both of his wrists. The thick curls of glossy black hair on his head could have disguised the bulges of small horns, Theresa supposed, but none were visible.

The Minotaur's arms, chest, abdomen and legs were matted with hair, but it definitely was hair, not fur. He was well-muscled and tall, well over six feet, with a rugged face and a classic Greek nose.

Theresa was surprised that he had no beard, not even the shadow of one. The nails on his fingers and toes were yellow, thick as horn, but otherwise his hands and feet looked nothing like hooves.

His huge penis, already half-erect when Theresa had turned into this branching of the labyrinth, was stiffening to its full length as she and the Minotaur regarded each other. Theresa stared as if hypnotized at that great, pulsing cock. Its head emerged from its leathery foreskin as it grew longer and thicker. The Minotaur's great balls hung heavily in his scrotal bag, one lower than the other.

Even when his swollen organ was upright and throbbing against his belly, the Minotaur still made no move toward Theresa. He seemed to be fighting to maintain control, waiting for her to come to him.

Perspiration had broken out on his face and torso. His sweat made a thin sheen on his forehead and sparkled like jewels in the coarse hair covering his massive chest.

He looked like a god compared to the men she knew back home, Theresa thought. No, not a god. He looked the way a real man should look, powerful and confident and untamed. Part beast.

He was nothing like Phil, so concerned with treating her respectfully that he never noticed she faked all of her orgasms when she was with him. Or Reggie, with his workout obsessions, who seemed to like his own body more than he appreciated hers. Or even Jonathan, so intellectual and sophisticated, but without a trace of real passion.

The Minotaur was staring at her tits. Theresa knew her nipples were erect, jutting against the rough cotton, leaving no doubt as to her state of arousal. She unconsciously moved her hands to cover the front of her blouse in modesty.

When she realized what she was doing, she took her hands away again. She wouldn't be modest here with this man, she thought. She would be just as primal and natural as the man-beast who wanted her.

She brazenly threw back her shoulders, pushing out her chest to display her oversized tits like some big-busted whore showing off her wares. Let him stare, she thought. He deserved to look at them more than any of the wimps out in the real world did.

He wouldn't try to bullshit her with witty conversation or flowers or candlelight dinners. The Minotaur didn't care if she knew that all he wanted was her body: her tits and her ass and her pussy. Everything about him was concentrated in his crotch, and his hard cock showed Theresa everything that was on his mind.

She liked that kind of honesty for a change.

Her mouth was full of saliva. She brought her hands to her chest and massaged her swollen breasts for the Minotaur's benefit, squeezing them roughly to tantalize him. All the while, she kept her eyes on his crotch. She couldn't take her eyes off of his thick, pulsing erection. It was so huge, so frightening and yet so...

The Minotaur lunged toward her and she stumbled backward in surprise, painfully twisting her ankle as she sprawled on the smooth marble floor. Before she could regain her feet she heard a jangle of metal and the Minotaur's cry of frustrated rage. She pushed her blond hair from her eyes.

A foot away from her, the Minotaur was straining against the iron chains that bound him to the far wall. They were attached to the manacles Theresa had mistaken for bracelets on both of his wrists. She realized that he must have been hiding the chains behind his body when she first saw him.

Now the Minotaur was so close that Theresa could smell his sweat. It was bitter and pungent, undisguised by the soap smells and deodorant scents of her civilized world.

His chains kept him from coming closer, no matter how savagely he pulled against them.

Even here, Theresa thought. Even a creature like this one in a place like this isn't free to do as he wants. Part of her knew she should be relieved. Another part of her couldn't help feeling disappointed.

She scooted away from the Minotaur and got to her feet, favoring her ankle. Two buttons of her blouse had come undone, exposing the deep crack of her cleavage. When she reached to refasten them the Minotaur let out a wordless bellow. Theresa let her hands hover at the front of her blouse and looked at him.

There was no anger in the Minotaur's expression, she thought. Only sexual heat. Animal lust. He was enraged by his bonds, certainly, but more of his passion arose from his desire for her body. His hard cock was at its full length now, its swollen head almost purple. His balls had drawn up snugly against the base of his shaft.

Theresa realized she could have what she wanted from him, even if he wasn't free. The chains only meant that she would have to take a more active role. She would have to assume complete responsibility for whatever happened.

Instead of fastening the button she held, Theresa moved her fingers down to the next one. She casually slipped it out of its buttonhole. She tugged her blouse up out of her shorts to undo the last remaining button, then let the sides of the blouse hang open. Her nipples remained covered, but the curves where her breasts met each other were plainly visible. So was her smooth belly, shiny with her sweat.

"You like that, don't you?" She wasn't sure if the Minotaur could understand her language, but she was positive he would respond to her tone.

The Minotaur grunted low in his throat, not taking his eyes away from Theresa's body.

Theresa pushed her blouse back from her shoulders without taking it off, completely exposing her breasts. Her heavy tits swayed slightly with the motion.

The Minotaur's arms still were straight out behind him, holding his chains taut as he leaned toward Theresa. His head was as far forward as he could manage. At least a yard remained between his face and her body.

Theresa took a small step closer. The Minotaur made an extra effort to close the gap. It was no use. Theresa pushed out her chest. Her nipples were thick and stiff, standing out at least an inch from her breast-flesh. Their tips were redder than usual, from where the rough cotton of her blouse had irritated their sensitive nerve endings.

The Minotaur snaked out his tongue toward them, but couldn't quite reach.

He looked up and Theresa saw intelligence in his eyes. Or was it animal cunning? The Minotaur suddenly backed away a few feet, letting his chains go slack, doing his best to look calm and disinterested.

"Oh, no," Theresa said. "I know what you're up to. I'm not getting that close. Not yet, anyway."

A hint of a smile crossed the Minotaur's face. He made a movement with his shoulders that might have been a shrug.

Theresa took another small step forward. "This is as far as I go...for now." She crossed her arms under her hanging breasts, squeezing them together to emphasize her cleavage. Teasing him.

The Minotaur stepped toward her and leaned against his chains again, arms stretched straight out behind him like before. Theresa had estimated the distance between them perfectly. She could feel his hot breath on her bare tits. She pressed them against his face. He sucked one of her erect nipples into his warm mouth. His tongue swirled around its tip.

He nuzzled it with his big teeth.

Theresa was sure he wouldn't bite.

She clutched the back of his head in her hands, running her fingers through his glossy hair while he nursed at one of her breasts and then the other. Her pussy was getting wet, very wet, and she felt hot between her legs. She wanted the Minotaur's huge, bull-size cock up inside her, stretching her pussy and fucking her. At the same time, she was determined to wring every tantalizing second she could from this exquisite foreplay.

All at once, the Minotaur threw his legs forward, using them to grab her around the waist. Pulling at his wrist chains for leverage, he dragged her close enough to the wall to get one of his chained arms around her back. While Theresa struggled against his grip, he used his other hand to tear her blouse from her shoulders, leaving her topless. Then his hand moved to the seat of Theresa's khaki shorts.

The Minotaur shoved his sharp, bone-hard fingernails through the material where it was stretched over the crack of Theresa's ass. The

34

khaki tore as easily as tissue paper. He ripped the shorts from her body and tossed them aside. Theresa's skimpy cotton panties may as well have been woven of spider webs for all the trouble they gave him.

Theresa felt faint, overcome with a delicious sense of exquisite helplessness. The Minotaur's cock was like a thick club against her belly, throbbing with the pulse of its hot blood. She buried her face in the Minotaur's neck and licked at his salty perspiration, whispering, "Fuck me, fuck me now, fuck me."

The Minotaur put his hands under her arms and lifted her off her feet. Theresa languidly spread her legs, wrapping them around the Minotaur's back. Her pink running shoes and white ankle socks were all she wore now. She toed off the shoes and they thudded to the marble floor.

The Minotaur slowly lowered Theresa onto his upright cock. She felt its swollen head push inside her pussy, stretching her cuntlips wide as it went in.

"Oh, yes," she moaned. "Oh, dear God." She let her head roll back in ecstasy.

Then the Minotaur's cock was completely inside her, filling up every inch of her slippery cunt. Theresa's sweaty breasts trembled as she panted through clenched teeth. A flush of heat appeared across her chest, reddening her shining tit flesh. She felt as if her entire body were nothing more than a living sheath for the magnificent erection impaling her cunt.

The Minotaur's coarse pubic hair teased at her sensitive clit as she was lifted and lowered, lifted and lowered on his hard staff. His chains clanked against each other as they moved, echoing off the marble walls. He shook sweat from his eyes and grunted.

Reggie the bodybuilder had been able to fuck her this way, supporting all of her weight in a standing position. Yet with Reggie, Theresa had felt as if she were nothing more than another set of barbells, a means to an end. She almost expected Reggie to ask her to count off reps each time he lifted her, or to grade his performance with a 9.9 card when he was finished.

For all Theresa knew, the Minotaur might not give a damn about her needs either, but there was a difference. Reggie only was interested in showing off, impressing her with his manly prowess. The Minotaur's attention was devoted to the experience of fucking for its own sake. He acted as if the fuck itself were the most important thing, the physical act of spearing his hard dick in and out of Theresa's sex.

She knew she was welcome to take as much pleasure as she could from the act, but it was the fuck itself that mattered to the Minotaur, and only the fuck.

She hunched her crotch toward him, bucking her hips. When she looked between her legs, the sight of that giant cock plunging in and out of her body was more than she could take. She clutched the Minotaur's head to her chest so he could suck her tits some more while he fucked her.

The Minotaur moved his hands down to cup her ass cheeks, squeezing them hard. Before Theresa knew what was happening, he had lifted her completely free of his cock and stood her on the floor again. The marble felt cool on the soles of her feet through her thin ankle socks.

The Minotaur turned her around and pressed down on her shoulders. Theresa obediently went to her hands and knees, tilting her ass upward toward him. She looked back over her shoulder to see the Minotaur kneeling behind her.

He quickly spread the round cheeks of her ass and buried his face in her crack, lapping at her pussy with his nose pressed against her anus. He speared his tongue in and out of her cunt, using it like a slippery miniature cock. Then he trailed its pointed tip up across the narrow bridge of skin that separated her two holes and began hungrily licking her asshole.

Theresa was so startled by this unexpected attention that she flinched, but the Minotaur held on tightly to her hips. He rooted deep in her anus with his tongue, salivating so much that he soaked her entire backside. He certainly wasn't like Jonathan, who once had let his tongue wander to Theresa's anus during oral sex, but then ruined that moment of rare abandon by hurrying to brush his teeth afterward.

The Minotaur seemed to enjoy licking Theresa's asshole as much as he liked eating her pussy. He alternated circling the flexing bud of her anus with plunging in and out of that small, sensitive opening. He was a beast in the best possible sense of the word, Theresa thought.

He took one last long lap from her pussy up to her anus before pulling his face away. Then he situated the club of his cock at her pussy's opening and thrust inside, going much deeper than before from this different angle.

Theresa cried out when his thrusting cockhead bumped against her cervix. She reached between her legs to wrap her hand around the base of his shaft, to keep it from going all the way in. The Minotaur seemed to understand and didn't push her hand away. His balls slapped against the protective collar of Theresa's fingers as he pumped in and out of her juicy pussy.

God, what a magnificent cock, Theresa thought as she grunted there on the floor, her big tits swinging heavily under her body with each thrust she took from behind. What a huge, beautiful, fantastic cock.

She wished she could stay in this place and spend her life fucking this way. She wished she never had to go back to the real world again, never had to make another long commute to her boring job at her goddamned office. This is what life should be, she thought. Animal sex and sweat, no thinking necessary. No morals, no ethics, no bullshit love or phony romance. Just a hard cock and a wet cunt. Fucking for fucking's own sake.

She decided to let herself be completely carried away by the sensations in her pussy, with no further thought for the outside world. Her orgasm seemed to build in the tips of her stiff nipples and spread to the depths of her cunt. She cried out with inarticulate release as wave after wave of her climax crashed over her body.

Then the Minotaur's dick swelled thicker in her pussy. Theresa knew her lover would be coming soon. She rocked forward enough to dislodge his cock, then quickly spun around to take its head in her mouth. It was slick and sweet with her pussy cream.

She jerked up and down on that mighty shaft with both hands, flicking its fleshy head with her tongue.

The Minotaur groaned loudly as the first thick jets of his semen spurted into Theresa's mouth. He tried to force his whole cock into her throat. She did her best to keep from gagging, but didn't pull away. Some of his thick load dribbled from her lips onto the marble floor and shone there like dull pearls.

When it was over, the Minotaur leaned back against the wall, his legs out in front of his body. Theresa lapped her way up his abdomen to his chest, then found his mouth. The heavy links of his chains rested against her back as he surrounded her with his arms. His chest hair was rough against her tender nipples.

But she liked the feeling.

His cock was still big against her belly.

In no time at all, it was hard again.

An hour later, Theresa emerged from the labyrinth wearing only her blouse, socks, and shoes. She held her shirttail over her bare crotch to hide her pussy. She knew she was blushing.

The Greek girl behind the anteroom counter retrieved Theresa's purse from the locker where she had stored it during her tour. Theresa purchased panties and a brightly colored wrap skirt from the girl, who didn't seem at all surprised that Theresa needed them.

No one else was in the room to see Theresa get dressed. She was pleased at the privacy of the expensive service.

"Did you find what you wanted within the labyrinth?" the girl asked in unaccented English. Her neutral tone implied neither judgment nor actual curiosity.

Theresa only smiled and looked away, wistfully gazing out the anteroom window. Beyond a stand of olive trees was the cruise ship in the Cretan harbor, an unwelcome reminder of the real world.

She almost hoped it would have left without her.

But that was unrealistic. She knew she hadn't been gone long enough. She was right on schedule, punctual and completely civilized.

The Greek girl gestured at a jeweled box on the counter with a slit on top. "If you were pleased with the service, you're encouraged to leave a tip for the performer, although this is not required." She smiled sweetly.

The last lingering wisp of Theresa's fantasy abruptly dissolved. The real world, as always, took precedence.

Theresa sighed, and took several colorful Greek bills from her purse.

Thanks for the Mammaries

"You've got to remember me. I'm Jennifer. Don't tell me you've completely forgotten who I am!"

"Jennifer?" I repeated, staring at her. She looked so damned good I should have just lied and said I remembered her perfectly. She had long blond hair, great legs and a pair of unbelievably luscious tits. They bulged up from the neckline of her black velvet cocktail dress as if they were trying to escape. The top rims of the pink circles around her nipples winked in and out of view as she moved.

Much as I hated myself for it, I couldn't recall ever seeing this beautiful woman before in my life.

"That's right, Jennifer," she said. "I'm your girlfriend, remember?"

I just sat there on the edge of the bed with my mouth hanging open, probably looking pretty stupid. I had no idea whose bed it was. It might have been mine, it might have belonged to the big-titted babe who said her name was Jennifer or it might have belonged to just about anybody in the world.

I had one hell of a headache, but I tried my best to concentrate. "I'm sorry, I don't..." The words trailed off. I shrugged apologetically.

Jennifer sat beside me and put an arm around my shoulders. The tit closest to that arm almost popped out of her strapless gown. It was round and swollen and perfect. The delicate traces of tiny blue capillaries were visible just under the surface of her pale tit-flesh.

What's strange is what those almost invisible blue veins reminded me of at that moment. They were like the anti-counterfeiting threads the U.S. Treasury puts in dollar bills. You've got to look extra close or you won't see them, but they're there: blue and red threads, made inside the paper.

And just like genuine American currency, there was no doubt that this babe's jugs were the real thing. The way they hung from her chest, the supple tautness of their skin and their distinctive shape were all tip-offs that these weren't silicone jobs. Jennifer's double D-cups were all natural, in this expert's opinion.

"You really must have slammed your head hard on that chin bar, Glen. Don't you remember anything at all?"

Chin bar? That sounded familiar. I saw it at the bedroom doorway, a silver metal bar wedged in the doorframe. I touched my forehead and felt the raised lump across it. A memory flitted across my mind: Jennifer running into her bedroom giggling, me trying to undo my pants and chase after her at the same time and then...slam.

"I must have run into it..."

"That's right. Oh, honey, I'm so sorry I put the thing there. I didn't even think about how much taller you are than I am. I feel so stupid." She gently pulled me sideways to cradle my head against her huge tits. They were fat and soft, like two warm pillows.

I may have forgotten a lot, but I sure remembered how much I liked big knockers. I wanted to yank down the front of this busty babe's dress and bury my face between her mammaries. I wanted to heft both of those massive milk-bags in my hands and run my tongue back and forth between their big nipples. Jennifer had the spread-out kind that took up almost the whole bottom halves of her gigantic tits, and I wanted one of them in my mouth ASAP.

I realized that part of my memory must have been coming back. How else could I know what kind of nipples Jennifer had without seeing them? Now I wanted to get her topless more than ever, to make sure I was right.

"I only put the chin bar there so I could keep my chest muscles strong," Jennifer cooed soothingly. "I read somewhere that doing pull-ups every morning would make my breasts firmer and tighter. I know how much you love them, after all, and I never want them to sag or get out of shape."

"When my head stops throbbing, I'll be sure to thank you," I replied. Trying to introduce the subject of getting her naked, I added, "I just wish I could remember you better."

"Think hard, Glen." Jennifer was running her fingers through my hair. "You know me. What's my last name?"

I nuzzled closer to her tits, letting my nose wander toward the crack of her cleavage. She had sprayed perfume down into the deep crevasse between her mounds. Her breasts rose and fell as she breathed. I resisted the urge to snake out my tongue and taste them. What the fuck was her last name?

From somewhere in the back of my mind, a word appeared. "Uh...is it Conners?"

"That's right!" she squealed, hugging my head closer to her boobs. "I'm Jennifer Conners. I knew you couldn't forget me that easily."

My next move was risky, but I couldn't help myself. I figured that if I had been chasing this top-heavy goddess into her bedroom, we probably were more than friends before I lost my memory. If I was wrong, she might scream. But if I was right...

I tugged down the strapless front of her velvet dress before she knew what I was doing. Her fat tits were revealed in all their naked glory, jutting out proudly from her chest. Their stiff tips were like inch-long pencil erasers. Just as I had thought, her areolas took up the whole bottom halves of her breasts.

Jennifer's eyes went wide, but she seemed happily surprised. "Glen, what on earth are you..."

I pushed her backwards on the bed. Her jugs were so big and swollen they stood out even when she was lying flat on her back. At the same time, they had spread out a little, lolling sloppily to either side of her chest.

"I think this will help me remember," I said, cupping her tits in my hands. "Your tits are so sexy they're all I can think about right now."

Jennifer gave me a smile that was so deliciously slutty I thought I would come right then and there. "All right, lover. Play with my big titties for a while, and we'll see if they jog your memory." She put both arms behind her head and pushed out her chest.

I lapped at the silky underside of one tit, licking and kissing that sweet, warm flesh. Although I only had used that line about her tits bringing back my memory as an excuse to get her topless, I actually did start to recall some of the forgotten bits of my past.

It was no wonder that the blue veins in her breasts had reminded me of the threads in dollar bills. I remembered all at once that Jennifer and I were a pair of high-tech counterfeiters. I recalled the months of planning we had put into our latest scheme.

The details came flooding back as I moved my mouth around to suck one of Jennifer's rubbery nipples. As I pushed it back and forth with my tongue, things started getting clearer.

Tonight was the night everything had come together. Jennifer had been the bait to seduce a certain member of Congress who could point us to a supply of currency-grade paper. Printing money was no problem for anybody with a high-quality color printer, but the paper quality always was the giveaway. Nothing else feels like the real thing, or shows those telltale red and blue threads.

I had been hiding in a closet of Jennifer's apartment, monitoring the feed from a pair of hidden video cameras while she and a certain

Congressman went at it earlier tonight. Although Jennifer had said she was sure the guy would come through with the goods, we had agreed it couldn't hurt to have a little insurance. Blackmail isn't pretty, but it's usually effective. Even in this day and age, the wives of high-placed government officials don't take kindly to seeing their husbands fucking other women in HD.

The guy was a real tit fan, just like me. And Jennifer was any tit-lover's dream come true. It was perfectly understandable why he would risk throwing away his whole career for a hot session with my bosomy babe.

I had kept my eye on the monitor as he pulled down the top of Jennifer's cocktail dress, baring her tits the same way I had done. Jennifer had been very accommodating with her wares. She held out both of her jugs for him to suck, pressing one and then the other against his open mouth. Her head was rolling back on her shoulders and she was sighing with pleasure as the guy tongued her tits, making them glisten with his saliva.

Maybe I should have been pissed off, watching the two of them go at it. But it was easy to keep from feeling jealous when I considered the potential payoff involved.

The guy took off his pants. I felt a pang of inadequacy when I got a look at his dick. The son of a bitch was hung like a horse, and I got the feeling that Jennifer wasn't exactly displeased. The look on her face as she took that big cock in her hands showed that she had no problem at all with mixing business and pleasure.

She tried her best to suck him all the way down, but she didn't quite make it. Then the guy had his fingers in her hair and was fucking her face. Jennifer's hanging jugs swung heavily against the crumpled velvet of her dress as she rocked back and forth with the motion. The guy hadn't let her take off the dress, he just left the top pushed down so her tits were exposed.

Jennifer's nipples had plumped out so stiff and long that I could see even on the small video monitor that they were erect. The guy looked like he would be coming in her mouth any minute.

He surprised me by pulling his cock free before the moment of truth. Jennifer looked up at him with a confused pout. Her expression indicated she was sorry if she had displeased him, but that she would do her best to make up for it if he gave her another chance. She tried to put her mouth back over his cock, but he quickly got on his knees between her legs where she sat on the edge of her living room sofa.

42

He pushed up the short hem of her dress and literally tore her lacy panties from her body. He tossed what was left of them across the room.

Jennifer realized that he only had pulled his dick out of her mouth because he wanted to fuck her pussy. He didn't even want to move to the bedroom, where we had another camera set up. He was in too big a hurry.

Jennifer pulled up her knees and held her cuntlips open for him. He wedged the fat head of his thick club into her fuckhole, then bucked his hips to drive it deep.

Jennifer happily wrapped her legs around his back and gripped him tight. I had a perfect view of his monster cock sliding in and out of her tight, pink cunt. She was groaning and bucking like a high-priced whore. Which I guess is what she sort of was, when all's said and done.

That fact didn't worry me much. Very soon, we would be able to print more cash than we could spend in a lifetime because of her performance tonight. Everything has its price.

Besides, I discovered that watching the two of them fuck actually turned me on. Instead of wanting to knock that bastard off my girlfriend and kick his ass out the window, I felt more like pulling up a ringside seat for a closer view. If you think that's kinky, maybe you're just leading a sheltered life. There's definitely something erotic about watching your girl sucking and fucking a stranger's foot-long cock.

The Congressman pulled out of Jennifer's box to tit-fuck her a little before he came. His cock was all shiny with her cunt cream. It slipped back and forth easily between Jennifer's jugs, even though she was holding them tightly around his meat with both hands.

I could see Jennifer fingering her stiff nipples at the same time, the little slut. I knew that I would have to show some kind of extra effort later that night in bed with her, if I wanted to give this guy a run for his money—so to speak. He had made her so hot she was creaming on the couch cushion.

He finished off by pulling free of her fat tits and gushing his load all over them and her pretty face. He rubbed his cockhead all over her breasts, making designs on them with his come. Jennifer seemed to be loving every minute of it.

Call me crazy, but I thought she looked more beautiful than ever like that. Her black cocktail dress was still pulled down from her tits and pushed up around her waist. It looked like nothing more than a thick velvet sash. Her jugs were covered with milky come, and her pink fuckhole still gaped open slightly from the hard plowing she had received. The dark hairs around her cunt glistened with her juices and sweat.

The guy got dressed pretty fast after that. He handed Jennifer a slip of paper before leaving. Behind his back, Jennifer gave the high sign to the living room's hidden camera lens, letting me know that it contained the information we wanted. Everything was going according to plan.

When I heard Jennifer let the guy out and close her apartment door behind him, I emerged from where I had been hiding in her cramped closet. Jennifer had pulled her top back up and wiped herself off. The hem of her skirt had fallen back into place around her knees. Except for the healthy glow of her skin and her slightly mussed hair, you never would have guessed that she had been fucked into a frenzy five minutes ago, right in this very living room. She looked terrific.

"He gave me the address of a guy who can get us the currency paper as soon as we want it," she squealed. "We're going to be rolling in dough, baby!"

I grabbed for her, but she playfully spun out of my arms. She was running toward the bedroom.

I tugged at my belt and ran after her. I never even saw that goddamned chin bar she had installed across her bedroom doorway.

Everything went blank.

But now I was sucking on Jennifer's tits, my own beautiful Jennifer's gigantic, gorgeous tits. I pushed up the hem of her velvet dress. She still was bare between her legs, just as I remembered, from where that big-cocked bastard had torn off her panties. I wormed two fingers inside her cunt. It still was juicy with her pussy cream.

"Oh, Glen, that feels so good," Jennifer sighed. "You know I was only faking it with that guy. Nobody's as good as you. Hurry up and take your clothes off, lover."

I stood up and pulled my shirttail out of my pants. I had the feeling that I should just jump into bed without asking any questions, but one thing still bothered me.

I stared at my reflection in the mirror over the dresser. Without looking back at Jennifer, I asked, "You called me Glen, right?"

"Don't tell me you can't remember your own name," Jennifer said from behind me.

"Well, now that you mention it..."

Jennifer got up on her knees in the bed, so I could see both of us together in the mirror. She reached around to help me undo the

44

buttons of my shirt. "You're Glen Gilroy, silly. As in Glenda Anne Gilroy. Remember?"

She pulled open my shirt and gripped both of my big tits in her hands, squeezing them through my satin bra. "Yeah, that sounds familiar," I replied.

Jennifer unhooked my bra's front clasp and pulled its cups away from my breasts, then went to work on the zipper of my jeans. I was so hot for her that my panties were wet. I couldn't wait for her to start sucking my hot pussy while I licked hers.

Everything was getting clearer by the minute.

I decided we would worry about my memory and making money in the morning. Right now, the night belonged to me and my girl.

A Certain Something

Caroline Redmont used two fingers to scoop some of the thick white moisturizing cream from a blue jar. Cupping one of her heavy breasts in the open palm of her other hand, she lifted it away from her body to lovingly massage the cream into its firm, warm flesh.

As she rubbed her fingers around and around her protruding pink nipple, she looked at herself in the vanity mirror. God, it was great to have a beautiful set of tits, she thought. She was sinfully proud of her oversized and attention-grabbing bustline.

She liked to watch herself as she touched her body. Sitting naked at her dressing table, she gave her reflection a naughty smile.

The soft curls of her light brown hair framed her heart-shaped face. She knew one of the things about her that turned men on was the irresistible combination of her innocent little-girl face and her almost obscenely large breasts. A girlfriend once told her that she looked like the perfect mixture of slut and schoolgirl, and Caroline knew she was right.

Caroline also knew exactly what effect her big boobs had on every man she met. First, they would look at them with undisguised appreciation, their eyes opening a little wider with lust. Then, if they were gentlemen, they would make a conscious but futile effort not to stare. When they thought she wouldn't notice, their eyes inevitably would wander back down toward her bustline.

Caroline knew that every man she met would find it impossible to resist imagining what it would be like to squeeze, suck or shove their big hard cocks up between her tits.

The thick white cream tingled on her breast, making it feel electric. Her nipple perked up to stand at stiff attention. She scooped out some more cream and lifted her other breast to give it the same treatment. Starting at its distended nipple, she rubbed her fingers around its surface in ever-widening circles until her entire boob glistened.

When she finished massaging the cream into her boobs, she supported them from underneath with both hands, holding them out from her chest and pointing their nipples directly at the mirror. Then she gently blew across their curved tops.

Her breath made her skin cream feel icy cold and red hot at the same time, and her stiff nipples hardened even more. She used her thumbs to push them back and forth, letting her head roll back as she sighed. Giving both breasts a loving squeeze, she felt herself getting moist between her legs.

Ever since her breasts had developed to their D-cup proportions in her early teens, Caroline had been able to get off just by playing with them. Now that she was 21, she'd had years of self-pleasuring experience. She knew just how to handle herself to maximize the intensity of her orgasms.

It was always best when she started with her tits before moving on to finger her sex. The little button at the top of her pussy slit was throbbing now. She knew it wouldn't be long before she would drive herself over the edge.

Looking back at the mirror, she saw that her nipples were a darker pink than before. Her entire chest was flushed with color. She held and squeezed her tits, tugging at them and loving the sensations running through her body. She kept thinking about how much she was going to enjoy getting fucked later tonight.

She'd only met Johnny Scofield two days ago. He was a deliveryman at the dealership where she purchased her new sports car, one of the all-electric Palominos that had just come on the market.

Someone in the service department had removed the car's antenna when the special paint sealant she ordered was being applied, but had forgotten to screw it back in place afterward. Caroline hadn't noticed until she was almost home and turned on the radio, only to hear static on every station.

The salesman on the telephone was properly apologetic, and said he would send someone over right away to set things right.

When Johnny showed up, he and Caroline hit it off right away, laughing and joking with each other. If she hadn't been late for an appointment, Caroline thought she probably would have fucked him right then and there. She wasn't sure exactly what it was about him that she liked so much, but he definitely had a certain something that turned her on.

They had set up a dinner date for tonight. He would be at her place to pick her up in an hour, but she already was so horny she knew she had better take care of herself before he arrived. Otherwise, she thought she might attack him as soon as she opened the door. And a girl shouldn't appear too eager.

The thought of what his cock would look like made her move one hand to her crotch to rub her clit. It always thrilled her to see a new man's cock. No two were exactly the same, but she never had met one she didn't like.

She imagined him shoving his big, hard dick in her mouth and between her tits and in her pussy, which she rubbed a little harder than before. She let out a little moan. Then she bent her neck and pushed one of her nipples into her mouth, so she could suck and lick it. It tasted slightly of the moisturizing cream she had rubbed into it, but she thought that only made what she was doing even kinkier.

Her pussy was so juicy that she slipped one finger up inside her box, then another. She worked them in and out of her tight hole while she sucked her tit. Then she was coming, hunching her back and groaning with sensations that overwhelmed her naked, sweating body.

When the waves of her orgasm subsided, she looked back in the mirror and gave herself a lazy grin.

"Johnny, you're in for one hell of a night," she said to the naked Caroline looking back at her.

Johnny ordered a screwdriver. Caroline told the waitress she would have a strawberry daiquiri. The dance music at Club Theodore was loud, but not too loud.

"So, what kind of business are you in?" Johnny asked. "Anybody who can afford a Palomino SX Turbo must be doing something right."

"Oh, God, let's not talk about work," Caroline replied. "I'm sure you would find me boring if you knew what I did for a living."

Johnny smiled. "You're talking to somebody who delivers car parts five days a week."

"Is it really all that bad?"

"Well, you do get to meet some nice people now and then."

Caroline smiled, squeezed his arm and said, "Let's dance."

Her white close-fitting top was so low-cut it barely covered her nipples. When she danced, the tops of her pink areolas slipped in and out of view as she moved. The top was a halter style that left her smooth stomach bare. When Caroline twirled on the dance floor, the red silk skirt knotted at her waist would part to reveal the tops of her garterless black stockings and her white satin panties.

Caroline knew Johnny could tell that every other guy in the place was looking at her. Some were sneaking looks when they thought their dates wouldn't notice, while others who were sitting or standing alone simply stared.

She liked Johnny knowing how much other men appreciated her body. What girl wouldn't like that kind of attention?

*

Johnny never had seen a sexier girl in his life, much less dated one. When Caroline opened the door to her apartment and he had seen how she was dressed, he popped an instant boner that hadn't quit since. He still could feel it as he danced, sticking straight up and slightly out of the elastic waistband of his jockey shorts. He hoped his condition wasn't too obvious through his pants.

A light sheen of perspiration was on the top curves of Caroline's gorgeous tits, which jiggled as she danced. Looking at the deep crack of cleavage between them, all Johnny could think about was how much he wanted to put his dick in there and tit-fuck her.

A middle-aged man in a suit touched Caroline on the shoulder. When she looked at him, he said, "Excuse me, but are you Caroline?"

Brushing a stray lock of hair from her forehead, she said, "Yes." Judging by her expression, Johnny though she seemed to be trying to place the man's face.

"I thought it was you," he said, giving her a conspiratorial smile. "I'm Mark Beatty. We had a session last week, remember?" Then he leaned close and whispered something in her ear.

"Oh, yes, I remember," she said, blushing slightly. "Well, uh, nice to see you."

"Maybe I'll give you a call again sometime," Beatty said. He gave Johnny a disinterested look, squeezed Caroline's shoulder, and moved off through the crowd.

"What was that all about?" Johnny asked back at their table.

"Oh, nothing," she said, looking away. "Business."

"The mysterious business you won't talk about."

"Yeah."

One word nagged at the back of Johnny's mind. He hated to think it, but there it was: *Hooker.* No wonder she looked so fucking sexy, he thought. She's a pro, one who is used to showing off the merchandise.

He pictured the two of them back at her apartment, and wondered how long she would wait before telling him her hourly rate.

Then it occurred to him that this wasn't the way whores operated. They wouldn't waste time on a date just to set up some john for a payoff back at the bedroom later. Maybe he was wrong.

One of Caroline's stubby nipples popped completely out of her top when she raised her arm to signal the waitress. It was so goddamned beautiful that Johnny wanted to lean over and suck it right there at the club.

He had a second thought about Caroline and her possible profession. Even if he didn't have to pay, she still might be a hooker. It was possible that she actually did like him and that this really was a date, not a set-up for a business transaction, because even whores had to have a personal life. But did Johnny really want to start a relationship with a girl who fucked other men for money?

Sitting across the street from Caroline's apartment building the next day, Johnny debated for the hundredth time about whether he should try seeing her again. He had told her at the club that he suddenly felt sick, and dropped her off at her place without even kissing her. He said that was because he didn't want to risk giving her whatever illness he had picked up, but he could tell she knew he was lying.

After that, he went home feeling like the world's biggest idiot. He convinced himself that he had judged Caroline unfairly and with no real proof. He tortured himself with the realization that he had just dumped the most beautiful girl he'd ever seen.

"Hell, I'm just wasting time sitting here," he muttered to himself in the car. Tucking the gold box of Godiva chocolates he had just bought under his arm, he crossed the street and took the elevator to the fifth floor.

He was just about to knock when he heard a phone ring inside Caroline's apartment. It apparently was on a table just inside the door. Footsteps clicked on the floor, the receiver was picked up and he heard Caroline say, "Hello."

A look up and down the hallway showed Johnny that no one could see him eavesdropping, so he leaned a little closer to the door.

Caroline said, "Mark Beatty? Oh, yes, hi, Mark. Sure, I can work you in today. I'll be there in an hour. I'm sure I still have your address in my book. Okay, see you soon. Bye."

Johnny heard her hang up and walk away from the phone. He knew what he had to do.

It was easy to tail Caroline. The Palomino line was still new enough that there were few of them on the roads, so her red Turbo SX was a cinch to follow.

She headed up Route 7 to Great Falls, a pricey Washington suburb. Johnny let her get pretty far ahead of him after she turned onto one of the small side roads where there wasn't as much traffic. When he saw her turn into a private driveway leading to a three-story mansion, he parked at the side of the road and crept to the house on foot.

Caroline looked in the mirror of her compact and touched up her lipstick before ringing the bell. She was wearing a clingy blue silk dress with a slit up the side. From his vantage point behind a nearby tree, Johnny could see Caroline's bulging tits lolling to the sides of her chest and her nipples making hard points against the fabric. She obviously wasn't wearing a bra.

He also noticed that he had gotten a hard-on again just looking at her. The whole time he had been following her car, he wondered why the hell he cared so much and why he was bothering. Now he was staring at the answer. He knew he never would be able to stop thinking about a girl with a body like hers.

The door opened and Caroline stepped inside the mansion. Johnny tried spotting them through other windows with no luck. He sprinted toward the back of the house to try looking through a few others. That's where he saw Caroline and Beatty emerge unexpectedly from a back door and cross a flagstone path toward a small guest house.

That must be the guy's fuck shack, Johnny thought from his vantage point behind a low hedge. Maybe Beatty didn't like fucking whores in the main house, where a servant, his wife or other family members might walk in. Or maybe he didn't trust any potentially sticky-fingered hookers around the kind of expensive antiques and other high-dollar crap that filled the mansions of rich pricks like him.

Instead, he had a little love nest out back for when call girls came calling. How nice.

The good thing about that much smaller building was its large picture window. Through it, Johnny could see Caroline casually toss her purse onto a chair. He couldn't see the rest of that front room from this angle. He knew Beatty must be in there with her, and not elsewhere in the place, because he could see Caroline talking to someone.

Then, with no hesitation or show of modesty whatsoever, Caroline reached behind her neck, undid the back of her dress and let it fall to the floor. All she had on now were a pair of black high heels and sheer-to-the-waist pantyhose, with no panties underneath. Her heavy tits hung halfway to her waist, but were firm enough to bulge out prominently from her chest without seeming to sag. They were sensational.

She suddenly extended an arm and caught something tossed to her just as Johnny felt the business end of a rifle press against the small of his back and heard a deep voice say, "Like what you see, pervert?"

As he slowly put up his hands, Johnny noticed that what Caroline had caught was…a bra?

The beefy caretaker pushed Johnny ahead of him toward the small guesthouse. He knocked at its door and said, "Mr. Beatty?"

Beatty, sounding annoyed, said, "Yes, Karl?"

"Mr. Beatty, I'm sorry to interrupt you, but could I see you for a moment out here?"

Beatty was completely dressed when he came to the door. Johnny saw that Caroline had put on a white terrycloth robe, but was turned from the doorway and not facing him. The half of the room Johnny hadn't been able to see turned out to be full of photography and lighting equipment.

"Caught this guy peeking in your window outside, boss." Karl gestured at Johnny with his rifle. "You want me to call the cops?"

"Peeking in the window?" Beatty said, looking disgusted. "Well, yes, I suppose so…wait a minute, don't I know you?"

Johnny wished he were dead, or at least a few thousand miles away. Before he could answer, Caroline turned and saw him. "Johnny! What on Earth are you doing here?"

Figuring he might as well tell her the truth, Johnny said, "Look, maybe I'm just jealous and stupid, but I wanted to see how you make your money before I let myself care too much about you. This set-up looks kind of kinky, but I guess I basically guessed right."

"You guessed that she was a bra model?" Beatty said, incredulous.

"A…what?"

"Well what did you think, Johnny?" Caroline asked.

"I…uh…I thought you were a hooker," Johnny mumbled.

Beatty very indignantly said, "Young man, Miss Redmont is a professional model whose physical attributes have made her one of the country's top bra models for catalogs and print ads. I'm shooting her for a lingerie fashion spread. I think you owe both of us an apology."

*

Caroline knew she shouldn't have forgiven Johnny so quickly for spying on her, but there was something so touching about his concern that she couldn't resist.

She had arranged for him to come over to her apartment after the photo shoot. Just like the night before, she noticed the erection bulging in his pants right away. The difference was that tonight they were going to put that hard-on to use.

They moved to the bedroom. In no time, Johnny was sucking one of Caroline's swollen tits while he squeezed and massaged the other. Caroline's pussy was starting to lubricate, making her feel deliciously slippery inside.

Johnny surprised her by straddling her chest, with one knee on either side of her body. "I want to fuck your tits, baby," he said with all-new assertiveness. "I've wanted to fuck your beautiful tits since the first second I saw you."

Caroline responded by pushing her two huge mounds together on either side of his Johnny's stiff dick. Johnny started pumping his hard-on between those soft hills while he thumbed their rubbery nipples.

"Oh, yes, yes," Caroline moaned, arching her back to push out her chest even more. "Fuck my tits, Johnny. Fuck my big tits." She reached down to slide two fingers up her cunt while Johnny fucked her incredibly sensitive breasts. She soon felt her pussy muscles clamping down on her fingers as she came.

Seeing Caroline writhing and bucking with her orgasm made Johnny thrust his meat even harder between her massive tits. Caroline put her chin down against her chest, which allowed her to suck the big head of Johnny's dick while he rutted in her cleavage.

"Holy fuck!" Johnny shouted, as the first long streamer of come spurted from his cock and into Caroline's waiting mouth. She swallowed every drop that gushed from his dickhead, then looked up at him with her best naughty little-girl smile.

She knew it would be hard not letting Johnny find out that she really was a hooker, and that she only did catalog modeling on the side. But there was a certain something about him that made her think it would be worth the effort to let him go on thinking she was as good as she looked.

Testing, Testing

When the phone rang, I was sprawled on the world's lumpiest couch with my pants around my ankles. I was fast-forwarding through a DVD called "Sufferin' Suck Attacks," trying to find a particular scene that had made my dick dance the night before.

What can I say, a guy's got to take care of his needs now and then.

Still shaking hands with my best friend, I used my other hand to thumb the pause button on the remote before I picked up the phone.

I didn't say anything at first. You never know when the fucker on the other end might be calling from a collection agency.

After a few silent seconds, a hesitant female voice said, "Hello? Is anyone there?" She had that perky coed optimism that probably comes from lots of fresh air and cheerleading practice. I pictured her standing atop a pyramid of other college beauties, legs spread wide and arms raised to hold her pom-poms high.

Just the thought of it made me start stroking again.

"Yeah, what's up?"

"Oh!" she squeaked, startled. "I'm sorry, I...well, anyway, hold on a sec..." I heard papers rustling and assumed that meant some kind of pre-scripted sales pitch was coming, but she sounded so cute so I didn't hang up. "I'm calling from Technology Institutes Testing Services, and we're doing a consumer marketing analysis. Do you have a minute to answer a few questions?"

"I like your initials. Is this some kind of sex survey?"

"Our initials?" she said, flustered. "T-I-T...oh my gosh, I never realized!" I could almost hear her blushing. "No, this is a vitamin survey, conducted for drug manufacturers and local pharmacies."

"Okay, shoot." What the hell, she probably was the best-looking girl I would end up talking to all day. No matter what she looked like.

"You'll really answer my questions?" Her sincere enthusiasm made it obvious that most people had hung up well before this stage of the conversation.

"Sure."

"That's wonderful! All right, here we go. First, do you currently use any vitamins or other dietary supplements on a daily basis?"

"Uh, could you repeat the question?" I had been tugging on my rod and was a tad distracted. Like I said, she had a great voice.

"Certainly. Do you currently use any vitamins or other dietary supplements on a daily basis?"

"Yep."

"Are these multi-purpose vitamins, individual vitamins, or other?"

"Other?"

"That's what it says here," she awkwardly explained.

"I guess they're multi-purpose."

"Could you tell me the brand name?"

"Do I have to?"

"Well, umm, yes, if you wouldn't mind."

"Frrmmstms."

"Excuse me?"

Oh, the hell with it. "Flintstones. You know, Fred, Barney, the modern stone-age family."

A moment passed before she responded. "Sir, are you pulling my leg?"

"I should be so lucky."

She giggled. "Okay, next question..."

"Don't I get to ask you one now?"

"I beg your pardon?"

"Come on, fair's fair."

"Well..."

"Would you go out with me tonight?"

After a pause she whispered, "I don't think we're supposed to have personal conversations, sir. I might get in trouble."

"All you have to say is yes."

"But I don't even know you!"

"Hey, you're the one who called me, not the other way around." Okay, that was stupid logic, but what did I have to lose?

"How do you even know we're in the same city?" she asked. "I might be thousands of miles away in another country."

I could tell from her Valley-girl accent that it was pretty unlikely she was in a Bombay call center. I confidently said, "I'm in L.A."

"Oh. Me, too." With a hint of hopelessness, she added, "Will you still answer the rest of my questions if I say no?"

I decided to try for a gratitude reward instead of an obligation pay-off. "Sure, that doesn't have anything to do with it. But I hope you'll say yes anyway."

"Wow, that's really nice of you. I guess I could see you tonight. What's your name?"

"Jack."

That's usually Jack as in "jack off," but tonight with any luck it would be Jack as in "Jack in the box."

Her name turned out to be Lisa. I was chanting a rather ungallant mental mantra—"please don't be a pig, please don't be a pig"—when she opened her apartment door that night and I got my first look at her.

Chill-forged iron. Tempered titanium steel. My dick. Get the connection?

The cheerleader image her phone voice had conveyed was right on the money. Bright blue eyes, honey-blond hair that curled around her shoulders, a friendly smile with perfect white teeth. And, oh wonder of wonders, great big tits.

She was wearing tight black jeans and a blue Polo shirt. The embroidered little man with the mallet looked like he was galloping up the foothills of a stretched-cotton mountain.

"Lisa?" I said, praying that the vision in the doorway wouldn't turn out to be my date's hot roommate.

"Jack?" she replied, sounding a little reserved. I might have resented her tone more if it hadn't been so obvious which of us was getting the way better end of this deal.

She also didn't look too impressed when she saw my car, which I affectionately refer to as "the piece of shit." But I think I made points when I remembered to open her door for her. From the outside, that is.

When I got in, she said, "Could I ask you a big favor?"

"You name it." Yes, yes, get into my debt right away, you magnificent busty Amazon.

"Could we stop by my office before we go to the theater? I think I left my purse there."

T.I.T.S. turned out to be in the Gelaquid Building at Warner Center. The company didn't really use its initials, possibly because it wasn't being run by somebody like me, but that's the way I thought of the place.

We both signed in and took the elevator to the fifth floor. The offices were deserted, but all the lights had been left on. Lisa worked at one of the dozens of orderly desks situated in the middle of a huge open area. Each identical workstation had its own phone.

"How can you remember which one's yours?" I asked, as she made a beeline to the fifth row.

She pointed at the back of a chair. "That helps." Stuck to the white plastic was a sticker of Hello Kitty talking on a telephone. Lisa was that kind of girl.

While she rummaged through her desk drawers, I glanced at the walled-in offices surrounding us. Signs on each door described what must have been various research specialties: Politics, TV Programming, Coffee/Soft Drinks and others. The one that caught my eye said "Sexual Response."

"Here it is," Lisa said, retrieving her purse from under a pile of papers.

"What goes on in that office?" I asked, pointing.

"I'm...not exactly sure." She sounded as if she wanted to change the subject.

"Want to go take a look?"

Her eyes got wide. "Oh, no, we couldn't do that!" But I already was walking toward the door, and she followed me.

It was unlocked. Inside were two desks and doors leading into other offices. Floor-to-ceiling shelves held hundreds of porn DVDs. I also saw neatly labeled binders filled with copies of every skin magazine title I'd ever seen, which would be a lot, and several more besides. There also were uniform rows of ultra hard-core publications, the kind you only find in sleazy adult bookstores, with titles on their spines in several languages.

I wanted to pull out some of those binders and catch up on my knob-kneading reading, but I realized Lisa might regard such behavior as somewhat crude. She probably already was forming an all-too-accurate opinion of me for wanting to check out this office in the first place.

I decided it might be a good idea if we left, before she lost whatever respect she might still have for me.

When I turned around to suggest this, I saw that Lisa had pulled out one of the stroke books herself and flipped it open. She was staring as if hypnotized at a full-page photo of two girls lapping the thick shaft of a spurting dick.

A thin line of saliva slowly drooled from the corner of Lisa's pink-lipsticked mouth to the page. When it touched that patently prurient printed image, the sight of my hand seemed to break her spell. She blinked twice, then looked up at me.

Naturally, like any thinking man in such a situation, I had my cock out by then.

A week later, I was being strapped naked into a vinyl-upholstered chair, a technician was pressing suction-cup electrodes to various parts of my anatomy and I was trying my best not to think back to that first incredible night with Lisa. But I just couldn't help it.

She had glanced at my cock, at my face, my cock, my face and then fell to her knees in helpless lust.

Maybe she had led such a sheltered life that something finally had to give when she got a look at that pornographic picture. Maybe she had a vision that I was destined to be the right man for her. Or maybe she sucked dick four times a day and I happened to be in the right place for her eight o'clock feeding.

Whatever the reason, I was getting my banana blown, and that's all that really mattered.

When I lifted her by the arms so I could unfasten her pants, she held on tightly to the waistband of her jeans. She silently shook her head "no," as if she weren't sure she really wanted to go all the way. She was pulling the jeans up so resolutely that their crotch seam was wedged between the thick lips of her pussy, creating a cameltoe that sort of defeated any attempt at modesty.

Undeterred, I licked and kissed the bulge of her cunt while she kept tugging upward on her waistband with both hands. Soon her breath was coming in little gasps and she was moving her crotch against my mouth.

She took her hands away and put her fingers in my hair. I took that as my cue to skin her jeans and her pink satin panties down her very womanly hips. She lifted one leg and then the other so I could take the jeans off and toss them onto a table.

The cleft of the immaculately shaved pussy she had tried so desperately to keep hidden was shining with wetness. When she saw me staring at her enticing cunt, she abandoned all of her defenses by leaning back against the table and spreading her legs.

"Mr. Lester, our readings show you have an erection." The crackling speaker in the corner of the testing room brought me back to reality.

"Uh, yes, as a matter of fact I do." I knew that I shouldn't have thought about Lisa. I had a feeling this would happen if I did.

"Please try to lose it, so we can begin fresh."

I looked down and saw my pocket pal standing at attention, one electrode stuck to its purple head and another down at its base.

Concentric flexible metal bands were spaced at half-inch intervals up the length of the shaft, each one attached to a wire that ran to a machine under my seat.

I closed my eyes and thought about how much I owed my bookie, due to some shockingly bad football picks last weekend. Thoughts like that always manage to make me go limp.

Five seconds later, I said, "All set, Doc."

It was lingerie day. A half-dozen live models took turns displaying lacy bras, skimpy panties, satin camisoles and stomach-cinching garter belts for my benefit. The fussy technicians in the next room were graphing my heartbeat, perspiration and penile stimulation responses as each of the leggy babes paraded in front of me.

Incredibly, I was getting paid for this.

Lisa had helped me get the job. To be honest, she probably did it out of pity. After she had cooled down from her fuck frenzy that first night, it apparently dawned on her that she was screwing way below her class. She didn't even give me a goodnight kiss when I drove her back to her apartment, even though I had been mining her motherlode an hour earlier.

The next day, someone from the Sexual Response division let it be known that there was an opening for a full-time male test subject at T.I.T.S. Lisa tipped me off by phone, and now I was going into my fourth day on the job. My specialty was apparel.

The ceiling speaker said, "Outfit number five seemed to get the most positive response from you, Mr. Lester. Is that correct?"

"Could I have another look?"

"Certainly."

A slender redhead with bright green eyes and alabaster skin walked back into the room. She was wearing a matching bra and panties set. The material was almost transparent, with little silver and blue flowers embroidered on the fabric.

The model gave me a proud and somewhat slutty smile, obviously knowing what the nerdy technicians hadn't figured out. She and I knew that any subject's reactions would be based as much on the model as on what she was wearing.

I thought it was odd that the fidgety geeks in charge didn't take that factor into account. Then again, most of the research staff looked as if they would rather spend time with a paramecium than a pussy.

"Yes, I definitely like that outfit the most," I said. The redhead gave a slight nod, acknowledging the implied compliment.

"All right, Mr. Lester, now let's move on to sleepwear," the ceiling speaker said.

Lisa was putting on a jacket at her desk when I emerged from the Sexual Response offices that night.

"Don't forget your purse," I said, walking up behind her.

"Oh, hi, Jack." She seemed a little uncomfortable.

"You're usually out of here by this time." I had the feeling she had been leaving early on purpose, in order to avoid me.

"Uh, yeah, I guess so. How's the work going?"

"It's great, really," I said. "I've been meaning to thank you again for..."

"No, it was nothing, really. Um, I've got to go now." She began walking away, but I grabbed her arm. Everyone else had left, so there was nobody around to see us.

"Lisa, even if you don't want to go out with me anymore, can't we just be friends? I know you've been avoiding me."

She looked at me as if I were speaking Urdu. "Don't want to go out with you? Jack, I'd love to go out with you again!"

"But I thought...I mean, you gave me the cold shoulder when I took you home, and..."

She looked down at her chair. She started picking at the Hello Kitty sticker there with a fingernail. "Look, I know how unattractive I am to men. I wanted to let you off the hook, so you wouldn't have to pretend to like me just because I got carried away that first night."

"What?"

"Don't try to make me feel better, Jack," she sighed. "I loved everything you did to me that night, but I know you were just doing your duty because you didn't want to hurt my feelings."

A glistening tear rolled down her left cheek.

"Lisa, what the hell are you talking about? You're the sexiest girl I've ever seen, and I'd give my left nut to fuck you again! Of course, that might make it difficult, but...well, you know what I mean."

"You really mean that?" she sniffed.

"Jesus, just look at yourself!" I turned her in profile so she faced a window. The darkness outside made the glass reflect Lisa in all her glory. Her breasts swelled under her ruffled silk blouse and short jacket, while her black miniskirt hugged the curves of her firm ass. Her hair had that tousled just-got-out-of-bed look and her full lips were shining with gloss.

"You look fantastic, Lisa."

She gave a reluctant smile and pushed her chest out. "I do look pretty good, don't I?"

"What gave you the idea you didn't?" I said, taking her in my arms.

"It's a long story."

It turned out Lisa had been a Sexual Response division model until six months ago. The guy who had my job before me apparently didn't like blonds, or big tits, or God knows what. Nothing Lisa wore ever managed to get a positive response out of him. The clueless technicians thought that must be because Lisa was bad at modeling, so they transferred her into telephone research at half her old salary.

Lisa took my predecessor's indifference to mean that she must be a sexual washout with no appeal to men. She had stopped going on dates altogether, until I asked her out over the phone. By the time she saw that photo of the spurting dick, she had gone without sex for almost a year.

When I took her home the night she told me all of this, I gave her another taste of what she'd been missing all that time. Between positions, we came up with a plan.

"I suppose it's safe to say that swimsuit number six was your favorite, Mr. Lester," the speaker crackled. "Your erection grew an extra two centimeters while you were viewing that one."

"Could I take one more look at it, Doc? You know, just so we can be sure."

"No problem."

The side door opened and Lisa walked back in wearing a hot pink thong bikini. As always, she gave no sign of recognition for the technicians behind the one-way glass to see, even though we had been living together for a month. Ever since she convinced the director to give her a second chance at modeling, we had kept our off-duty relationship a secret.

She turned on her heel, so I could see the sweet cheeks of her tanned ass hugging the narrow crotch strap of the suit. When she faced me again, my heart did an abrupt staccato. Her cunt lips were so clearly outlined against the material that she may as well have been bottomless. The bikini's top pushed her bulging tits up so far I could see the tops of her nipples.

Then she cocked her head to one side and took a deep breath.

I could hear applause from the monitoring room as my dick began jerking and spurting. Doctor Sifert sounded practically giddy when he came on the intercom. "Mr. Lester, I think Beach Bitch swimwear definitely has a winner with that style, judging by your reaction! This should make the client very happy indeed!"

I gave Lisa a quick wink before she left through the side door.

We both know the lab boys will catch on eventually that their system is flawed, but we're not about to be the ones who tip them off. Some pretty goofy items of feminine apparel are probably showing up in stores based on my test reactions, but I can't help it if Lisa looks good in everything she models.

As for me, I figure I can keep up with the draining demands of scientific research for quite some time to come...as long as I keep taking my vitamins.

Words and Music

Despina swayed seductively in the studio control room, moving her magnificent body to the loud playback from the ceiling-mounted monitors. I tried not to stare, but I couldn't help myself.

That's because being completely irresistible was part of the secret of Despina's success.

Her black leather miniskirt was so enticingly short that it revealed the bulge of her pussy mound in her black satin panties. Her garterless stockings only came up to mid-thigh, and their opaque whiteness contrasted starkly with her dark olive skin. The outfit was topped off by a red spandex halter with a frilled neckline, like the one she wore on her first album cover. The material was stretched tight, barely containing her perfect breasts.

Almost every teenage and 20-something girl in the country has an outfit like that one by now. None of them can pull off the peasant-slut look as well as its originator, though. Despina was simultaneously a whore, a goddess and a work of art as she danced to the bass-heavy backing tracks and the vocals she'd just recorded.

Her latest song was as catchy and commercial as her previous hits, but with some changes it could be even better. That's why I was around.

Up to that point, Despina's fans were almost exclusively 12-22 year old females. Research showed that a significant segment of the adult music-buying public regarded Despina as just another bimbo pop diva, the kind who churns out throwaway top-40 fodder between soft drink commercials.

Those people were wrong.

Sure, Despina was as sexy and popular as all of her big-voiced, ass-shaking contemporaries. But she had something more genuine than any of them under all the fluff. It was there in her offbeat dance melodies, in her languid but intense delivery and in the sensuous way she moved.

Her only problem was lyrics. Her words got in the way.

"So what is it that you are thinking?" She was looking at me, smiling. Her teeth were brilliantly white against her Mediterranean skin and the glossy black curls that spilled to her shoulders. Her tits were so magnificent they were distracting, so big and firm that she always seemed to be thrusting them forward.

Despina had a habit of using inappropriate word choices, sloppy grammar and awkward clichés in her songs. Born in a remote Greek village, she hadn't learned English until her teens. And it showed.

"It's really good," I said, nodding my head with the beat. Barry Allantine, Despina's producer and manager, gave me a skeptical glance.

"But how is it that the words are sounding?" Despina had danced behind me and put her hands on my shoulders. She smelled like exotic spices. "Are you thinking it needs any changing?"

This was where I had to earn my keep. Barry had twisted some label exec's arm to put me on the payroll for this album.

Despina's first record had consisted of ten songs she wrote by herself and recorded for next to nothing. Originally an indie release, it went on to sell triple platinum when a major label picked it up for distribution.

But teen audiences are fickle, and Barry realized that Despina's core fans would outgrow their affection for her. In order to keep his star act from being a one-album wonder, he knew Despina would have to gain enough credibility to attract older listeners. More mature lyrics and subject matter would go a long way toward making people forget Despina's illiterate teenybopper image.

Just as movie studios hire script doctors for problem projects, I'd been tapped as a song doctor. My name doesn't appear on writing credits for these kinds of jobs, but the money helps take the sting out of anonymity.

Besides, like every other straight man on the planet, I was nuts about this big-busted Greek beauty. Not many grown men would admit to being fans of Despina's music back then, but any guy with a working dick was in love with her body. I had jumped at the chance to work with her.

She danced back around in front of me again. She had big, dark nipples, clearly outlined where they pressed against the thin fabric of her stretchy top.

As the playback faded, I decided to go for broke. "You've got a great melody here, but the words are just too plain. You should put more of yourself into your songs. They'll mean more to other people if they mean more to you."

Despina looked puzzled, cocking one of her trademark dark eyebrows quizzically. "What is it exactly you are meaning?"

"Start with the title of this song, 'I Love You So Very Much.' Instead of that kind of typical boy-girl thing, it would work better if you changed it to 'I Love You Selassia,' making it more personal."

Her eyes lit up. "I love you Selassia," she repeated, intrigued. I could tell my homework had paid off. Selassia was the Greek village where Despina had been born.

Suddenly, she lunged to where I was sitting in front of the control board, threw her arms around me so her world-famous breasts were pressed against my face and kissed the top of my head. "I love it!" she squealed. "You are right, absolutely, and it is perfect. We will be rewriting the rest of the whole song, right now, top to bottom. You and me."

Barry winked at me from the couch. This looked like the beginning of a beautiful partnership.

Three hours later, I wondered what the hell I had gotten myself into.

"You are not Greek, you do not know the Greek people, how can you be telling me what are the things I should be writing?" Despina shrieked. Her hands were balled into fists, her dark eyes were full of fury and her mouth was set in an expression of sheer rage.

We had relocated to her rented Santa Monica beach house. Barry, quite reasonably, had objected to paying overtime rates at the studio for a writing session that didn't require any technical equipment other than pen and paper. He and Kevin the engineer said they would see us tomorrow at noon, by which time we were all sure that Despina would have some new lyrics to record.

"Look, I'm just saying you'll sound like an idiot if you sing, 'I'm still always loving you after falling off your shore.' I know what you're trying to say, but it doesn't make any sense like that!"

Her breasts were heaving in her red halter-top. I was surprised to see that her nipples were very stiff now, jutting out prominently. "And just how is it that you would say what I am saying?"

I read from the yellow legal pad in my hand. "'I know I'll love Selassia, now and forevermore.' You know that's better, Despina. Hell, Selassia doesn't even have a shore! It's in the goddamned mountains!"

She stuck out her bottom lip and crossed her arms under her big breasts, knowing perfectly well that I was right but not wanting to admit it. By this time, we had argued about every line of three different songs. Now we were going back over the first one again because of her stubbornness.

Yet although she seemed frustrated at every suggestion I made, I could tell that she was beginning to respect my opinions—and me—a little more after each of these battles.

"Maybe you are right. This time, anyway." She looked like a pouting little girl, tapping one sandaled foot on the floor and fuming. At the same time, she looked like a big-busted, slender-hipped slut. She was petulant, immature, impossible...and delicious.

That was when Adonis, her live-in boyfriend from "the old country," came in through the sliding patio doors that looked out on the beach. Adonis wasn't really his name, but it may as well have been. He had the look of your basic bronze god.

He said something to Despina in Greek and tossed his towel on the back of a leather chair. She responded in kind and gave him a sexy smile, all red lips and fluttering black eyelashes. The way she glanced back over her shoulder as she went to him made it obvious she was being extra nice to the half-naked stud just to taunt me.

She put an arm through one of his and addressed me dismissively. "I suppose I am liking your idea more, now. Try to write some more lines and I will be back soon." Then Adonis was pulling her toward the bedroom. She laughed as she half-stumbled after him.

For the next fifteen minutes, I was treated to a chorus of his grunts and her cries of passion amid a melody of syncopated bedsprings. I knew that a lot of Despina's vocalizing was for my benefit. Why else would she be moaning "fuck me" and "eat me" and "suck my tits" in English to a Greek lover?

I was pissed off, but I also had an insistently throbbing hard-on as I slammed her front door behind me and headed for my car. I was just turning the key when Despina came running from the house. She was holding Adonis' towel in front of her naked body, but it wasn't covering much.

"Don't go, Marty," she breathed, leaning in the open passenger side window. She was glistening with sweat. Strands of her long, dark hair were plastered against her forehead, her cheeks and the tight flesh of her tits. "Please don't be so mad at me."

A car going past honked and its driver whistled. I could imagine the view he must have had, since Despina's entire backside was uncovered.

"Either get in the car or go back in the house, don't just stand there like that," I said.

To my amazement, she opened my car door and got in, flashing a generous expanse of ass and thigh as she settled into the leather seat.

Adonis appeared in the doorway of the house, his hard cock standing out from his crotch like a glistening club. He looked distinctly annoyed.

I floored the accelerator and sped off down the Pacific Coast Highway. Despina didn't say a word.

It wasn't a long drive to where I lived in Venice, Santa Monica's slightly funkier next-door neighbor. The aroma of Despina's sweat and musk kept my dick hard the whole time. She had hunched down in the passenger seat so other motorists wouldn't recognize her. I gave her a pair of sunglasses from my glove compartment, so she could hide her distinctive dark eyes.

She tentatively stroked the back of my hand a couple of times as I shifted gears, but kept quiet. I couldn't keep my eyes off of her long, bare legs, the soft line of her chin or the swell of her breasts above her white terrycloth towel.

After I pulled in my carport, she grabbed my key and said, "Which one?" I pointed out the front door key. She rushed into the house ahead of me, not bothering to cover the firm, perfect cheeks of her ass. The deep split between them left just enough space between her firm cheeks to reveal her meaty pussy lips and the tiny notch of her asshole.

She didn't have any trouble finding her destination. By the time I caught up, she was spread out in a seductive pose on my bed, with her legs tucked under her body and her arms thrown out to either side on the pillows behind her.

She had lost her towel somewhere along the way.

Almost every man in America has seen the nude telephoto shots of Despina sunbathing in Europe that turned up in a certain men's magazine last year, or at least the black-barred versions that ran everywhere else. But seeing her naked in person made it obvious that no photo could do her justice.

Her swollen breasts bulged out from her chest with the ideal shape that sculptors, painters and plastic surgeons all hope to capture in their work. Her nipples were as raised, puffy and pink as a pair of macaroon cookies against her dark tit flesh. Her belly was a swell of softness above her well-groomed and jet-black pubic bush.

"I want you now in my pussy," she said, parting her legs and drawing her knees up to show me her sex. She pointed at the protruding lips of her cunt. "Right here." Her little opening was gaping open slightly, all shiny and wet inside.

If the Greek loverboy she left back at her beach house was Adonis, then I felt like Zeus. She had left him literally hard up so she could

69

come with me, a guy who only had fantasized about her before today. I might not be sure why any of this was happening, but I wasn't in any hurry to analyze the situation.

After I stripped, I couldn't resist kissing and licking her warm pussy before shoving my cock between its lips. It turned me on that she was fucking another man half an hour ago who hadn't been able to satisfy her. It turned me on even more to know she apparently thought I would do a better job.

I loved the feel of her swollen tits against my chest as I pumped in and out of her tight slot. I loved seeing her sigh underneath me, licking her lips and moaning. This writhing, sweating beauty was the ideal dream girl of millions of men, but for that moment she was all mine.

"Suck my titties," she groaned, wiggling under me. "Suck them while you are fucking me so good."

Keeping my cock embedded in her body, I grabbed both her tits and let my tongue dance over their tips. When I sucked her already thick nipples, they plumped out even more, standing out at least an inch from her breasts. They were so sensitive that Despina shuddered with pleasure when I nuzzled them with my teeth.

After I shot my load inside her juicy cunt, I ran my tongue over nearly every square inch of her body, licking and sucking and tasting every part of her from her nipples to her pussy to her asshole.

And then we were fucking again.

Two weeks later, Barry shouted, "That's fucking fantastic!" Despina had just laid down a first-take vocal for a new song called "The Oracle." She was coming into the control room from the studio as Barry added, "You really must have knocked yourself out on that one, Marty. Terrific lyrics."

Despina and I exchanged a look, then she started to giggle. "I wrote that one all by myself, Barry," she said.

It was true. She'd sent Adonis packing and I had moved into her beach house the day after our first fuck. Since then, Despina had been as eager to improve her songwriting skills as she was about demonstrating her lovemaking talents.

She told me it was the way I used words that made her choose me over her old boyfriend. He only loved her for her body, she said, while I seemed to know what was in her secret heart.

I wasn't about to argue.

"Jesus, I'm sorry, Despina," Barry apologized, sounding surprisingly sincere. Then he looked at both of us. "I don't know what you two have got going, but I sure hope you keep it up. This album's going to knock everybody flat on their asses."

When I woke up the next morning, Despina was sitting cross-legged in bed, naked and radiant. She tapped an eraser against her chin as she stared at a notepad in her lap. She looked like a sculpture of Aphrodite made flesh, framed by the bright blue sky outside her floor-to-ceiling bedroom windows.

I scooted behind her so I could put my legs on either side of her body. I cupped her heavy breasts in my hands, rolling her nipples between my thumbs and index fingers while I nuzzled the back of her neck. "Need any help, beautiful?"

She put her hands on top of mine. "This is another one I've got to write all by myself," she whispered.

Then she turned to kiss me. At the same time, she guided one of my hands down between her legs. I let the middle finger of that hand trace the protruding lips of her warm pussy, then gently wedged it inside her tight little fuckhole. It eased open for me gradually. As I worked my finger in and out of that snug opening, I soon felt the familiar honey of her pussy begin coating the silky inner walls of her cunt.

I slipped my finger in as far as it would go, then pushed a second one in beside it. Her clit stiffened against my palm, which I was grinding against her mound while I finger-fucked her slippery snatch. I knew Despina could feel my erection throbbing against her bare back.

She pushed out her chest and I squeezed her left nipple with the hand that still cupped her breast. Despina tossed the notepad she had been using to one side of the bed. I saw the title "Marty My Love" written across the top sheet.

Then she squirmed free of my grip, flipped onto her stomach and grabbed my hard cock in both hands. She slipped her lips over its head, then lapped up and down its rigid length with her pink tongue. Her heavy breasts were against the tops of my legs. Her ass was as hard and flawless as marble.

I grabbed her shoulders and rolled her onto her back, so I was straddling her chest. She looked up at me and gave me her famous million-dollar smile. She knew what I wanted.

She took both her tits in her hands and pressed them close around my erection. My dick was still wet with her saliva, so it slipped easily back and forth against the silky smoothness of her breasts. On each of my up-strokes, Despina lapped at my cockhead, sometimes getting her lips completely around it before I slipped free again.

71

Her delicate fingers kneaded her tits savagely, squeezing them so they felt as tight as a virgin's pussy around my cock. The sight of my hard-on plowing the valley between her big-nippled breasts was too much to take. I shoved my dick up between her pouty lips and pumped my load into her mouth.

She swallowed in big gulps, not losing a drop, and tried to suck even more out of me after I stopped coming. It was paradise.

"Despina 2" shipped triple-platinum. The critics promptly fell all over themselves saying how much Despina had improved since her freshman effort, and retailers predicted the new album easily would surpass her previous sales.

The best part was that Despina actually ended up doing most of the songwriting herself. Once she was on the right track with an idea, I was only there to clean up her grammar. I was proud of her, and she was proud of herself.

Barry threw a release party at the China Club in Hollywood. Despina was radiant in an off-the-shoulder Armani gown with a simple pearl necklace and white heels. So much for her former peasant-slut look. I had a delightful image of high school and college girls across the country attending class in similar high-fashion finery, emulating their queen's new style.

When we got back to the beach house, Despina seemed abnormally quiet. Instead of going directly to the bedroom, she strolled into the den I had made into my office. She leaned on the corner of my desk and looked at the framed celebrity photos I'd hung on the wall. You would be surprised how many movers and shakers a songwriter gets to meet.

I put an arm around her. "What is it, beautiful? Something the matter?"

"No, not exactly. I just have something to ask, and I don't know how it will come out."

"You're not still worried about using the wrong words, are you?"

She smiled. "I want to keep working with you, Marty. Always. But I also want to get another...what's the word...perspective. I think I would like a woman's help, too. Do you know what I am saying?"

I hoped she meant what I thought she meant. Before I could say anything, she pointed at one of the pictures on the wall. It showed me standing beside a willowy Eurasian knockout who was widely known to swing both ways. Somebody had snapped our picture at a post-Grammy party.

"Someone like her, together with you and me," Despina added. "Together, here, with both of us. You know?"

As she said it, she looked like a hopeful innocent. At the same time, she looked like a randy, big-busted bitch in heat. I knew that irresistible look.

It was part of the secret of her success.

The Wedding Party

This story started out as a very different one titled "Member of the Wedding." When that torrid tale tragically failed to catch the fancy of the fine folks at Penthouse, I retooled it to enhance the main character's bustline and submitted the result to the big-boobs mags Hustler Busty Beauties, Juggs, Bust Out *and* Gent.

After that foursome likewise failed to be won over by the story's charms, I completely rewrote it by changing its narrator from a woman to a man, creating a new second half and calling the result "The Wedding Party." I also made the object of desire not only stacked but short and sweet, so I could send the remake to a Gent *sister magazine called* Petite.

Then a weird thing happened. A new editor at Gent *said he wanted that revised version of the story for his own magazine. That was more than three years of submissions, rejections and rewrites after I started sending out the original.*

The lesson here: Never give up!

In the acting biz, a guy without a lot on his résumé learns to take whatever jobs are out there, even if what's available ain't exactly Shakespeare. That's how I ended up in the role of a horny partygoer in an audience-participation play called "The Wedding Party." Ticket-buyers got to wander around a theater that was decorated to look like a reception hall, where they could interact with performers playing the guests and relatives of a pretend bride and groom.

Personally, I was amazed people would pay good money to see that kind of thing. But until a better gig came along, I was happy to put in an appearance every night, especially since Carly was part of the deal.

Carly was a petite cutie cast as a shyly innocent bridesmaid. Over the course of each evening, she had to lose her inhibitions after repeated trips to the punch bowl. That's because her character wasn't supposed to know the punch had been spiked.

As Carly pretended to get looser and looser, she also had to start getting friendlier and friendlier with yours truly. By the end of the second hour, she had to be making out with me like a complete slut under a banquet table.

I remembered the day we first auditioned for our parts. We didn't know each other. Neither of us was sure how intense we should make things look, but when the director shouted "action," we knew we had to impress him if we didn't want to go back to our day jobs.

I knew I wouldn't have any trouble convincing anyone that I was hot for Carly. Something about her less-than-statuesque size turned me on so much that just looking at her made my dick hard.

That surprised me a little. I was used to fucking tall, willowy dancer types, or stage actresses whose bodies were as big and dramatic as their gestures. Carly wasn't like them at all. She was a perfectly formed doll: all woman, but in three-quarter scale. Except for her tits, that is.

Carly's delicious D-cuppers would have looked big even on a normal-size girl. On her, they looked positively huge, nicely rounded and sticking out from her narrow chest without a bit of sag.

Since this was only a try-out, she wasn't wearing the purple taffeta bridesmaid costume she would have to don for an actual performance. Instead, she was dressed in a skin-tight black leotard with a scoop neck that showed off the deep cleavage between her impressively oversized breasts.

Her big tits were firm enough that she didn't need a bra, and she plainly wasn't wearing one. Her stubby nipples poked out against the nylon of her top. Everyone in the rehearsal space could see the thick nubs of her nips, and the halo-bumps surrounding those thick points.

Below the waist, she wore a snug pair of cut-off jeans that were rubbed white where they covered her compact butt cheeks. Her clothes were almost too casual, as if she didn't think she had to bother dressing up to impress anybody.

I approached her with the scripted line, "Hey, baby, how's about you and me giving each other some mouth-to-mouth?" She tried politely fending me off, pushing at my chest with her tiny hands and turning her heart-shaped face away. She even managed to blush, which I thought was an example of some damned fine acting ability.

Until then, I had thought of myself as a complete professional. But the first time Carly touched me, it felt like a jolt of electricity. She was so sexy that I knew I wouldn't be happy just acting like her lover. I wanted to be the real thing. I wanted to take her home, strip her down, suck her melon-sized tits and pump her little pussy all night long.

As she pretended to get loaded and started hanging all over me, I knew she could tell my dick was hard. A few times, she even "accidentally" brushed a hand against my bulge.

As for me, I copped more than a few feels, squeezing her braless tits through the thin material of her leotard top. Her nips were as hard as bullets.

The director eventually spoke up. "You two don't have to get quite so touchy-feely, you know. I don't want the audience thinking this is some kind of live-sex show!"

Everyone laughed. Inside, though, I wished that was exactly the kind of show we would be doing. I thought about how great it would be to bend Carly over the phony reception hall's gift table, push up her floor-length bridesmaid gown and tug her little cotton panties down around her knees. Then I would spread her ass cheeks and stick my hard-on deep in her honey-hole for all to see.

She was small enough that my dick would feel huge in her petite pussy. She would groan with pleasure, biting down on her plump bottom lip, while a hundred shocked audience members watched me fuck my rod in and out of her creamy cunt and rub her flexing asshole with the pad of my thumb.

"Whash in this punch?" Carly slurred, bringing me back to rehearsal-hall reality. She pretended to take another drink from her empty cup, then started kissing me again. I reached behind her and squeezed her ass.

"Okay, that's enough practice for you two, you're both hired," the director said.

As good as that made me feel, I would have been happier about getting the job if I didn't get the distinct impression that the director didn't care much about this particular production. Maybe he was like me, and thought he was cut out for better things.

After all, the only thing lower than this kind of gig probably was circus work.

Now that the focus was off of us, Carly turned and walked away from me without a word. I caught up to her and grabbed her elbow. Trying to sound charming, I said, "Hey, I thought maybe we could do some more rehearsing on our own before showtime. Like back at my place, I mean."

The look she gave me is one that every guy on earth gets from a hot girl at one time or another. She cocked an eyebrow in a way that said, "You must be joking."

It should have been a look that pissed me off. But coming from a sexy blond bombshell who was a head shorter than me, it only made my dick stiffer.

"My drama coach said I never should mix my professional life with my personal one, or I never would get anywhere as an actress," she said. "Sorry."

I couldn't believe she was serious. From the way she had used her tongue in my mouth and pressed her stiff nips against my chest, I thought she was genuinely turned on during our audition.

I tried to argue, but she just walked way, swinging her lovely little ass like she just couldn't help it. She apparently had a genuine superstition about mixing business with pleasure.

I put a hand in my pocket to stroke my boner as I watched her go. I would do anything to get my tongue and my dick between her legs. That meant I was going to have to do my best to make her appreciate my talents.

Opening night was Saturday, which also was the first time I got to see Carly in costume. Her purple gown's puffy sleeves and floor-length hem made her petite body look even tinier. But the elastic bustline of the gown only emphasized the outrageous size of her knockers.

Anyone looking at the two of us that night would have thought we were in love, or at least in lust. Carly did things like put her legs on either side of one of mine and hunch her pussy against my thigh. She threw back her shoulders and rubbed her huge tits from side to side against my ruffled tuxedo shirt. And she didn't pull away when I ran my middle finger up and down the crack of her ass through her dress.

A leering slob who was watching us said, "Hey, buddy, why don't you just go ahead and fuck the bitch?" His hard-on bulged in his polyester pants. I swear I could see the thing throbbing. It was nice to have an appreciative audience, but this was ridiculous.

The guy's wife tried to tug him away, but he said, "Not now, honey, this is just getting good. Maybe the little bimbo will start sucking the guy's dick or something."

Carly flashed me a funny expression when she heard that. For a second, I swear she looked as if she might do exactly what the guy suggested. Then she went back to necking with me and making improvised "drunken" wisecracks.

The next few nights went the same way. Carly didn't seem to mind when I did things like rub her nipples or massage her crotch through her dress. It got to the point where I was surprised the director didn't ask us what the fuck we thought we were doing and fire us both.

He must have known a good thing when he saw it, though. We obviously were the hit of the show. People gathered around us to watch our steamy make-out sessions. The guys egged me on, telling me to put my hand down Carly's top or finger her snatch. The women wondered why Carly didn't slap my face, but they didn't look away.

After every performance, I had a raging case of blue balls. It got to the point where I started jerking off in the men's room before leaving the theater, because I couldn't wait long enough to get my rocks off at home.

Fortunately, Carly seemed to be warming up to me. She had turned down my offers to drive her home for four nights in a row, but I had the feeling on the fifth night she would agree. With any luck, she might be willing to give me at least a quick blowjob in my car.

"So, is tonight the night you finally let me drive you home?" I asked, crossing my fingers.

She hesitated, then said, "Actually, I've got to head over to another job right now. But you can take me there, if you want."

"Another job? But it's already after eleven."

She gave me a bad-girl grin that looked bitchy and sexy at the same time. "That's right. I go on at midnight." Another pause, then she added, "I can get you in free if you want to watch the show. But only if you don't ask any more questions."

Ever have a hunch that you're in for a real treat? That's how I felt at that moment. I knew that any show starting after midnight was likely to be of the "adults-only" variety. Maybe Carly was a showgirl in some kind of topless review. Or maybe it was something even better.

She told me to park in the lot of a building that didn't have any kind of sign out front. We went inside together. Carly told a burly guy who stood in front of another door that I was a friend of hers. He looked me up and down, then held the door open for us.

Inside was a high-dollar gentlemen's club, all polished oak and brass, with topless waitresses making the rounds. Their G-strings were so narrow that their pussy lips surrounded them in the front the same way their ass cheeks did around back. On a small stage, a naked girl was on her knees sucking a man's cock while she fingered her own cunt.

I had been to plenty of strip clubs, but I never had seen that kind of action at one of them. Obviously, this was a very "private" establishment.

"The drinks here are pretty steep," Carly said, "but the show makes up for the prices. I have to go change, but I'll be on in a few minutes." She headed toward a side door marked "Performers Only."

I took a seat. A waitress appeared at my elbow and said, "Welcome to Pixies. May I take your order?"

That's when I noticed what else was special about this place besides the show. Like Carly, none of the waitresses were taller than five-two. All of them had slender frames like Carly's, and all of them had oversized jugs that swung from side to side when they walked. The busty girl on stage was at least a foot shorter than the guy whose dick was in her mouth. This place was like a paradise full of petites.

The guy grimaced, took his cock out of the girl's mouth and aimed it at her bare tits, which she held from underneath with both hands. Vigorously stroking his pole, he let fly with several jets of come that striped her breasts and dripped from their stiff tips.

Staring at this display in delighted disbelief, I distractedly ordered a beer. The girl on stage waited for her lover to finish shooting his load, then she put her mouth back on his cock to suck him some more, an act that received a quiet round of applause from the room.

My beer arrived just as the girl and guy left the stage and Carly strolled onto it, bathed in a single pink spotlight. She was wearing a flimsy see-through white robe. Her dark nipples and the split of her shaved pussy were plainly visible through the material.

A red curtain behind her opened, revealing a bed covered in shimmering silver sheets. It was tilted so that its head was higher than its foot.

Carly casually let her robe drop to her feet while exotic music thumped from the room's speakers. That meant she was completely, gloriously naked. Her perfect skin looked radiantly flawless in the spotlight.

She danced a little, swinging those big tits and that firm ass of hers. Then she sat on the bed and started caressing her breasts, delicately at first. She used her long fingernails to tug at her nipples. Then she lay back, extended both of her short legs in the air and parted them in a wide "V," giving everyone a good view of her thick pussy lips and her tiny pink asshole.

I thought I would come in my pants when she went to work on herself with her fingers, fucking them in and out of her hairless snatch.

This was better than I possibly could have imagined. I had heard of girls who worked in conventional strip clubs while they waited to get a break in the acting biz. I even had met a few of them, who said they started out as waitresses but couldn't resist a chance to make more money by getting on "stage."

I never had been lucky enough to meet one who worked in a place like this, though. To be honest, I couldn't believe an establishment like this could exist without getting shut down. How much payoff money must the owners be slipping to the local police and the city council to stay in business?

Carly got out of the tilted bed and prowled naked along the edge of the stage. She waved her pussy-scented fingers under the noses of several red-faced men. She thrust her glistening crotch forward, taunting them.

Then she looked directly at me. She put one hand on a slender hip, extended her other arm and crooked a finger. She was beckoning me to join her.

I smiled, realizing what was going on. This was her way of giving me what we both wanted without violating her drama teacher's rule about dating a co-worker. Just like at the fake wedding reception, where she pretended to be a horny guest every night, Carly could let me do things here as part of her performing duties while remaining "professional."

Every other man in that club must have simultaneously hated my guts and envied the hell out of me as I stepped onto the stage. Since this seemed to be the kind of underground club that didn't worry about indecency laws, I realized Carly might do just about anything with me. I hoped she wasn't into any kinky dominatrix stuff, but at that moment I probably wouldn't have run away even if she pulled out a whip, a pair of nipple clamps and a studded strap-on dildo.

I thought about the fact that she probably had done this with lots of other guys before me, and that most of them probably had been strangers. That only made me hotter for her. The thought of this precious little pixie fucking and sucking different men on stage every night was dirty, nasty and erotic as hell.

How many big dicks had she stretched her pretty little mouth around? How many hard-ons had filled her tiny pussy while a hundred other men watched?

Carly knelt before me, unzipped my pants and pulled out my cock. The thing was so hard it was bouncing up and down with every beat of my heart. She opened her red-lipsticked mouth wide and sucked me inside, using her tongue all around my cockhead.

I was onstage getting my cock sucked by the sexiest girl I ever had seen in my life. It was without a doubt the greatest moment of my career. I decided that I had an obligation to Carly and to my profession to help her put on a show that no one ever would forget.

I pulled my dick out of Carly's mouth. She looked at me in confusion as I gestured for her to stand up. Then I took hold of her narrow waist with both hands, lifted her 90-pound body off the stage and flipped her completely upside-down in one smoothly acrobatic motion. That way, her face ended up at my crotch and her bare pussy was in front of my mouth.

Carly wrapped her legs around my head and sucked my rod while I gave her a stand-up eat-job, mouthing her meaty cunt like a guy who had been on a desert island for the past 10 years.

The crowd applauded. Carly's pussy was good and juicy, and tasted as sweet as vanilla icing. I sucked and nibbled her clit, occasionally going deep in her fuckhole with my tongue, while she blew me. She was so lightweight that supporting her upside-down body was no trouble at all.

"Fuck her!" yelled a guy in the crowd. A few other spectators took up the chant. "Fuck her, fuck her, fuck her!"

I gently deposited Carly on the bed. She pulled up her knees, reached under her butt to hold her pussy lips apart and looked hungrily at my stiff cock. If this was acting, she deserved a goddamned Oscar.

"Do it," she said. "Fuck my little pussy, right here in front of everyone. I want that big dick in my cunt."

I pressed its swollen head against her tiny opening. When I pushed inside, her fuckhole opened up for me like a wet, hot mouth. Carly groaned with pleasure, bucking against me and writhing on the bed.

The crowd went dead silent, watching me screw this adorable, undersized nymph. My balls slapped the firm cheeks of her ass with each thrust.

She was so tight and hot that I was ready to gush in less than a minute, but that obviously wouldn't do. I paced myself by pulling out and eating her pussy some more. I pushed up her thighs far enough that I also could get at her dainty little asshole with my tongue.

That's how fucking crazy I was about her. I didn't care how many men she fucked every night. I considered it a privilege to suck her pussy and tongue-fuck her asshole in front of a room full of strangers.

I put my cock back in her snug love-box and fucked her harder, making the bedsprings squeak as if they were going to give out. Carly's tongue was in my mouth, her nipples were stiff against my chest and her pussy was so juicy we made slurping sounds as I pumped her.

Covered in sweat, I pulled out and shot my load up across her belly and her jiggling tits. Carly rubbed my come into her skin as if it were body lotion. Then she raised up to put her arms around my neck and kiss me. This wasn't like the kisses she had given me at the wedding reception play earlier that night. These were real. I could tell.

We've fucked onstage at that nameless club every night since our first appearance there last week. Carly still won't screw me except when we're working together, but I don't mind all that much.

So long as we get to follow up every "Wedding Party" appearance with an on-stage honeymoon, I'll be a happy guy.

Special Request

"Good morning, Miss Seligman, my name is Ron Wexler. I'd like to come in and suck your breasts."

Cathy Seligman was too shocked by this shameless pronouncement to say anything, or even to slam her apartment door in outrage.

Ron quickly continued, "I hasten to inform you that I am neither a doctor of medicine nor a sexual deviant. And although I will do my best to coerce you, I will not use force, and I most definitely will commit no crime. Furthermore, I will endeavor to give you as much pleasure as I am sure you will be giving me. Now, may I come in?"

Cathy knew she must be crazy for continuing to listen. But she had to admit that the stranger was kind of cute, in a wholesome way that his outrageous request seemed to contradict.

As for his apparent fascination with her breasts, Cathy was used to guys ogling her oversized bustline. She had become accustomed to the way men "accidentally" managed to rub against them on elevators or in crowds. And it had become a given that any member of the male species would stare at her boobs while talking to her, all the while thinking that she didn't notice where their gaze happened to be focused.

Still, she couldn't remember ever hearing a line as direct as this guy's.

Finally, she overcame her sense of utter flabbergastedness and said, "You've got a lot of nerve, you know. What makes you think I won't just call the police?"

"I hope you won't, Cathy. I'm really only being honest. I find you extremely attractive, especially your magnificent breasts. Believe me, I'm very embarrassed telling you all of this, but I find I can't be silent about the way I feel any longer."

The way he talked was so awkwardly formal and precise he must either be a virgin or the next best thing, Cathy thought. That was hard to believe, though. He had to be at least in his mid-20s, with thick blond hair and a pretty-boy handsome face. He was wearing a yellow Polo shirt and jeans with what looked like tan cowboy boots. From his decent build, it looked like he worked out regularly.

As for Cathy, she had been sunbathing on her balcony when the doorbell rang. Her red bikini was so skimpy she had wrapped a fluffy blue towel around herself before answering the door. Her light brown hair was pulled back into a high ponytail with a silver bar. The earbuds of her iPod still hung around her neck.

"You're really not some kind of weirdo?" she asked, looking deep into his eyes. "Come on, be honest."

"Cross my heart. Look, here's my driver's license so you can see that I'm who I say I am." He had it ready and handed it to her. When she took it, her towel slipped a little, exposing more of her tanned tits.

"Okay, I know I must be crazy, but come on in." She stood back from the door. "How did you know my name, anyway?"

"I asked around at the park where I've seen you jogging." Ron took a seat on the white leather sofa. Cathy sat across from him in a matching chair.

"Why didn't you just talk to me there?"

"I wanted to, really, but you always were listening to music. Besides, I'm kind of shy."

Cathy laughed. "I wouldn't call someone shy who comes to a girl's door with the kind of request you just made."

"Yes, well." Ron shifted his gaze to stare at the cleft between Cathy's jugs where they bulged above her towel. "How about it?"

"My God, you really do have a one-track mind, don't you?" Cathy moved a hand to cover her cleavage, but she obviously was flattered. She also had to admit that she was getting more than a little turned on.

Ron's tight jeans made it obvious that he had a hard-on. And a big one, at that. Okay, so maybe this wasn't exactly a conventional way to make contact with the opposite sex. But what was so bad about a guy who got directly to the point, instead of wasting a lot of time beating around the bush?

Ron got up from the sofa and knelt in front of Cathy. "Believe me, you won't regret this. It'll be great."

She looked in his eyes again and decided he actually was sincere—or at least as sincere as any of the other guys she'd been with. Letting her hands rest at her sides, she pushed her chest out a little and gave him a coy smile.

"I suppose since you asked so nicely, it would be terribly rude of me to turn you down."

Ron tugged open the towel that encircled Cathy's breasts, revealing the tiny red bikini top that squeezed her fat tits together. The swimsuit

86

material was the next best thing to transparent, and Cathy's dark nipples sat up high. Their stiff tips pushed the fabric out at least an inch.

Her bikini cups also had ridden up a little, so Ron could see the undersides of her tits where they swelled out from her body. Those bottom crescents of her boobs were enticingly untanned.

Ron placed his hands on the sweetly swollen hills of her hooters, feeling the soft weight of them. He nuzzled the tops of her jugs with his mouth, giving her nipples gentle pinches through the bikini. Then he hooked his thumbs under the thin straps that supported her top and pushed them off of her shoulders.

Cathy let out a sigh when Ron pulled the straps down far enough to expose her nipples. She sighed with pleasure as he began sucking one of them while gently rubbing the other with the flat of his palm.

Three loud knocks followed by two soft ones on the door startled both of them.

"Jesus, it's my fiancé!" Cathy whispered in a panic. "That's his knock!"

"Fiancé?" Ron asked. "But...but..."

Cathy pushed him toward the balcony, her heavy tits swaying from side to side as she crossed the room. A deep voice on the other side of the door said, "Honey, it's me. I got back early. Come on, let me in."

Cathy quickly told Ron, "Look, I want to see you again, but you've got to go now, and fast. We're only on the second floor, and there's a drainpipe you can use to help you climb. Hurry!"

Ron looked decidedly pissed. "Why can't you just tell him to go away?"

Cathy darted a look at the door, which resounded with three more loud knocks and two soft. In a burst of words, she said, "He's been out of town for a week, he won't take no for an answer and he has a key he'll be using any second now. Also, he's a former all-pro linebacker. Any more questions?"

The door opened behind her just as Ron's blond hair dropped out of sight below the balcony. Cathy closed her towel over her bare breasts, turned around, and exclaimed, "Teddy! You're back!"

"Honey, I've been knocking and knocking," grumbled the six-foot-seven bear of a man who lumbered inside. "You deaf or something?"

"Sorry, hon, I had on my music and must not have heard you." She was glad she hadn't taken off the earbuds in the heat of the moment earlier.

"Come here and give me a kiss, beautiful." Teddy held out his arms. When Cathy came close, he reached for her towel and whipped it off in one quick motion. Cathy hadn't pulled her top back up, so both of her massive tits still hung out over her bikini cups.

Before she could think of some way to explain her appearance, Teddy said, "Going for one of those all-over tans, huh, baby?" He insolently tweaked her left nipple and added, "Better watch out for sunburn."

Then he scooped her up in his arms and made for the bedroom, where he dropped her on the satin comforter. Her heavy breasts lolled to either side of her chest as she watched him undress. Then he was on top of her and doing it, but all Cathy could think about was the man who had come to her door with a very special request.

"Ron? It's Cathy. I found your number online. I'm sorry I couldn't call before now, but I really would like to see you again."

"You sure you really want to?" Ron asked, sarcastically. "I mean, I don't want to come between you and your loving fiancé or anything."

"Stop it," Cathy pleaded. "I have to see you because I'm not sure I even want him for a fiancé anymore. Last night when he fucked me, all I could think of was how sweet and funny you were."

"I'm surprised you even remembered my name."

"Your driver's license helped. You forgot to take it back from me yesterday."

"I left in kind of a hurry."

"If you come over right now, I'll be glad to return it. And that's not the only thing I'll give you."

"I'll be right there."

Cathy was wearing a simple white cotton sundress when she opened the door. It hugged her slender waist and pushed up her sun-browned breasts above its low-cut neckline. She had a feeling Ron would like it a lot. From the look on his face and the bulge that quickly appeared in his pants, she saw she had guessed correctly.

Ron didn't even pretend to be shy this time. He couldn't wait to get her stripped. He undid her first two buttons, but popped off the other three. "I'll buy you a new one," he whispered.

Shoving the front of the dress open and pushing it down, he squeezed Cathy's heavy, swinging breasts in both hands while he licked their nipples.

"That feels soooo good." Cathy stretched her arms above her head and luxuriated in the attention Ron was giving her breasts. He seemed to know just how to squeeze them, just the right pressure to use to make her nipples get harder and her pussy get wet.

She pushed his hands away and held both of her tits out for him, pushing one and then the other into his open mouth. As he tongued one of her nipples, she purred, "There wouldn't happen to be any other parts of my body you're interested in, would there?" Then she wriggled so her dress dropped to the floor. She wasn't wearing panties.

Ron pushed her against the wall and got on his knees to push apart her thighs and eat her pussy. Cathy watched him lapping her and moaned. Feeling slutty, she reached down and held open the lips of her cunt to make it easier for him to suck her swollen little clit.

Finally, she couldn't take it anymore. "Come on, let's get on the bed before my knees get any weaker."

She soon was on her back with her legs locked around Ron's body as he plowed her creamy slot, watching her big tits shake with every thrust. Then he rolled onto his back and pulled her on top, so Cathy could ride his cock like a naked cowgirl, grinding her clit against his thick pubic hair.

When she knew that he was about to come, Cathy slid up and off his hard dick. Then she scooted down in the bed to put her tits around his meat. She moved her whole chest up and down, squeezing him between those two soft but firm mounds, until his tool began jerking and spurting its load.

After Ron finished shooting, Cathy slid her mouth down over the head of his prick and sucked out the last precious drops of his warm come.

Two months later, Cathy couldn't believe how completely her life had changed since that day, all because a complete stranger had come to her door with a rather unusual request.

She had dumped Teddy the same day she first fucked Ron. She and Ron moved in together soon afterward. Ron still was her favorite bed partner, but she had so many other lovers now that it was getting hard to squeeze him into her busy schedule.

Ron seemed to understand. In fact, he actually encouraged her to have sex with other men, and especially with other women. Cathy couldn't help thinking how wonderfully different he was from tight-assed Teddy, and how lucky she was to have met him. Ron had opened up a whole new world of sexuality for her.

Today, for example, she was going to do something she couldn't have imagined trying when she was with Teddy.

Her high heels clicked on the black granite flagstones of the mansion walkway. She slipped the butler a fifty to make sure the owner came to the door. A minute passed, during which she touched up her lipstick and fluffed her hair. Then the darkly handsome multi-millionaire man of the house appeared, the one she had seen out walking the two big Alaskan Huskies yesterday when she drove past this street.

Cathy tilted her head to one side, gave him a less-than-innocent smile, and said, "Good morning, Mr. Elkins. My name is Cathy Seligman. I'd like to come in and suck your cock."

It might not be subtle, but it worked every time.

Writer's Block

I was just sliding my dick into Beverly Morrison's tight little teenage pussy when I thought of Laura Elmont. The only thing the two girls had in common was the size of their huge tits, but that was enough.

Beverly was a high school cheerleader who had just turned 18, blond and big-titted and brazen. I'd had my eye on her since the beginning of her senior year, but I wasn't about to mess with her while she was jailbait. A lot of people might think gym teachers like me aren't too bright, but we're not completely stupid.

I saw her drinking at Triggers, my favorite bar, on her birthday. She was celebrating by making use of a false ID that said she was three years older than she really was, which I thought was kind of charming.

She was downing beers with some other students, so I didn't want to be too obvious about checking her out. But we made enough eye contact to know what was on each other's minds.

She showed up at my office next to the gym this afternoon between classes. She made it so clear what she wanted that I had to tell her to keep her clothes on, because I sure as shit wasn't going to fuck her on school property. So now here we were, fucking like a pair of crazed minks in my apartment.

Laura Elmont, on the other hand, was an old college classmate of mine who got her degree the same year I did. We didn't have a hell of a lot in common back then, what with her majoring in English Literature and me in Physical Education, but somehow we had become friends.

I remembered Laura was good-looking, but in a bookish kind of way. She was one of those girls you knew would look a hell of a lot better if she would take off her glasses and let her hair down.

She couldn't disguise her tits, though. She may have dressed and acted like a librarian, but she had a pair of jugs that would do a porn queen proud.

"Yeah, coach, fuck me like that," Beverly grunted as she squirmed underneath me. "Real hard. I like it hard."

As I slammed my cock in and out of that sweet little mouth between Beverly's legs and watched her fat tits shake, I caught myself imagining that I was looking at Laura's big boobs.

I never did get a look at Laura's tits back in college, and neither did anyone else, as far as I know. She was a strict Catholic who insisted that she would remain a virgin until she married. Meanwhile, I was banging every slut who would spread her legs for me, which turned out to be quite a few.

Don't ask me why the two of us got along. Maybe opposites really do attract.

After we graduated, I headed right back here to my hometown high school to teach gym. The last I'd heard from Laura was that she was working as a sales clerk at a bookstore in the next county, which must have been a real comedown for somebody with four years of college bills to pay. We pretty much lost contact about a year ago, just by drifting apart.

Teenage Beverly was sweating and moaning like a whore under me while I fucked her. With all that energy and spirit, it was easy to see how she'd made head cheerleader.

She had her knees pulled way up, so I could push my cock as deep as possible into her slippery cunt. My balls slapped the pink cheeks of her ass with every thrust. Her hands were on her tits, squeezing them so hard she left red finger marks on them.

When she pushed one of her tits to her mouth and started tonguing its big, swollen nipple, I thought I would lose my load right there. She ran her pointed tongue around the whole raised halo, making it shine with her saliva. Finally, she used her fingers to push the stiff nipple into her mouth and suck it. As she nursed at her own swollen breast, she looked at me with a dreamy expression.

All the while, I was imagining Laura Elmont doing the same things. I pictured prim, proper Laura sucking herself while she got fucked, moving her ass like a horny slut, groaning with lust and basically loving what my big cock was doing to her.

"Let me turn you over, baby," I said to Beverly, pulling my meat out of her juicy twat. "Let me fuck you from behind, so I can see your pretty ass spread open wide."

Beverly rolled over with a giggle and stuck her butt in the air. She held her cheeks apart so I could see everything she had, from her little pink asshole to her fuck-stretched pussy. "How's this, coach?"

She didn't know the real reason I wanted to fuck her that way, of course. From that angle, it was easier to pretend that she was Laura.

I positioned my dickhead against the outer lips of Beverly's sopping wet pussy. I moved it up and down those thick lips, caressing the soft folds that surrounded her pink, shining hole. In my mind, this was Laura Elmont's virgin cunt before me, and I was about to be the first man to impale it.

"Umm, that feels nice, coach, really nice," Beverly sighed. She wiggled her hips while I moved my dick around her crotch. I imagined Laura kneeling that way, Laura on her elbows and knees, offering up her body for my pleasure.

Beverly suddenly bucked back against me, stuffing her cunt full of my cock, and we were fucking away again. I squeezed her heavy, hanging breasts while I boned her.

In my simultaneous fantasy, I was pushing one of Laura's plain woolen skirts up around her hips. Her cotton panties were stretched tight across her crotch. A narrow line of moisture on the material defined the slit of her pussy.

I pumped Beverly with long strokes, pulling my cock almost completely out of her cunt each time before shoving it back in balls deep.

At the same time, I was thinking what it would be like to kiss Laura's panties and smell her pussy through them. I would push aside the material to see that pristine, perfect, unfucked cunt. It would be gaping open slightly. Laura would blush with embarrassment, because of how vulgar and slutty it looked. But then my tongue would be lapping it and she would give herself up to the feeling and...

"Jesus, oh Jesus, oh my God," Beverly groaned, panting. I was holding onto her hips and fucking her hard and fast. Her cunt muscles squeezed my cock in waves as she came. Then I was pumping my load into her, shooting it out in long spurts and shuddering with how good it felt.

It had been a perfect fuck. And the girl who had made it perfect was somewhere in the next county.

In my office the next morning, I looked up Laura's number. I'd been thinking about her all night, wondering how weird she would think it was that I suddenly had an overwhelming desire to fuck her. I guess it was one of those cases where you don't know what you've got until it's gone.

"Hello?"

"Hi, Laura. It's Jim. Jim Ellison, from college?"

"Come on, Jim," she said with a sweet lilt. "I know it's been a while, but of course I remember you! How are you doing?"

"Okay, I guess. Still teaching. Are you still at the bookstore?"

"Yeah, but I've got the noon to nine shift today, so I'm at home. I was writing when you called."

"Still working on that novel?"

"Yeah." She sighed. "It's taking a lot longer than I thought. I've kind of hit a writer's block."

"What's the problem? I remember you used to be typing away on your laptop all the time."

"Uhh...it's kind of embarrassing. I'm writing a love scene, but I'm not sure that I'm getting the details right."

I felt my dick getting hard in my jock. Talk about your goddamned golden opportunities! With any luck, the one thing more important to Laura than her vow of virginity might be her goal of finishing her great American novel.

All through college, she had talked about wanting to be a published writer, how it meant more than anything else in the world to her. She was a big Hemingway fan, too, so she believed writers should write about things they actually have experienced.

This was going to be a piece of cake.

"Laura, listen, I was calling because I'd really like to see you. You're not married yet or anything, are you?"

Laura laughed. "No, not married. Or anything."

"Well, how about a date?"

There was a pause. She probably was thinking back to college, when we had been good pals but never actually dated. Because we talked about everything then, she knew I was a total horndog who was fucking girls left and right the whole time I knew her. That meant she might be wondering what she would be letting herself in for if she said yes.

Finally, she broke the silence. "Sure, Jim, that would be fun."

She was wearing a grey pleated skirt with a matching blazer when I picked her up. The blazer was buttoned, hiding the swell of those magnificent breasts I remembered. Her gold wire-frame glasses were a little severe, and her hair was up in a bun. She looked more like she was heading to work at an accounting office than going on a date.

So why did I have a hard-on within two minutes of seeing her? Maybe it was because she was something different from my usual conquests. Maybe it was because she really did have a pretty face behind those glasses, and her business suit couldn't hide all her curves. Hell, maybe it was just because it was Saturday night and my pecker was a creature of habit.

We went to dinner at a decent restaurant, then took in a movie that was her choice. It was a little highbrow for my tastes, but she seemed to enjoy it.

Back at her apartment door, she said, "Tonight was fun, Jim. I really enjoyed seeing you again." She put out her hand for me to shake, as if we had just finished a business lunch.

I knew I had to make my move, and now was the time. Holding onto her hand, I put my other arm around her shoulders to pull her close, then leaned over to kiss her.

"No, Jim, I...," she began, but then I was giving her one of my best efforts. Her lips were parted just enough for me to find her tongue with mine before she could draw away.

She blushed and gave me a little smile. "I wasn't expecting that," she said, but she didn't seem offended.

"Do I get to come inside?" I nodded toward her door, but hoped the double meaning of my words wasn't lost on her.

She looked down, then fumbled in her purse for her keys. "Sure, I guess."

We made a little small talk on her sofa, then I decided to go for the gold.

"Listen, Laura, I don't want to sound like a jerk or anything..."

"There's that 'or anything' again." She gave me a grin.

I smiled back. "Listen, I know we're friends, and I don't want this to come out wrong, but I'm really attracted to you. What I'm getting at is that I'd really like to go to bed with you."

She looked very surprised, but didn't say anything, so I went on. "I know that vow you talked about in college, but I also know how important your writing is to you. I remember you always said people shouldn't try to write what they don't know. Then you told me on the phone that you were having trouble with a love scene. Well, I want to give you some first-hand experience."

She looked at her knees, straightening a pleat of her skirt. "So you want to have sex with me for the good of my writing, is that it?"

Here was where I either was going to get laid or get the door, but I had practiced what to say and was pretty sure of my game. "No. But I would say anything to convince you to do this, because I want you so much. You're all I've been thinking about lately, even when I'm in bed with other girls."

I knew that last part was dangerous. It would either piss her off, or flatter the hell out of her.

"Really?" she said, looking at me with a funny grin.

Score another one for the coach.

Her bedroom wasn't what I expected. Somehow I thought she would go for straight lines and functional furniture, but she had a big polished brass bed with fluffy pillows and white lace ruffles all around. The wallpaper was pale pink roses and sky blue stripes, like what you would expect to find in a little girl's room.

We sat on the bed and I kissed her, tasting her tongue while I pushed her jacket off her shoulders. Her nipples were hard, poking out against the fabric of her white silk blouse. When she noticed I was looking at her chest, some color came into her cheeks. She kissed me again in a way that I sort of thought was meant to block my view of her breasts. But when I started massaging one of her big tits through her blouse, she didn't pull away.

"Here, let me do this first," she said, putting her glasses on a nightstand and reaching for the bun on her head. She pulled out four pins and her hair fell around her shoulders. She fluffed it out with her fingers. It had that wavy, funky look from being up all day. It looked sexy the way it was all messed-up now.

Before removing her blouse, I got on my knees on the floor and pushed her legs apart, living out my fantasy of the previous week. When I pushed up her skirt, I got my first shock of the night.

Although she was wearing what at first looked like sensible pantyhose, they were the crotchless kind—and she wasn't wearing panties. The pink flaps of her pussy hung from either side of her fuckhole, which was glistening with a little drop of moisture.

I cupped her ass in my hands and pulled her crotch close to the edge of her bed so I could eat her box. She moaned with pleasure while I licked her. She unbuttoned her blouse and unsnapped her bra. Her fat, gorgeous tits were so big they spilled over the sides of her chest.

I held the flaps of her pussy open with my fingertips, making it easier for me to spear my tongue into her musky cunt. Before long, she started coming, grunting low in her throat while an all-over shudder went through her body.

When I looked at her face, her expression made me want to jump up and fuck her as fast as I could get my pants off. She looked more like she wanted it than any other girl I've ever been with.

I threw off my clothes and climbed onto the bed, but she stopped me before I could slide my dick into her home plate. I thought at first that was because she might want me to put on a rubber, which I was

96

hoping to avoid. I hate the fuck out of those goddamned things. But I would go along with even that requirement if I had to.

Instead, she caught me completely off guard by saying, "Let me look at it first, Jim." She sat up and put a hand on my cock. "I want to remember everything about this night, especially the way your penis looks."

Somehow, she made the word "penis" sound unbelievably hot.

She ran a pink fingernail up and down the sides of my hard shaft, then cradled my balls in her palm. She stared at my cock in fascination, examining every detail.

"Put it in your mouth, Laura," I said. "Put it in your mouth and suck it."

And she did. Not slowly, or with any hesitation. She obediently slipped her lips over my cockhead and started blowing me as if it were the most natural thing in the world.

I reached down and cupped her big globes in both hands, tugging her thick nipples with my fingertips. Her tit flesh was warm and smooth, stretched tight over her firm breasts.

I pushed her mouth away before she could make me come. She lay back and opened her legs, her eyes half-closed. Before I could put my dick in her, though, she said, "Jim, I'm not on the pill or anything. Do you have something?"

Damn. Of course, I had a rubber in reserve, just in case. But I couldn't help showing my disappointment. The hell with safe sex. When I fuck, I want to feel wet, silky pussy around my dick, not a damned latex sausage casing

Seeing I was annoyed, Laura said, "Please use one for me, Jim. Believe me, I really do want you to fuck me."

She must have seen how much it turned me on to hear this strait-laced beauty say the word "fuck," because she added, "Please hurry, so you can fuck me right away. I want to fuck so much I feel like I'm burning up inside."

I got the rubber out of my pants pocket and rolled it down over my prick in two seconds flat. I teased her pussy lips with the head of my now-covered dick, then pushed it all the way in with one hard thrust. She squealed with surprise, holding on tight while I plowed that virgin furrow between her legs. She was so juicy we were making slurping sounds.

She came again, clawing at my back and panting. I started feeling the pressure building in my balls and said, "Laura, I'm going to come."

"Pull out quick and let me see," she said, looking down at where we were joined. "I want to watch it happen. Don't take off the rubber, just let me see you filling it up."

I thought that was kind of weird. I would have preferred snatching the stupid thing off and shooting on her belly and up onto her tits. I wasn't going to ruin the moment, though, so I did as I was told.

I slipped my cock out of her cunt and started spurting. My semen quickly filled the reservoir tip of the rubber, making it stand out from my dick like a long white nipple. More of my come backed up to surround the head of my cock.

Laura scooted down between my legs to get a better view. Impetuously, she grabbed my sheathed dick and licked her pussy juice off the latex. Then she put her lips around the full tip of the rubber. She amazed me by biting down hard on that protruding tip and shaking her head from side to side, tearing the whole end of the rubber open so semen spilled out onto her face and mouth.

"Mmmmm," she sighed, licking the stuff from her lips. "It tastes wonderful."

I felt like kicking myself for wasting all those years I could have been fucking what turned out to be a wild bitch in librarian's clothing. She started sucking my dickhead where it bulged from the torn rubber, drawing out even more of my come.

Laura scooted up in bed so her head was nestled in the crook of my arm, and kissed me while I played with her tits. "Well, was it anything like what you thought it would be?" I asked.

"You were better than any of the others, Jim. You were fantastic."

My eyes popped open in surprise. "Better than the others?"

"Definitely. Of all the guys I've fucked, you're the best. And you eat pussy like a champ."

"But I thought...I mean, what about your vow?"

She put her hand on my cock. "Come on, Jim. I broke that vow as soon as I got out in the real world and realized what I'd been missing. But thanks for thinking I still was a good girl. It made tonight pretty interesting, didn't it?"

"But what about that trouble you said you were having writing a love scene?"

"Oh, that. There's a scene in my book where a couple of girls are in bed with a guy. I'm not the delicate virgin I was in college, but I haven't had that particular experience yet. You can't help me out, can you?"

"Let me think about it," I said, rolling on top of her so I could put my dick between her big jugs. "I just might have somebody in mind."

I sure hoped Beverly Morrison didn't have cheerleading practice tomorrow night.

The Milk Wagon

I was the set-up crew's most recent hire and it was my first day on the job. That's why I thought the other guys had to be kidding when they told me about the milk wagon. I assumed it was just another one of those hazing things, like telling the new guy to find a left-handed screwdriver.

"You think we're just pulling your leg, don't you?" Randy, the beefy crew supervisor, was squinting at me in the bright sun. We were standing in the parking lot of a just-built shopping center. He had been telling me and the other guys where to put sections of metal shelves in an otherwise empty grocery store. We were taking a break before starting on another pallet's worth of the things.

I put on my best shit-eating grin. "Yeah, I definitely think you're pulling something." I looked around at the other guys for their approval. A couple of them smiled.

Randy wiped his sweaty forehead on the sleeve of his T-shirt. "Okay, pal. Feel free to stay right here when the wagon comes around, then. You'll just be leaving more for me." Then he gestured at the pallet of shelves and addressed all of us. "Now let's get this stuff inside, before it gets too much hotter out here."

As I helped carry the six-foot shelving sections, I thought about how ridiculous Randy's story had sounded. Did he really expect me to believe that the women who ran the mobile food van would...nah, it was just too ridiculous. I would look like a damned idiot if I asked them about what Randy called their "special services." I figured that probably was the point. I would look stupid, and all the guys would get a good laugh at my expense.

But what if Randy's story actually were true?

About an hour later, I heard the bells of the roach coach as it turned into the parking lot. It was just in time, too. I felt like I had worked off five pounds since morning, and I was starving.

When the big side panel of the van opened up, I stared in disbelief. Just as Randy had said, the three women behind the counter were all big-busted and really good-looking. One was blond, one redhead and one brunette. And none of them had a bust size smaller than a D-cup.

The list of food prices seemed high, but these girls probably didn't have any trouble getting customers to pay them. Then I saw something at the bottom of the list that shocked me: "Special Services: Inquire."

My dick started stiffening in my jeans. I tried casually putting a hand in my pocket to shift my cock to a better angle, giving it room to grow.

Randy gave me a smug look, then whispered something in the redhead's ear. She whispered something back. Randy checked his wallet. He nodded at her and headed for the rear of the van. It was longer than any roach coach I'd ever seen, more like a Winnebago or a mobile home, with lots of room beyond the food serving area up front. A side door opened. Randy went inside.

"And what'll you be having today, handsome?" The blond was talking to me. Her big tits were practically hanging out of the low-cut neckline of her tank top. It was real damned obvious she wasn't wearing a bra. The sides of her swollen jugs bulged out of the shirt's big armholes. Her nipples looked like two stubby fingers pushing against the stretched material.

I made a show of scanning the menu again, but I knew what I wanted. And I wanted it bad enough that I didn't mind the risk that I might be making a fool of myself by asking for it.

I stepped close to the van. "Uh, could you tell me about your...special services?"

She gave me a slutty smile that made my dick get harder. "Sure, handsome. Those are special things some guys like to have for lunch. What did you have in mind?"

I leaned close to her, so none of the other guys could hear. "How much for some milk?"

She gave me a figure that was roughly equal to half a day's pay. But when she took a deep breath that made her mammaries swell even bigger, I didn't feel like haggling.

The side door of the van opened and I stepped inside. The place was decorated like a plush whorehouse on wheels, with embroidered red carpet and dark wood paneling. The blond was waiting for me in the narrow hallway.

She didn't have on anything below the waist, not even underwear. Her light blond pubic bush was trimmed way back, exposing the thick pink lips of her cunt. Now that I was inside the van, I could see that the brunette up front was bottomless, too. No one outside could tell, because the side panel window wasn't low enough to show anything below the girls' waists.

"I'm Robbie, by the way," I said.

"I'm Tammy," she said, holding open a door that led into a small bedroom. "We're going to have a really good time, Robbie. Come on inside."

She entered the room ahead of me. Her ass was perfect, hard and firm, with a deep crack. The double bed in the room had a blue silk spread. She sat down on it and casually pulled her tank top over her head.

Her oversized globes hung halfway to her flat belly. They looked like they were full of what I had come here for. Their nipples had deep indentations in their tips, making it obvious they were there for more than just show.

"Why don't you pull out your cock, Robbie? I can see it bulging in your pants. Go ahead and take that big prick out for me to see." As she said it she started massaging her tits, squeezing them roughly. She took each of her nipples between a thumb and index finger, tugging them.

I dropped my pants and jockey shorts and kicked them aside. My boner swayed in front of me like a club as I watched Tammy play with her tits. I grabbed my cock down at its base and stroked myself while I stared at her.

She had her head thrown back, obviously enjoying what she was doing to herself. I watched as two thick drops of milk appeared at the tips of her oversized nipples. Then she cupped both of her breasts from underneath and held them away from her body, as if offering them to me for my approval. The thick drops of milk hung from their tips like perfect white pearls.

"Your milk is ready, Robbie," she breathed. "I think you'll agree you won't find any that's fresher than mine."

I dropped to my knees, put my mouth on one of her big nipples, and started to suck. A gusher of warm, thick milk filled my mouth. All the while, I kept tugging my cock, which felt like it was ready to start shooting at any minute.

I have to confess that I love the taste of mother's milk, fresh from a girl's swollen teats. It was my one fetish, the thing I always wanted that almost none of my girlfriends could provide.

I had been fortunate enough to meet one girl who was a milker the year after I graduated high school. She wasn't knocked up or anything, just one of those girls with a weird metabolism who always was lactating. I'm not kidding, girls like that really do exist, but they're damned hard to find.

This one loved to be sucked dry, and I was always more than willing to accommodate. But then she went away to college, and I hadn't heard from her since. I always half-assumed she was using her deliciously milky jugs these days on her professors, to help her grade-point average.

Then there was the young mother I was banging last year. Her husband was away on business a lot at the time. But she was permanently horny, and loved having a man drink the milk from her heavy, womanly breasts. After hubby stopped going on the road, she decided to play the faithful spouse and cut me off.

There had been a couple of others, but they never seemed to be available for long. Milkers know exactly how rare and precious they are. They also know they can pick and choose from the multitudes of men who adore their special talent.

I gently squeezed Tammy's huge breast, increasing its milk flow into my mouth. I flicked at her spurting nipple with my tongue, which made her shudder with pleasure. Like most mothers' milk, hers was very sweet. But unlike the milkers I had tasted before, her breast beverage was almost as thick as cream.

Also, none of the titters I'd known before were able to produce more than a half-pint at a time from each jug, and usually a lot less. But I was sure that I already had swallowed more than that from Tammy's left tit alone. She was a genuine dairy queen.

When I moved my mouth over to her other milkbag, I noticed that her left tit had lost only a little of its round firmness. It still jutted out from her slender chest like a pretty pink torpedo.

"Oh, yeah, that feels great," Tammy moaned. "Keep sucking my big titties. Drink all the milk from by swollen breasts, lover." She pushed her chest against my mouth. Some of her milk spilled down my chin and onto her smooth belly.

She found the hand I was using to jerk myself off and took over for me, encircling my stiff cock with her delicate fingers. I still was nursing at her breast, slurping down her chest cream. Her fingertips caressed my dickhead.

"Come on and fuck me with this, Robbie. Fuck me while you're sucking out my milk. God, I need your dick in me now."

She sounded as if she actually meant it, not like a hooker saying what she thought a customer would want to hear. I knew that some milkers got really turned on during feedings, because their nipples were such powerful erogenous zones. I never expected that I would get to fuck this big-titted beauty as well as drinking her milk, but I sure as hell wasn't going to turn down the opportunity.

Tammy scooted back on the small bed and spread her legs. The way she looked at that moment is burned into my brain for life. Her huge, sloppy tits were hanging to either side of her chest. They glistened with my saliva and the milk that had dribbled down over her taut tit-skin. Her nipples stood out at least two inches from her dark pink halos, with milk drops bubbling from both of their tips.

Her belly was smooth and flat. Her nicely toned legs were bent at the knees and splayed, completely exposing her well-trimmed crotch. Her sex slit was gaping open, its fleshy lips parted to reveal her shining pink fuckhole. An inch below it, her dainty pink anus peeked out from the shadow of her deep crack.

And on her face was the dirtiest "fuck-me" expression I'd ever seen.

I climbed on top of her and shoved my cock into her cunt. She gripped my dick with her pussy muscle each time I pushed inside her, like she didn't want to let me go. She was tight as a virgin, as far up as my cock could reach, and she gave a little gasp each time I lunged inside her body.

"Yeah, fuck me good," she moaned. "Suck my milk while you're fucking me, Robbie. I want to give you my warm milk."

She held up her right tit, pushing it toward my mouth. When I put my lips on its nipple, she craned her neck to lick it along with me. Both of our tongues swirled around her milky nipple while I plowed her gripping love hole.

I couldn't take any more. I pulled my cock out of her pussy and knee-walked up the bed to her face. "Stop sucking that and suck this, baby," I said. "Suck it hard!"

Tammy opened wide and engulfed my stiff dick. I loved watching her blow me. I loved knowing that she was tasting her own pussy juice as she sucked my rod. She was tugging her nipples the whole time.

"Yeah, that's it. Eat that cock, Tammy. Suck my dick milk right out of me."

She made little mewing sounds as she nursed at my pole. My balls drew up tight. I felt my load start pulsing up the length of my cock and shooting into Tammy's mouth, gushing in long, thick spurts. She gulped it all down, and kept sucking even after I was drained.

For the rest of that day, I wanted to kick myself for not trying to get her phone number or address. After shooting my wad, I had kind of half-stumbled out of the van in a daze. A minute later, it was gone.

Randy told me it wouldn't have mattered anyway. "They never let anybody know how to get in touch with them," he said. "My theory is that they're all married with kids, and picking up money on the side this way. Or maybe they're a bunch of rich society girls getting their thrills from banging us sweaty blue-collar types."

"Do you always take the redhead?" I asked.

"Yeah, pretty much. I like to fuck her in the ass after I've sucked the milk out of her tits. The other two aren't as good at taking it up their back door as she is. But that redhead...she practically uses her asshole like a second cunt, the way she can clamp down on a cock."

"And all three of the girls give milk?"

"That's the one specialty they have in common, just like I told you this morning. I don't know if they're pregnant, or if they all just had kids, or what the fuck their story is. But any of them can give a guy more sweet milk than he can handle. Now, aren't you sorry you doubted me?"

"I sure as hell am. But I'll go broke if I keep paying that blond's price."

Randy gave me a philosophical look. "Would you rather spend your money on meaningless things like beer, food and shelter?"

"I guess you've got a point."

Every day for the next two weeks, I blew a generous portion of my salary milking Tammy's teats in the back of that van and fucking her creamy cunt. Just like Randy said, she never would give me her phone number or address. Hell, maybe I was better off, I thought. This way, I could only pay once a day. If Tammy were available around the clock, I probably would go bankrupt sucking her sweet sweater-melons.

On Monday of my third week on the job, I popped a bone as soon as I heard the roach coach ringing its bells on its way into the parking lot. But when the side panel went up, I was shocked to see three guys behind the food counter.

A bunch of my fellow crewmembers started grumbling. Randy spoke up. "Where the hell are the girls?"

"Sorry, guys, but they hired us to run the van for them. They said they had made enough money to start being bosses and stop being workers."

My hard-on wilted. I felt like hitting somebody, or breaking something, or maybe just sitting down on the asphalt and crying.

The sound of a close-by car horn made me jump. A snowy white Lexus braked to a stop next to me.

Tammy was inside. Her fat knockers pushed the front of her dress out so far that it was obvious she needed a good milking. She leaned out and said, "You didn't think I would forget about you, did you?"

"Well, I..."

"Here," she said, smiling. She handed me a card with an address on it. "Come see me sometime, Robbie. And make it soon. My titties are full of milk, and they need lots of attention."

"Tammy, I..."

"And by the way, there won't be any more charges for my special services. The girls and I have decided to put pleasure before business, now that we've moved from labor to management."

She stepped on the gas before I could say anything.

I yelled to Randy that I was taking the afternoon off as I ran to my car. All of a sudden, I was dying of thirst.

Crack Reporter

The rookie detective moaned softly as I flicked the tip of my tongue up and down the length of his hard, pulsing cock. We were in the back of his unmarked Dodge. I had convinced him to move it a discreet distance from the crime scene.

He had his pants open to give me easy access to his hard-on. I was sideways on the car's floor with my knees on the mat, low enough so nobody could see me from outside. The red and blue lights of the nearby patrol cars made a light show through the windows as I bobbed up and down on his stiff dick.

"Oh, yeah," he sighed. "You really know how to do it. Just like that. Don't stop, keep sucking my dick that way."

My blond hair grazed teasingly against his tight ball bag. My mouth was full of saliva, making his thick cock nice and shiny and slippery.

He liked it when I took his whole dick in my mouth at one time. Then I would let my lips rest against his springy pubic hair, with the swollen head of his cock way back in my throat, so he could get the full effect. Like most guys, he probably never had been deep-throated before. Hell, most guys probably count themselves lucky if they get decent head, period.

He hadn't seen anything yet.

With his entire dick still in my mouth, I began swallowing, over and over. My throat muscles tugged insistently on his cock, making it grow even bigger.

He made whimpering sounds when I did that. I knew he was close to coming. But I didn't want things to reach their climax until I was sure that I would get what I wanted out of the experience, too.

I backed off with my mouth, but gripped the base of his cock with my thumb and index finger to keep the pressure on. I knew I could keep him rock-hard forever that way, if I wanted.

"Are you going to give me the suspect's name?" I whispered. "Are you going to tell me what you've got on the guy, or am I going to have to find out from somebody else?"

I gave his cockhead a tantalizing lick, then waited.

I didn't have long to wait.

"The suspect is Brian Albarn, we found his prints all over the house and a neighbor IDed his car," the detective breathed.

"You mean the same Albarn who's pushing the anti-crime initiative in the state senate?"

"Pretty fuckin' ironic, huh?" He pulled my head closer to his cock. "Now hurry up and finish me off, because I'm ready to explode. Suck my cock some more, beautiful. Put those red lips around my dick before the cops at the scene wonder what the fuck I've been doing over here for so long."

"My pleasure, detective." I took his rod in my mouth again and really started working it, rubbing the flat of my tongue all over the underside of his cock. A few more deep-throat moves and his dick was jerking in my mouth. His come slipped down my throat like a warm oyster.

I straightened my hair and hurried to my car, getting out my phone. Now I had a story to call in to my editor that would make every other newspaper's coverage of this murder look pathetic.

Another suck, another scoop. At this rate, I would have a Pulitzer in no time.

The large metropolitan daily where I work would fire me in a second if the publisher knew the real secret of my success. I didn't get where I am in the newspaper biz by busting my ass and beating the bushes. I've gotten my stories because of my bust, my ass and baring my bush. You might say that I've uncovered my biggest stories from under the covers.

To say that I know my sources "intimately" would be putting it mildly. I've spread my legs and opened my mouth for the cocks of firemen, cops, accident investigators and bureaucrats. I even did the county coroner once, when I was on a hard deadline.

The *Washington Journalism Review* might not think too highly of newsgathering techniques like mine. But I've enjoyed every wicked minute of getting my sources to reveal more of themselves—so to speak.

Want to know what a female reporter really goes through to get a good story? Well, don't believe all that crap about research and perseverance and luck. For me, getting facts has always meant giving fucks.

On one occasion, letting a security guard have his way with my neatly shaved pussy gained me instant access to a locked file room after hours. Guys like that can get pretty lonely in an empty municipal building at night. Believe me, they don't ask any questions when a pretty girl knocks on the door and asks if she can use the phone because her car broke down. And if that same oversexed girl happens to start doing a slow striptease in the lobby once she's inside, you can bet that he's not going to get all official and ask her to leave.

I took everything off, watching him break a sweat and run a finger around the inside of his collar. He started to say something a couple of times, but nothing came out. When I was completely naked, I scooted my butt up onto his desk. Then I slowly spread my legs, leaned back against the screen of his security monitor and said, "Come on and eat me out. I want you to shove your tongue all the way up my hot pussy."

It wasn't all work and no play, either. The guy really knew what he was doing down there. As he ran his tongue up and down the pink folds of my cunt, I felt my honey start to flow. He lapped it up and kept coming back for more. An electric current seemed to be running directly from my clit to my hard nipples. Before long, I was bucking against his mouth, in the throes of an orgasm that echoed off the empty lobby walls.

I hadn't planned on letting him fuck me, but at that point I was so worked up I found myself begging him to do it. Still sitting on his desk, I reached down and held open my cunt with my fingers.

"You've got to give it to me now," I said. "I'm so hot I've got to have it. Give me your cock, ram it deep in my cunt and fuck me hard."

I gave a little cry as I watched his big, beautiful dick slide all the way into my little pussy with one hard thrust. I reached down to rub and squeeze his balls as he pumped my cunt. The buttons on his shirt-pocket flaps were rubbing against my hard nipples as he slammed his hot cock in and out of my clutching, hungry hole.

He cupped my ass cheeks and lifted me up off the desk, with his cock still embedded in my cunt. I held on tight, loving his heat and his strength and his big, hard dick up inside me. He slipped one of his fingers down my crack. Then he rubbed that finger in circles around my asshole, while we fucked. We were both trembling and panting, and he shouted out when he came.

He didn't give a damn when I told him that I had lied about my "car trouble" and that I was really a reporter. In exchange for his midnight snack and after-hours workout, he was more than happy to let me rummage in the file room to my heart's content. I found enough dirt to put three not-so-dedicated public servants away for five years. Not a bad night's work.

On another occasion, sucking an arson investigator's cock until it exploded in my mouth enabled me to be the first to report that a building bombing was arranged by its bankrupt owner. At first the crime-scene investigator seemed annoyed when I remained in his office after his "official" press briefing ended. He didn't seem so annoyed when I locked his door, came around his desk, unzipped his fly and fished out his cock.

"What are you…" he began, but I put a finger on his lips to shush him. Then I wrapped my own lips around his dick. It lengthened and stiffened in my warm, wet mouth. Instead of resisting, he put his fingers in my hair to hold my face close to his crotch.

Still on my knees, I unbuttoned my blouse and unsnapped the front clasp of my bra. The whole time, I was looking submissively up at him with his cock still in my mouth. You should have seen his eyes light up when I started tugging on my nipples, getting them nice and hard. Then I took my mouth from his meat, pushed out my chest and pressed my soft titties around his hard-on.

With my hands at their sides, I pressed my firm tits snugly around his cock, like I was making a surrogate cunt with my breasts. His tool was surrounded by my smooth, warm breast flesh. He started pumping his cock between my tits. I bent my neck so I could suck his cockhead each time it emerged from that soft valley.

Not a whole lot of conversation goes on when a guy unexpectedly gets the chance to use his dick for something other than taking a piss. It's almost like a man thinks he might break the magic spell if he says anything, and that I'll vanish in a pink puff of smoke. That's okay with me, so long as the silent treatment ends when I start asking questions later.

This guy's dick must have been starved for attention, because he was shooting his load in no time. I swallowed every hot gusher. A dedicated reporter knows the importance of doing good follow-up work, after all.

At that point, he had a lot to say about things he wasn't supposed to reveal. You would be surprised how forthcoming a guy can be when he's finished coming.

Surprisingly, some of my biggest stories have required the least effort on my part. For example, uncovering the mayor's cocaine habit was a snap, thanks to my snatch. All it took was a quickie with his executive assistant on a day when I noticed that His Honor was looking a little shaky.

The flunky and I did it on the sofa of the mayor's own office while he was at lunch. Funny thing is, the guy actually seemed pleased that my dripping-wet pussy and his spurting cock made such a slippery mess all over the mayor's imported leather upholstery. So much for political loyalty.

After he finished plowing my cunt, he told me where the mayor was meeting his dealer that night. I was there with a photographer, who got the whole transaction in living color.

Don't get me wrong, I didn't start out knowing these unwritten tricks of my trade. It took me a while to learn the ins-and-outs. My journalism professors didn't teach me how to use my hot tits and body to get hot tips and bylines.

When I was an idealistic cub reporter straight out of college, I tried the traditional route of cultivating sources: taking them to lunch, interviewing them by phone and making appointments to visit their offices. I got the basics that way, but never anything special.

My editor eventually called me into his office to say I would have to digging up better stuff if I wanted to get anywhere in this profession. I took that as a warning—and a challenge.

At my apartment that night, I thought about my situation as I took a shower. I knew I would have to think of something that would give me an edge, but what? When I turned off the water and reached for a towel, the answer was right in front of me.

I had been working out at a health club twice each week since graduating, trying to lose some of my baby fat. Until the moment I stepped out of the shower, I didn't realize how good a job I had done. I'd transformed myself from a chubby undergraduate into the voluptuous woman who stood naked before me in the full-length mirror.

I took note of my rounded, firm breasts, my flat stomach and my long legs. Droplets of water glistened in my neatly trimmed pubic hair. My skin was pink and flawless and free of any swimsuit lines, thanks to my nude sessions on the club's tanning bed. I turned in profile to check out the smooth, tight curve where my ass cheeks met my well-toned thighs. Like my tits, my butt didn't show even a hint of sag.

I turned my back to the mirror, then looked back over my shoulder at myself. A wave of pride came over me as I surveyed the hard, round globes of my ass. Feeling more than a little naughty, I bent at the waist and leaned away from the mirror while holding my cheeks apart. That way, I could see the puckered little rosebud of my asshole and the puffy, soft lips of my pussy from behind. Moving my fingertips to my cunt, I held my labia open to look at the pretty pinkness inside.

I decided it was time to put all of my previously hidden assets to work. The next day, I arrived at the police station as usual to go over the police blotter with Sergeant O'Reilly. He was beefy and bald, in his mid-50s, with a gruff voice. In the past, I had dealt with him the way I would any other authority figure: with deference and humble gratitude for whatever scraps of information he would throw to me. Today was going to be different.

I was wearing an ensemble that I thought he wouldn't be able to resist: a pleated plaid skirt, a button-up white cotton blouse, knee socks and black patent leather shoes. Call it a professional hunch, but I had a feeling he would go for the Catholic schoolgirl look. What red-blooded Irishman wouldn't?

I sat with my note pad on my lap and my bare knees pressed together demurely. I could tell he was eyeing my legs and breasts as he went over the details of the previous night's drug bust.

Finally, he couldn't resist commenting on my appearance. "That's a nice outfit you have on today, Melissa." His voice was lower than usual, and a thin sheen of sweat glistened on his bald head. His eyes were doing a full-perimeter assessment of my body. It was obvious that he wanted to take his investigation further. The term "full cavity search" came to mind.

I had wondered when I put on this "jailbait of the month" outfit that morning whether the kind of lewd attention I was getting would make me feel uncomfortable. It had exactly the opposite effect. As I watched the nervous way he tried to avoid staring, I actually started getting excited.

I was getting wet between the legs, and I'm sure my face was flushed. The pup tent rising in the sergeant's pants showed that he was getting aroused, too. When our eyes finally met, I gave him an innocent smile and slowly opened my legs.

Silly me, it seems I had forgotten to put on any panties. My cunt was lubricating so much that the tops of my inner thighs were wet and shiny in the fluorescent light.

The sergeant maneuvered from behind his desk with the agility of a 22-year-old street cop, dropped to his knees, pushed up my skirt and buried his face in my bare crotch. I scooted my butt to the edge of the chair, giving him easier access to my slick, hot pussy. He licked me like his tongue was on loan from the K-9 corps.

"Why, sergeant," I said coyly, rubbing his shiny bald head. "I never thought you were such an animal."

The next thing I knew, we were on the floor and I was helping him get out of uniform. His cock stood up like a billy club when I freed it from his underwear. My right hand worked his thick shaft as we played tongue tag. He was fondling my firm C-cuppers and nuzzling my neck. He seemed particularly to enjoy squeezing and tugging my nipples, which were getting very stiff from the attention.

"You know," he said, "I've been imagining what these tits of yours would look like since the first day you walked in here with that goddamned notepad. They're even nicer than I expected. Especially these pretty little nipples." He covered one of them with his mouth. He slipped a finger inside my cunt and worked it in and out while he sucked me.

"You know," I said, imitating him, "I've been imagining what this penis of yours would look like since the first day I walked in here with that goddamned notepad, too. And believe me, sarge, I'm not disappointed!"

I was jerking up and down on his hard tool so hard it's a wonder it didn't come off in my hand. He reached around and lifted me from the chair, put me down on my back on the industrial carpet and got between my legs. He'd had the good sense to close his office door before he began filling me in on the police report, and filling me up now.

He grunted as if he didn't give a damn who might hear him in the waiting room as he thrust his baton in and out of my body. My cunt muscles were as well-toned as the rest of me. I squeezed down on his cock with my pussy like I was putting it in a chokehold. He grunted like…well, like a pig, actually…when he came.

I didn't waste a second. While he was basking in the glow of a job well done, I found my notepad and pen. Still lying beside him on the floor, I said, "Now about that drug bust…"

"The stuff was planted," he said in a dreamy whisper. "That schmuck who owns the store wasn't paid-up on the protection money he owes one of the captains here."

As the post-fuck fuzziness cleared from his brain, he started to look uncomfortable. "This conversation is all off the record, right?"

I just smiled. The next day, my series on "Bad Cops" started running. It was good enough that my editor entered it in a state journalism contest.

I knew I didn't have any real competition for the award when I got a look at the other reporters whose stories were up for it. Two of them were old guys with potbellies. The other two were old broads who probably hadn't seen a hard dick since the turn of the century. It was a safe bet that they couldn't get their sources to open up by opening up, the way I could.

I can only laugh when I think of the emcee's words when he handed me the top prize.

"Congratulations," he said. "It's obvious from your work that you're a crack reporter."

If he only knew.

The New Girl

An Interactive Erotic Tale In Which YOU Pick the Ending!

Ms. Reynolds simultaneously slammed down her telephone receiver, swiveled a quarter-arc in her chair and barked, "You're the new girl, right?"

Just as she had planned, she caught the Brentline Company's newest employee completely off-guard. The baby-faced secretary was so startled by the abruptness of the question that she dropped a sheaf of papers.

Red-faced, the younger woman started to squat and pick them up. Then she froze in mid-motion and looked up questioningly, biting her full bottom lip, unsure whether to proceed.

Ms. Reynolds waved her hand dismissively and sighed. "Yes, yes, go ahead, by all means."

The new secretary began gathering the sheets from the carpet. "Thank you, ma'am," she whispered. "I guess I'm a little nervous. First-day jitters, you know."

Ms. Reynolds permitted herself a tight smile. This was going perfectly, she thought. Looking down her nose, she asked, "Do you have a name?"

"Cassie...I mean, Cassandra McBride, ma'am."

"You can lose the 'ma'am.' Just call me Ms. Reynolds."

"All right, Ms. Reynolds."

This...*Cassie*...must have made it a point to wear her most businesslike outfit today, Ms. Reynolds surmised. She undoubtedly was trying to make a good impression on her first day, with her expensive charcoal skirt and jacket. Her shining blond hair was pulled back in a tidy bun. She apparently had heard that Brentline was a conservative firm, and had made an effort to dress the part.

But there was nothing conservative about this little 18-year-old bitch's body, Ms. Reynolds noted. Even though the young tart had tried to disguise her bust and rear end with the straight lines of her business suit, her lush figure still was obvious.

Her jacket was buttoned as if she wanted to avoid drawing attention to her chest, but her big bustline was much too prominent to hide.

The fresh-faced teenager reached behind herself to pick up another stray sheet of paper. Her jacket gapped open, revealing the swollen profile of her left breast. Her blouse was stretched so tightly across her bosom that the fine lace pattern of her bra was clearly visible. So was the stub of her nipple.

She was trying to keep her knees together in a ladylike fashion. Her legs had the sheen of real silk stockings.

"You are already proficient with our spreadsheet program, is that correct?"

"Oh, yes, Ms. Reynolds. I've worked with a number of those programs, on both PCs and Macs. Plus I know... "

"Fine, I don't need to hear your whole résumé. I wish Personnel would consult me before making their hiring decisions, but they apparently think they know what they're doing."

Cassie stood, straightening her papers. She gave a quick smile of apology. Her teeth were perfect. Her cheeks still were flushed, giving her the look of a mischievous girl trying to play grown-up.

Ms. Reynolds drummed her fingers on the desktop. Finally, she pushed her chair back. "Very well, come with me and I'll show you to your work station."

Cassie dutifully followed her down a hallway illuminated by tastefully recessed lighting.

Ms. Reynolds had a good idea of what probably was going through the new girl's mind. She probably was naive enough to think that she could use her secretary's job as a stepping-stone to a Vice President position and a corner office. Growing up with a body like hers—with that more than ample bustline and those long legs and that perfectly innocent face—she probably has gotten whatever she wanted all her life.

It was high time that she learned a little lesson about how things worked in the real world.

"You'll be Mr. Kegren's secretary, but like all of the girls you will report to me," she said. "I'm the Office Manager here. Don't forget that."

"I won't forget," Cassie answered quietly.

"Here we are." Ms. Reynolds stopped at an open doorway. Windows with mini-blinds separated a secretarial anteroom from the hall. An inner door led to Mr. Kegren's private office. As Cassie took a seat behind her new desk, Ms. Reynolds knocked on that inner door. No answer.

"He must still be at his staff meeting," Ms. Reynolds said. "That's good. This way we can clear up a few things about your background before he gets back." She closed the door to the hall.

Cassie shifted her feet, but her face remained blank. "What exactly did you want to know?"

Ms. Reynolds thought she detected a hint of annoyance in Cassie's voice. She probably thinks questions about her skills are a waste of time, now that she has the job. And was the arrogant little bitch sitting that way on purpose, with her shoulders thrown back to emphasize the proportions of her oversized tits?

Ms. Reynolds cleared her throat. "Firstly, I would like to know exactly how much practice you've had at cocksucking."

Cassie's eyes went wide. When she finally managed to open her mouth, nothing came out.

"Come now, Cassie, it's not that hard a question." Ms. Reynolds sat on a corner of the desk and glared down at her new underling. "Exactly how good are you at giving head?"

Cassie remained silent. Her face was red again, much redder than when she had dropped her papers. It was funny how many of the new girls blushed that same way, Ms. Reynolds thought.

She wondered what went through their minds at this point. Maybe they thought the question was part of some strange psychological test, or perhaps it reminded them of the truth-or-dare questions they asked each other at slumber parties. Some of them might wonder if this was the Brentline Company's method of spotting overly sensitive employees who might make harassment complaints. Or maybe they thought Ms. Reynolds was a domineering sicko who got her kicks hearing about their sexual exploits.

Ms. Reynolds didn't give a damn what they thought.

She delicately plucked a piece of lint from the padded shoulder of Cassie's jacket. "Don't be afraid to answer, dear," she said. "Just be honest."

"I...I don't really like talking about those kinds of things."

"About what kinds of things, dear?"

Cassie folded her hands in her lap and stared at them. "Please, could we talk about something else?"

Ms. Reynolds got off the desk to pace like a determined trial lawyer. "All right. If you don't want to talk about sucking cock, how about describing something else you did the last time you had sex. Was it with a man? With two men? Or maybe with a woman?"

When she didn't get an answer, she leaned across the desk to put her face directly in front of Cassie's. "Let me phrase that differently. I want to know all about the last time you used your cunt, your mouth and that fat pair of tits you're trying to hide behind your prim-and-proper dress-for-success jacket."

Cassie's mouth was set in a straight line. Her big bustline was rising and falling with each of her quick, shallow breaths. Her eyes were so wet that tears might roll from them at any second.

She has to say something, Ms. Reynolds thought. She's afraid of me, afraid to speak up to her new supervisor on her first day at her new job, but she can't just ignore me.

Or can she?

They stared at each other. Ms. Reynolds felt a frisson of pleasure as she basked in Cassie's wordless contempt. Such delicious resentment! The pouting little tramp must be agonizing over the thought that working for me will be a living hell, but she still won't speak up.

Ms. Reynolds grinned, revealing tiny cracks in her rose petal lipstick. "What's the matter, Cassie? Don't tell me you're actually embarrassed about the things you do with your sexy little body."

Cassie said nothing.

Ms. Reynolds came even closer, so close she knew Cassie could feel her breath on her full lips. "And surely you're not ashamed of what you let your dirty boyfriends do to you with their big, stiff dicks? Don't you have anything at all to say for yourself, you stupid slut?"

That last word seemed to hit Cassie like a slap in the face. Something in the younger woman's expression changed from fear to naked hatred.

Bingo, Ms. Reynolds thought.

"I'm not ashamed of anything I do in bed," Cassie said hotly. "Why the hell should I be?"

Ms. Reynolds' cocked an eyebrow appreciatively. "There, that's more like it. Now, what exactly is it that you're not ashamed of doing?"

Cassie leaned back in her chair. She crossed her arms under her breasts in a way that made it obvious she was emphasizing them.

"I'm not ashamed of the way I suck men off and let them fuck me. I'm not ashamed of how I use my tits and my ass and my pussy to please my boyfriends."

"And when was the last time you…"

"Yesterday afternoon I got fucked good and hard," Cassie interrupted. "A guy I've been seeing came over with a movie he had rented, but we didn't bother watching it. I was so horny I already had masturbated that morning in the bathtub, just thinking about him. He's got a long, thick cock, with a head that's bigger around than the shaft. We call it his baton. That's our name for it, because his dickhead's like the thick rubber bulb on a twirling baton."

Ms. Reynolds was nodding slowly. Her sneer was still in place, but her head was trembling slightly. This was working out even better than she had hoped.

Cassie had to know that even if she shut up now, the damage was done. There was no way she could possibly take back what she had said.

She didn't look as if she cared. On the contrary, she looked like she was glad for the chance to stand up for herself.

Ms. Reynolds idly wondered how many times Cassie had been called a slut—or treated like one—for the word to elicit such a swift and delightfully crude reaction. "Don't stop there," she said. "I'm all ears."

"I'll bet you are," Cassie smirked. "When's the last time you got any dick, Ms. Reynolds? Is this your kinky way of getting off?"

"I'll ask the questions around here, young lady."

"Yeah, whatever. I'll play your little game." Cassie unbuttoned her jacket, letting her bustline swell even bigger. "My boyfriends usually like to fuck my tits before they put their cocks in me. I like it, too. I like to push my big titties together around a hard dick that's pumping between them. Sometimes guys squirt baby oil all over my tits to help their dicks slide better. But most of the time, I'm so hot and sweaty they don't need any help."

Cassie smiled smugly. "It's really so goddamned nice to have a big set of tits, Ms. Reynolds. All day long, I know men are staring at me. They think I don't notice, but I do. They all want to touch and suck and fuck my beautiful tits. They probably try to imagine what kind of nipples I have, the big, sloppy kind or the dainty, gumdrop type. When I wear a swimsuit, they don't have to wonder. That's because I only wear the styles that show off everything I've got. I'll bet you think that's pretty immodest, don't you?"

"Looking like common trash? Yes, I do think that's immodest."

"Big fucking surprise. You flat-chested bitches can't stand to see a busty girl flaunting her assets, can you? Christ, you should see the nasty looks I get from women when I go braless, with my big nipples sticking out and my tits bouncing. To tell the truth, it's pretty fucking satisfying to get those kinds of looks."

The phone on Cassie's desk chirped. Cassie calmly lifted the receiver and dropped it back in place without looking at it. Ms. Reynolds was horrified. Before she could say anything, Cassie was talking again.

"Every dog who got shortchanged in the looks department wishes she had my face, my legs and my ass. But they especially wish they had my tits. The desperate ones pay for fakes, but mine are 100-percent real. And don't think men can't tell the difference." She casually gave both of her breasts a loving squeeze. "Every woman wishes she had a pair like mine. You certainly wish you did, don't you, Ms. Reynolds?"

Ms. Reynolds drew a sharp breath. "I'm not the issue here, you impudent bitch."

Cassie ignored her. "You wish you could feel a pair of big, heavy breasts swinging back and forth under your body when you're on all fours and a man is fucking you from behind. Or that you could sit on a man's cock and slap his face with your swollen tits while he thrusts in and out of your hot cunt. You wish you could hold your breasts up and share them with a man, both of you running your tongues all over your nipples at the same time. Isn't that right?"

Ms. Reynolds narrowed her eyes. "You're really quite a foul-mouthed little slut, aren't you?"

"Men like foul-mouthed little sluts, Ms. Reynolds. In fact, they absolutely adore us. Or haven't you noticed?"

*

And now, dear reader, it's your turn to choose the last act of this torrid tale!

ENDING A:
AN OMINOUSLY EROTIC OUTCOME

Ms. Reynolds gave Cassie an evil grin. "Oh, yes. I've definitely noticed. That's why I wanted to have this little discussion with you."

"How come? Are you afraid that I'll fuck a few Vice Presidents and have your wrinkled old ass fired? Come to think of it, that's not a bad idea. Maybe I'll start with Mr. Kegren when he gets back from his meeting. He probably could use a quick hand job this morning at his desk, or maybe a nice, long blowjob. Perhaps I'll even let him fuck these big titties of mine."

"You're very self-confident, aren't you?"

"I get by. And don't even think about trying to fire me. As soon as Mr. Kegren walks through that door and gets a look at my body, I'm pretty sure that I'll have instant job security."

Ms. Reynolds gave a short, humorless chuckle. "You're really very confused, Cassie. After what you've just told me, firing you is the furthest thing from my mind."

Cassie looked puzzled. "Then why..."

The office door opened behind Ms. Reynolds. A fiftyish man with dark eyes and a thousand-dollar suit came in from the hall. He didn't make any reaction when he saw Ms. Reynolds, but smiled broadly when he noticed Cassie. He clearly liked what he saw.

Ms. Reynolds spoke up. "Mr. Kegren, this is Cassie McBride, your new secretary. As you can see, Personnel was able to accommodate your request for a large-busted blond. In addition, I've learned that Cassie enjoys giving head and especially likes to be tit-fucked. She also knows several spreadsheet programs."

"I'm sure she'll work out just fine, Ms. Reynolds." He extended a hand toward Cassie.

Cassie gave it a hesitant squeeze.

She even managed a weak smile.

*

Say, was that ending a little dark for your tastes? Then maybe you would prefer:

ENDING B:
HAPPILY EVER AFTER

Ms. Reynolds' eyes were full of fire. "I can have you fired for talking to me like that, you goddamned teenaged whore!"

Oh, is that so?" Cassie leaned way back in her chair and locked her fingers behind her head. Her nipples were hard as bullets now against the front of her white silk blouse. Her defiance clearly excited her.

"Never underestimate the power of a foul-mouthed little slut, you pathetic old wreck," Cassie hissed. "Otherwise, I might just end up having you fired. In fact, that's not a bad idea. I'll bet there are plenty of other young sluts around this office who wouldn't miss seeing your ugly face around here every day."

The office door opened behind Ms. Reynolds. A tall, fiftyish man with dark eyes and a thousand-dollar suit came in from the hall. He seemed engrossed in what was written on his yellow legal pad. Cassie quickly assumed a more businesslike position at her desk before the man looked up from his notes.

He didn't make any reaction when he noticed Ms. Reynolds, but smiled broadly when he spotted Cassie. He clearly liked what he saw.

Ms. Reynolds cleared her throat. "Mr. Kegren, this is Cassandra McBride. She's just joined the firm, so she will be on probation for the next…"

Mr. Kegren cut her off by extending a hand to Cassie and saying, "Hi, I'm Peter Kegren, glad to meet you. Really glad to have you on board here. And don't let old Ms. Reynolds here scare you. Her bark's a lot worse than her bite."

Cassie gave Mr. Kegren's hand a ladylike squeeze. She noticed out of the corner of her eye that Ms. Reynolds was doing a poor job of attempting to smile.

"Oh, I'm sure Ms. Reynolds and I will get along fine," Cassie replied. "Just fine."

The Teaser

I had heard that girls in L.A. would turn out to be dumb, shallow and materialistic, with a certain percentage who were genuinely kinky or otherwise weird. But they also had a reputation for being world-class sluts, which trumped all other considerations. So when I hit it big with some software stock, it was "California, here I come"—in more ways than one.

I'm proud to confess that I quickly turned into the sort of shiftless party-addict reptile that every working stiff hates. I leased a Hollywood Hills house with an infinity pool, bought a silver BMW and started making the club scene bigtime. It was no big surprise that a guy who flashed a big enough wad could end up with some amazingly slim-and-stacked girls to take home.

That's my "type," by the way: girls with slender bodies, flat stomachs, legs that look great in skinny jeans and bustlines so big they look completely out of proportion to the rest of the package. Since implants are an art form in this area, I was in heaven. It's sometimes impossible in these parts to tell oversized all-natural beauties from a pair of A's or B's that have been enhanced with world-class "special effects."

I met plenty of huge-knockered Amazons fast, and more than a few of them definitely qualified as beach-bunny space cadets. But the strangest turned out to be a girl who gave me the best sex I almost never had.

By that time, I already was up to my ears in top-heavy babes who happily would service me at a moment's notice. Did they only love me for my money? What the fuck did I care?

If I felt like a nice, long tit-fuck, I would ring up Jennifer in Studio City. She was a veterinarian's assistant with a firm pair of 38s that she loved to squeeze around my cock.

I liked to jugfuck her big rack on the redwood deck of my house. Knowing that it was possible for nearby neighbors to see us only added to the fun.

Jennifer's mammoth melons were so sensitive that she could orgasm from titty stimulation alone. Her moans of pleasure would echo up and down the canyon when I pumped my meat between her pillowy pontoons.

When I was in the mood for a three-way, I knew a couple of sweater-stretching roommates in Westwood who always were ready for love. Those two really knew how to show off their main assets. They never wore bras, and their saucer-sized nipples seemed to be erect constantly.

I never was completely sure what Cindy and Patricia liked more: getting fucked by me or eating each other. The best of both worlds was when I mounted one of those overblessed beauties from behind while she leaned forward to lick and suck her special friend's shaved pussy.

Then there was Serena, who had a wonderful habit of sucking her own nipples while I fucked her. And Karen, who liked to let her big, hanging tits swing free under her athletic body when I boned her doggy-style. And Colleen, who had a tattoo of a rose on one of her titanic tits and a tattoo of a honeybee on the other.

After a year on the West-is-best Coast, I was so used to having bra-busting babes at my beck and call that I almost was bored with my good fortune. Then I found a mysterious CD-R that made everything naughty new again.

I had spotted something on the roof of my car when I came out of my house for a drive to a Beverly Hills party. When I got closer, I saw that it was a fancy bra, all black satin and red lace. There was no tag, but my educated guess put its cup size at upwards of DD, which in my book was the same as "just right."

Nestled in one of its cups was a silver CD-R with no writing on it.

Intrigued, I popped it into my car's player and listened while I drove. The woman's voice that came over my speakers was seductive, almost whispering. This is what she said:

Hi, Rick. You don't know me, not yet, but I've had my eye on you. I thought I would take this occasion to tell you a little about myself. So just sit back and enjoy.

Some guys think I'm a spoiled little rich bitch, just because I've got lots of daddy's money in a trust fund, a red Porsche Boxster and a beach house in Malibu. But you know what? None of that stuff matters to me as much as an afternoon of hot, sweaty sex with a stud who can ride me hard.

I'll bet that got your attention, didn't it? Well keep listening, because you ain't heard nothing yet.

I like the way guys look at me when I sunbathe on the sand. Some girls act offended when a guy checks them out. Not me. If I didn't want attention, I wouldn't wear a string bikini with a thong for a bottom. And I sure wouldn't undo my top and rub suntan oil all over my big tits if I didn't want guys to stare.

If one of them has the balls to approach me, he usually ends up getting what he wants. Does that make me a bad girl? Sorry, Rick, but I can't help it. Maybe that's because I've got more sex hormones than other gals. After all, one look at my big tits makes it obvious that I'm a lot more woman than most.

Did you like my bra, by the way? Trust me, I can fill its big cups with no room to spare. And that's not because I'm some disgusting fat slob, either, in case you're thinking I might be one of those "more to love" types.

Let me tell you a story about what happened on the beach today. I was lying in the sun with my boobs practically spilling out of my skimpy bikini top. I was wearing one that didn't even cover my nipples all the way. The top halves of my pink haloes were plain to see, with my stiff tit-tips poking out against the shiny material.

A muscular guy in Ray-Bans and a "Surf Naked" T-shirt wandered over. His dick was so hard from looking at me that I could see it bulging in his baggy swim trunks. He asked if I lived nearby.

I nodded, but didn't say a word. Instead I got up, took him by the hand, and led him to the back door of my beach house. He didn't make any conversation, either. We both knew what we wanted.

He got a good look at the cheeks of my ass as I entered the house ahead of him. I know he liked the way my narrow thong disappeared between my butt cheeks. I put a little extra swing in my hips as I walked, showing off.

From the way he looked at the expensive paintings and designer furniture in my house, I could tell what he was thinking. He probably thought I would be too snotty and stuck up to really get down and dirty with him. He probably expected that I was just a princess in the mood for a quick screw, but that I wouldn't bother giving him any attention in return. Wrong!

I turned on some music and tossed my bikini top aside, letting my big tits swing free. Then I put my arms over my head and swayed from side to side, letting my boobs shimmy and shake like a strip bar dancer's. He stared at my swollen tits as if he were hypnotized. I reached under my beautiful balloons and held them toward him, licking my lips.

"Come on and suck my tits, baby," I told him. "You know you want to."

He put an arm around my waist and leaned over to fill his mouth with my right nipple. He alternated sucking it and running his tongue around its stiff tip. At the same time, he reached between my legs to rip my thong from my crotch. He rubbed his fingers up and down my slit until I was nice and juicy. Then he slipped two of his them inside my tight snatch and finger-fucked me while he kept licking and sucking my tit. At the same time, his little finger pressed against my asshole, rubbing all around. Jesus, it felt good.

I pushed him away long enough to lie back naked on my white leather couch. He knelt next to me and fingered my cunt some more while he licked sweat from my oversized breasts and my flat stomach. He gradually worked his way down from my tits to my sex. He covered the whole slit of my pussy with his open mouth. I reached down and held my lips open for him, exposing my little pink clit. He knew just how to eat me to drive me wild.

When I pulled my knees up, he took the hint and let his tongue trail around to my asshole, where he gave me an equally good licking. When he returned his attention to my neglected clit, I was bucking my hips against his face and coming in no time.

Then it was his turn. He climbed onto the sofa and straddled my chest with his knees. With his heavy balls rubbing against the tops of my tits, he pushed his hard-on into my mouth. I savored the taste of that thick, hot club. It was salty from the ocean water and his sweat. I made it get even harder with my lapping tongue.

We rolled onto the floor and he moved into position between my legs. I cried out with nasty pleasure as he shoved his rod between my slippery pink lips. He rode me like a pile driver, slamming me hard with every thrust. At the same time, he was sucking and biting my tits like a fucking animal.

I loved every dirty, sweaty, noisy minute of it. I dug my manicured fingers into his back and wrapped my long legs around his waist while he pumped me, pumped me and pumped me. I bit his shoulder as I climaxed a second time. Then I felt him gush his hot load up inside me.

I really can't begin to tell you how wonderful it is to be a rich bitch who gets to act like a cheap whore, Rick. But I'll show you, and soon. You can take that to the bank.

By the time her story ended, I was in no shape to make an appearance at that party I has set out to attend. I had come in my pants, leaving a spreading wet stain at the front. The anonymous girl's voice was so sexy that she could have been a phone-sex actress.

I'm no dummy. This girl probably had seen me out living it up and pegged me for an easy mark. That Malibu beach house of hers could be a shitty efficiency apartment in Reseda, for all I knew. Or maybe she was some goofy college girl whose sorority hazing assignment was to give a rich prick like me a raging case of blue balls. Maybe she was a pissed-off feminist neighbor of mine who resented seeing me bringing home different big-busted Barbie dolls every night and wanted to fuck with my head.

Or, hell, maybe she actually was telling the truth. It was possible. After all, I was in L.A.

I looked all over the CD-R for some clue as to its maker's identity, but there was nothing. I almost was crazy enough to try getting it fingerprinted and hiring a private investigator to track the sender down, but I thought that might be taking things a little far, even for a guy with way too much money to burn.

Two days later, another disc just like it was on my car, wrapped in a tiny pair of pink cotton panties. When I got into my car, the first thing I did was bring those panties to my nose, hoping they had been worn recently. They possessed the faint scent of female musk, just enough to be exciting. Inhaling the delicious aroma of an anonymous girl's fragrant pussy, I put the CD-R in the slot and listened:

Hi, Rick. It's me again. I hope you enjoyed my first message. You're probably wondering why I don't just come right out and introduce myself to you. You might even think that I'm lying about what a great body I have. But I can assure you that I am being completely, 100-percent honest.

I'm making these little love notes because I want you to be really worked up when we meet. I never played a sex game like this before, but I kind of like the mystery of it, don't you? No, maybe you'd better not answer that! Maybe you think it's wrong for me to be such a tease. Too bad!

Let's see, what can I talk about today? I know. I'll tell you a special secret. It's a bedroom secret, about something I do when I'm fucking. But first, I'll tell you a few more things that I like a guy to do to me.

I like a man who knows how to appreciate my big tits instead of going straight for my pussy. Some guys think that I want gentle licking and sucking, because I'm so pretty and feminine and delicate. But the truth is that I like a guy to play rough sometimes. My nipples like to be squeezed and twisted and sucked and nibbled. That makes their tips stand up nice and stiff.

I'll bet you're feeling that way yourself now, aren't you? Nice and stiff? Go ahead and jerk off, Rick. Pretend it's my hand around your big, hard cock while you listen to me.

Only after a guy has pleasured my breasts sufficiently will I allow him go down on me. As soon as his mouth is on my pussy, I can't help putting my hands in his hair and holding his head close to my crotch. I just love oral sex, especially when a guy keeps playing with my tits at the same time. I like that a lot.

No, that's not the secret I said I would tell you. Be patient!

My pussy gets wet fast. As soon as I'm juicy, I need to get fucked in a hurry. I love feeling a new man's cock pushing inside my slippery fuckhole and getting into the rhythm of a good screw. I love the way my stiff nipples feel when they rub against a new lover's hairy chest. I'll bet your chest is nice and hairy, isn't it, Rick?

And my little secret? Sometimes, I can't help laughing when I come. I know that sounds crazy, but I often find myself laughing with sheer joy when I climax. Some guys have called me a goddamned slut for getting so much pleasure out of sex, but I know you will understand.

You can tickle me that way whenever you want, Rick. I just know that we're going to have a lot of laughs together.

After that second recording ended, I got on the phone to a home-security company. I made an appointment for a guy to come over and set up a closed-circuit camera system at my house. Whoever this horny, nasty, enticing stranger was, I wanted to be sure that the next time she dropped off one of her audio enticements I would be able to catch her—on video, if not in person.

The teaser was too quick for me. Before the security guy arrived the next day, she already had put another CD-R on my car's roof. No bra, no pair of panties, just a silver disc with no writing. It went like this:

Rick, I can't tell you how much I'm looking forward to giving you everything you want. And that might just end up happening sooner than you think. It might even be today.

My firm tits can't wait to feel your strong hands on them. I'm touching them right now, just thinking about you. Mmm, they really are warm and soft. If I push my nipples up with my fingertips, I can reach them with my mouth. You won't mind if I suck my own tits when we're together, will you? Don't worry, there will be plenty for both of us.

Or maybe you would prefer that I sucked something else, like your big, hard dick. Do you like it when a girl runs her tongue all over the head of your fat cock? I'll bet you do. And I'll bet you like to have her jerk on your shaft and squeeze your balls, too.

You know, I have a confession to make. I'm tired of sending you these silly messages. Just making them gets me so horny that I have to play with myself. I had planned on sending you at least a week's worth, but fuck it. I'm too hot to keep playing this game. I guess maybe I'm too much of a slut to keep pretending to be a tease.

Instead, how about if we play a brand-new game that I just made up. It's called "Heaven or Hell." At noon today, I'll be sitting in the lobby of the Beverly Hills Hotel. You should have a pretty good picture in your mind of what I look like by now. Just look for the girl with the best set of tits you can imagine.

What you have to do is walk up to me, pull out your cock, and say, "Did you order room service?" If you guessed right and it really is me, I'm all yours. But if you guess wrong, you probably will be in really deep shit. Well, unless that other girl turns out to be as big a slut as I am, that is!

But be warned: If you're too chicken to whip out your dick in public when you walk up to me, I migh just pretend that I don't know what the hell you're talking about.

I'll be waiting, lover. Don't be shy, or I guarantee that you'll regret it every day for the rest of your life.

The recording ended. I looked at my watch. I could make it to the hotel in time without any trouble. But did I have the nerve to yank out my crank in front of what might be a lobby full of strangers?

I thought about the stranger's oversized bra and the sweet-smelling little pink panties. This was a definite no-brainer.

On the way out of my driveway, I began listening to my little teaser's unbelievably sexy voice again, feeling my cock get longer, thicker and harder. After all, I wanted to be sure that my exposed dick would make a good first impression.

Roughly a dozen people were in the hotel lobby. Four were young women. Every one of those slim, long-legged blond beauties could have been a runway model, except for the fact that their bustlines were far too big for their bodies.

This is California, remember?

One stood near the front desk. She had big, pouty lips and a miniskirt so short that I could tell she was bare underneath.

Another waited at the front windows wearing skin-tight jeans, a sleeveless ribbed blouse that showed off the side-swells of her breasts and a charmingly blank expression.

The third and fourth were in chairs at opposite corners of the room. The cat-eyed one who was filing her long nails glanced at me and looked away. The other, whose sweetly innocent face was directly contradicted by her lush body, was reading a magazine.

I walked toward my choice. Keeping my back to the rest of the room, I fished out my semi-erect cock so it was sticking straight out of my open fly. Then, without a hint of uncertainty, I confidently asked, "Did you order room service?"

She opened her mouth as if she were about to scream, but I resisted the urge to panic. Sure enough, she leaned forward in her chair to take the head of my stiff prick between those red cupid's-bow lips.

"Congratulations," she whispered when she backed off of my rod. "How did you know?"

Maybe she had been holding the magazine upside-down on purpose, or maybe she was as big an L.A. airhead as she looked. Either way, I was not about to risk telling her the truth.

"Are you kidding?" I replied. "You're obviously the sexiest girl in the room."

She swallowed it. And that wasn't all she ended up swallowing.

Chairman of the Broads

And now, another look under the sheets at the anatomy of a porn story.

At the end of the original version of this diary-style tale, I have included two new endings that an editor requested I write. She said the first one turned out to be more downbeat than she expected, even though it incorporated a plot development she specifically suggested.

Fortunately, she liked the second new ending much more...and so did I! In what turned out to be a win-win situation, I actually think the story works better with that extra bit attached than it did without it.

I realize this goes against the stereotype of writers being diva-like egomaniacs who regard their words as perfect pearls that are above all criticism. But sometimes miracles do happen.

FRIDAY, MAY 31

Mathilda was instructing our two most top-heavy maids, Alice and Bonnie, on how to prepare a stuffed goose when I walked past the kitchen. Their pretty faces were blankly attentive, even though I daresay that either of them probably knows more about the culinary arts than my strident shrew of a wife ever is likely to learn.

Thankfully, those two big-busted bitches are similarly tight-lipped about the numerous times I have fucked them behind Mathilda's back.

Delicious, dark-haired Alice, with her cantaloupe-sized breasts, has professed a fondness of anal sex since the first time I requested it from her in exchange for a slight salary increase. Whether or not she actually enjoys getting buggered, she has become remarkably good at taking my bone up her backside.

Her alluring anus is so well conditioned to being invaded by my cock that it automatically dilates to the size of a half-dollar whenever she strips for me. I adore wedging my erection into that irresistible opening.

She likes to have her oversized tits licked and fondled before I sodomize her sphincter. I bury my head between those blue-veined whoppers while I twist and tug their stubby nipples. Her jugs are firm and round and quite distractingly huge, even to a breast connoisseur such as myself. The sight of those swinging, soccer-ball-sized sacks covered with a thin sheen of my saliva is enough to make my cock so hard it throbs.

She also likes having her asshole licked. Sometimes I indulge her, but often I simply tell Bonnie to tongue Alice's backside while I watch, and then for Alice to return the favor. The two of them pretend that eating out each other's assholes and pussies gives them a thrill, but the truth is that it probably embarrasses and disgusts them. I like that. I also like seeing the awkward way they avoid looking at each other when they put their uniforms back on afterward.

In some regards, I take even more shameful advantage of blond Bonnie than I do of Alice. Bonnie is adept at offering up her udders for an energetic jug-fucking. She places her hands over mine when I squeeze her meaty mammaries around my hard tool. The valley between her titanic teats is silky smooth. On my upstrokes, she takes my dickhead into her mouth and sucks.

These breast-banging sessions often culminate in an extended round of deep-throat action. It excites me to hear the wet sounds of Bonnie's mouth on my dick. But what I enjoy almost as much as the physical sensation is her expression when I tell her to swallow my load.

She would be surprised to know that I always detect her look of fleeting resentment, which she quickly attempts to replace with an expression of enthusiasm before I notice. I have considered telling her not to bother pretending to be so eager to receive my sexual attention. I would take as much—or possibly more!—pleasure from the act of fucking her 20-year-old face with my 60-year-old cock if she appeared repulsed instead of receptive.

But enough about those two trollops.

Reynolds and his new bride are joining us for a dinner party tomorrow, featuring the aforementioned goose. I look forward to seeing just how far Mrs. Reynolds will go to ensure her husband's future with the firm.

SUNDAY, JUNE 2

Fucked Reynolds' wife. She showed up in a modest dress that she probably hoped would disguise the stripper-like proportions of the huge-breasted body it covered. Her name is Janet. During dinner, Reynolds mentioned that he had met her poolside on a business trip.

I imagined this beautiful, busty bitch lounging in a skimpy bikini that barely covered her nipples and bush, lying in wait for a well-to-do man.

I felt like laughing in Reynolds' face. I wanted to tell him he was a fool to marry a young slut who clearly only wanted him for his money.

I admit that part of my resentment was based on the fact that I am saddled with my own mirthless and menopausal Mathilda, the wrinkled crone. God, how I have come to loathe that woman over the past 30 years. Unfortunately, our combined share of corporation voting stock is what keeps me in place as chairman of the board. That is why I remain locked in unholy matrimony with her, and why I don't flaunt my affairs.

Janet laughed at every witticism Reynolds uttered, making her balloonish breasts jiggle enticingly. Reynolds clearly adored her. Mathilda was her usual babbling, prattling self.

Everything Janet did put me in mind of some new humiliation to which I wanted to subject her. When she spread her linen napkin, I pictured her lifting her dress and fingering her pussy. When she sipped wine, I imagined my hard cock plunging into her red-lipsticked mouth. As she chewed a mouthful of goose, I pictured her nude body smeared with warm gravy, from her saucer-sized nipples down to her hot cunt.

After dinner, I got her away from Reynolds and Mathilda by saying, "I'd like a few words in private with this lovely creature, to welcome her to the corporate family."

I knew that Reynolds wasn't about to object. I also knew Mathilda would keep him occupied with her non-stop nattering.

Behind closed doors in my den, I got straight to the point. "Janet, would you like to help your husband get ahead in his career?"

"Yes, certainly," she replied.

"Then I suggest you see how quickly you can remove that party dress to show me your tits and pussy."

Her eyes popped open. She blushed as deep red as the room's leather sofa. But she didn't storm out.

Women can be so fucking stupid. If she didn't want things to go any further, all she had to do was leave. But that would have meant risking the economic future of the gullible meal ticket she had married.

She gave a little laugh. "You had me going there for a minute. I thought you were serious."

135

I unzipped my pants. "I'm very serious. I want to see you naked and I want to fuck you. If we hurry, your husband and my wife won't have to wait any longer than necessary."

"But, I mean..."

"You do realize that I can fire your husband?"

She looked sick, disgusted and unmistakably defeated. Christ, but I do love the moment when they know they're going to give in to my dirty demands.

She tried to strike a bargain. "Look, would you be happy if I just sucked you off?"

"Goddamn it, take off your fucking dress!"

She looked away as she unfastened her hooks and zippers. She wasn't wearing anything under her pantyhose. Her bush was jet-black. Her big tits were snugly encased in a satin bra printed with flowers.

She looked straight into my eyes as she skinned down her pantyhose, as if she expected to embarrass me. I disabused her of that silly notion by saying, "Get the bra off, too. I want to see those fat tits in all their glory."

She flipped down her shoulder straps and undid the front clasp. Her tits blossomed out like a porn star's. She obviously had breast implants, but somebody who was very good at his work had done them.

"Now sit down and pull up your knees." The fleshy lips of her pussy were pressed together. I told her to use her fingers to separate them. She reached under her ass and held her fuckhole open wide.

I tugged my pole out of my fly and stepped in front of her. "Suck it," I said.

She opened her mouth and put it over my dickhead.

"Who do you think you're kidding?" I asked as she blew me. "I'm not the first rich prick whose cock you've sucked. You're not impressing anybody with the innocent act."

She glanced up with a look of sheer hatred, but kept her mouth on my meat.

"Now lean back so I can fuck you," I sneered.

She wasn't too wet, but I was hard enough that it didn't matter. As I rammed my cock home, I leaned over and mouthed her oversized tits. When I was ready to come, I pulled out and shot my load all over her belly and jugs, just to be a complete bastard.

She got some tissues from next to the couch and began wiping herself. I couldn't resist saying, "Congratulations on your marriage, whore. I'm sure you and your new husband will be very happy."

MONDAY, JUNE 3

My model-gorgeous assistant Tonya may not like her extracurricular duties, but I pay her well enough to put up with my demands. This morning, she was bent over a file drawer when I arrived at the office. I patted her ample, heart-shaped ass. She looked up with fire in her eyes. Seeing it was I, she relaxed and produced a tight, artificial smile.

In my office, I turned on my wall-mounted TV and flipped the hidden A/B switch under its shelf. That let me watch closed-circuit video of the comings and goings in the ladies room. Wiring hidden cameras into the toilet stalls there had not been a cheap proposition, but it was worth every penny in entertainment value.

There was Miss Watkins, sitting with her panties and hose around her ankles and her skirt bunched up around her waist. Very nice.

In the next stall, Miss Bartlett was tending to her monthly necessities. I smiled at how completely mortified she would be to know that she was being observed while in such an awkward and unglamorous position.

Later, one of the few board members I can tolerate asked if I felt like a lunch-hour trip to Club Kelman. It was his idea to get a private dining room there, and to tip one of the staff to bring us a woman. "A nice black one," he said.

The dark-bronze beauty showed up when we were on our second cognacs. She said her name was Sharita. She was conservatively dressed, in a maroon jacket and skirt with a white blouse, but her tits were remarkably large. While her nose looked European, her thick lips were decidedly African. She asked what we had in mind.

"First, I want to see those big tits of yours," Carson barked, refilling his glass.

Sharita calmly removed her jacket and blouse. She wasn't wearing a bra. Her dark-brown nipples were like chocolate silver-dollar pancakes. She fingered her tits a little, making their tips get stiff.

Carson leaned forward in his chair to suck her left nipple. I availed myself of the opportunity to suck her right. She cupped both breasts from underneath, holding them up and out.

"Now suck my dick," Carson said.

Sharita obediently unzipped his pants and fished out his cock. She put her thick, luscious lips around its bulbous head.

I told her to stick her ass in the air so I could push up her skirt. She had on stockings and a garter belt. Her white panties looked shockingly bright against her dark skin. I pulled them down and slipped my middle finger into her pussy as I undid my pants.

Sharita reached between her legs to guide my cock into her pussy's opening. She was nice and tight. She stroked my balls while she continued licking up and down Carson's rod. I reached around her body to squeeze her gorgeous jugs while I boned her bushy love nest.

"This is the life, ain't it?" Carson said, letting his head roll back. "This is the fucking life."

At the moment, I couldn't disagree.

SATURDAY, JUNE 8

I called Tonya into my office yesterday when I heard about the hostile takeover attempt. I wanted to fuck her in the ass, the same way I was about to get metaphorically screwed by our biggest competitor.

At first, Tonya balked at the idea. She never had a problem with me fucking her mouth or pussy, but always drew the line at anal sex. I had never pressed the issue in the past, but suddenly it seemed important.

"Either get your panties off and bend over, or I'll fire your ass instead of fucking it!"

She called me a dirty old bastard, but she did as she was told. Hey, it was her choice, right?

There's no lovelier sight than a pretty 21-year-old with her Chanel skirt around her waist, her white cotton panties at her knees and her cheeks spread wide to expose her asshole and cunt. Tonya's face and elegantly styled hair could have belonged to a refined heiress, but her readily accessible anus revealed that she was just another whore.

I played with her cunt long enough to get my fingers juicy, then shoved two of them up her asshole to lubricate it with pussy cream. That made it easier for me to ram my dick up her coal chute, making her grunt. My knees trembled as I pounded in and out of that wonderfully tight sheath. I was so turned on that I reached around to undo her blouse and get her big tits out, so I could knead their doughy flesh. Two hands full of tit and my cock buried in a hot cherry asshole—by Jove, who could ask for more?

I shot my load deep into her squishy bowels. Sighing with satisfaction, I pulled out and wiped my dick with a monogrammed handkerchief. Then I threw the soiled thing on the desk for Tonya to use. It seems that I had made rather a mess of her pretty crack.

She stormed out of my office. When I buzzed her later, she wasn't at her desk. I got a call from personnel. The little bitch had squealed on me and threatened to sue!

I asked the corporation's personnel director to come to my office so we could discuss my options and the company's strategy for handling the lawsuit. When she showed up, I was pleased to see she was a good-looking redhead on the right side of 30. She had brought along one of the attorneys from Legal, so I didn't get a chance to try anything cute.

But come Monday, I expect to have the bitch on her knees in no time.

*

The preceding story originally ended on that nasty note of malevolent misogyny. The editor said she wanted my protagonist to receive a comeuppance. Here is what I came up with:

WEDNESDAY, DECEMBER 17

My lawyers keep saying they will have me out of this godforsaken hellhole "in no time" on appeal, but I am beginning to have my doubts. The unanimous "guilty" verdict at my first trial, on charges ranging from sexual harassment all the way to extortion, landed me in this prison cell. Making matters worse, my bitch of a wife exercised her share of the corporate voting stock to handpick the new board chairman who replaced me. The spiteful old crone actually gave the job to Tonya, my backstabbing Judas of an assistant!

I think I should finish this entry quickly. My cellmate, a muscular sociopath named Henry, has a funny look in his eyes. I remember giving that look to plenty of women in my time, women that I wanted to strip down and bend over and...

Oh-oh.

*

Regarding that wrap-up as too downbeat, the editor asked me to try again. Below is the second new ending, which appeared in print. This ending replaces the final two paragraphs of the original story. (In other words, this new ending picks up right after the line "The little bitch had squealed on me and threatened to sue!")

The personnel director asked if she could come to my office with Tonya. It seems the two of them had some sort of "settlement" in mind that would keep this matter from going to the courts.

I quickly agreed. With a little luck, I thought I might end up rogering both of their ripe rectums before the afternoon was out.

How wrong I was!

SATURDAY, JUNE 15

It has taken me a week to put on paper the sordid details of last Friday's ordeal. The personnel director, a big-titted redhead named Claire, arrived carrying a flowered dress on her arm. Tonya and more than a dozen of the corporation's other female employees crowded into my office behind her.

"Put this on and do as we say," Claire instructed, "or Tonya and these other women will file a class-action lawsuit that will destroy the corporation and land you in jail."

I looked at the dress. "But...but..."

"That's for later," Tonya said, rather enigmatically.

While the women watched, I reluctantly removed my shirt, shoes and pants and slipped on the dress. When I looked up, Tonya slowly lifted her skirt. Strapped to her crotch was a frighteningly lifelike black dildo.

"Now, Mister Chairman, you are going to bend over that desk and get a taste of your own medicine," Claire said.

"You must be joking!" I shouted, fidgeting nervously with the lace ruffles at the front of my dress. "I will never..."

"Listen, douchebag," Tonya interrupted. "If you don't take this rubber dick now, you'll be taking plenty of real ones up the ass in prison. Your choice."

My face burning with rage, I leaned over the desk. I felt Claire lifting the hem of my dress. I felt Tonya tug down my boxer shorts. And then I felt the head of that monstrous fake cock pressing insistently against my shitter.

"This one's for all of us, girls!" Tonya shouted. Then she plunged the entire length of her strap-on dick up my asshole. The spiteful little minx didn't even have the common courtesy to use lube!

I grunted and choked while the women laughed. Tears rolled down my face as Tonya pumped her foot-long dildo in and out of my

140

straining crapper. Every female in the office wore a smile of smug superiority.

But then their expressions changed. They gradually realized that my groans of agony had changed to moans of pleasure. God help me, I actually was enjoying this!

One by one, they filed out in disappointment. When Tonya finally slipped her rubber dong out of my ass in disgust, I begged her to shove it back in. "Fuck you," she said, undoing its straps and throwing it in a corner.

I should have felt triumphant when she and Claire shuffled out of my office, grumbling under their breath about how "it's a goddamned man's world." But what the women didn't realize was that they were the real winners.

Because ever since that day, all I have wanted is another dick in my ass. A real one. Maybe even more than one.

Perhaps if I start acting like an even bigger bastard than usual at work, the girls will go ahead and file that lawsuit after all.

The Bitches
of Mammary County

My battered Ford pickup hit the pothole so hard that several dozen gorgeous tits fell off the passenger seat and tumbled to the floor. Those bouncing boobs were only on rolls of film, but they were as precious to me as the genuine items. That's because I knew there was mucho moolah in those 35mm mammaries.

Call me a Luddite, an old-fashioned purist or just an eccentric throwback, but I never got aboard the digital photography bandwagon. When it comes to taking pictures, I like the touch and feel of the real thing, the same way I like my favorite kind of tits.

I tried to keep my tires out of the gullies while I righted my tipped-over camera bag. I had spent the past month driving around the remotest areas of southwest Virginia, photographing the finest photogenic floppers I could find.

My publisher had given me the go-ahead and a big advance to do a sequel to my last hardback picture book, the bestselling "Bosoms of the Blue Highways." Page after page of that collection featured authentic country cuties showing off their overdeveloped udders against bucolic backdrops.

That dream book of doe-eyed Daisy Maes displaying their delicious dugs was dirty enough to make a dead man's dick dance. It was filled with shots of heavy-hootered Hatfields, mega-mammaried McCoys, gigantic-jugged Jukes and keg-knockered Kallikaks.

I had captured stacked rural sluts fingering and sucking their jutting nipples. I'd shot them massaging their heavy, hanging breasts with both hands, seemingly oblivious to my camera. And I had thrown in plenty of cock-hardening "candid" pix: freckled farm girls soaping their breasts in the creek; cream-complexioned nymphs lounging topless in forest glades; rustic lesbians licking and sucking each other's all-natural hangers.

The critics weren't exactly kind to my sexy shots of top-heavy tarts. They called me everything from a raunchy Herb Ritts to a no-talent Helmut Newton. Their nasty reviews didn't keep big-bust fans away from the stores, though. Even at 50 bucks a pop, the book stayed on the bestseller lists for almost seven months.

Like most men, I've had a fixation with titanic tits all my life. I started out as a portrait photographer, but kept losing jobs because of my tendency to zoom in on some of my subjects' milk bags.

I was flat broke when I got the idea to put together a high-priced coffee-table hardback that would appeal to Yuppie tit-hounds. I knew exactly how to get those snobs to pull out their wallets: I would head for Appalachia and shoot in black and white. The crowd I was targeting thought color nude shots were porno, but black-and-white ones were "art."

They also regarded buck-naked backwoods bimbos as more "innocent" and "natural" than sophisticated city girls. Translation: These guys worked beside brainy broads all day at the office, so their fantasies were about big-titted barefoot bumpkins who were dumb as rocks and horny as toads.

My grainy close-ups of hundreds of hefty hillbilly hooters ended up making me a big pile of dough. I was more than happy to repeat myself this year by heading back to old Virginny with my Nikon in my hand.

Here in the hill counties of the Dogwood state, the girls always seem to have a little something extra going on in their blouses. I had developed something of a talent for getting them to unbutton their gingham dresses, unsnap their catalog-ordered bras and bare their bovine bustlines.

Best of all, most of these earthy beauties wanted to do more than just pose once their tits were out of confinement. After a sitting, they often end up sitting again. On my face, that is.

Their cunts always were as sweet as honey pots. Their asses were as firm as Virginia hams. And I had sucked and squeezed enough ripe mountain titty to spoil me for life.

I noticed a shack high up on a cliff as I bounced along in my pickup. Then it was hidden behind a stand of pine trees, but I had fixed its location in my mind. I parked in a ditch and started hiking.

The odds of finding a female subject up there were in my favor. Most mountain men usually are out of the house from sun-up to late afternoon, off shooting game or making whiskey or stealing chickens. That meant their women were left by themselves a lot, alone and lonely.

A clothesline stretched from the dilapidated shack to a leaning outhouse. Hanging from it were a checked shirt with patches on the

144

elbows, a shapeless dress, a pair of pants that looked big enough for two men and a somewhat dingy bra. My dick stirred in my Dockers. The cups of that tit-sling would have fit comfortably over a pair of good-sized watermelons.

I adjusted my boner so the pleats of my pants made it a little less obvious before I knocked on the shack's weather-beaten door. If some bearded yokel happened to be home, I always could use my "lost tourist" line. But if not...

The door creaked open. I nearly dropped my camera bag. Framed in the sagging doorway was a twentyish, raven-haired beauty. Her cans were more than big enough to fill the massive bra on the clothesline.

That boulder-holder might well have been the only one she owned, because she sure as hell wasn't wearing one now. The tips of her saucer-sized nipples poked out through frayed holes in her dress, which was so worn and threadbare it left nothing to the imagination. A glossy curl of pubic hair that protruded from a rip near her crotch made it plain she wasn't wearing panties.

She had a slender waist and a perfectly flat belly, which made her overstocked top shelf look even bigger. There was no one behind her in the one-room shack. The only furniture I could see was a bed in the corner.

"Uh, my name is Richard, Richard Kinslow," I stammered. "I'm a photographer, and I'd like to take your picture."

"Is that right?" she drawled. "Well my name's Freda, Freda Jackson. And what's that supposed to be in your pants, Mr. Kinslow, your zoom lens?"

I glanced down. My boner was so hard it looked like a piece of pipe I had shoved in my crotch. "Uh..." I began.

She pulled me inside, threw me against a wall, and picked up a hunting rifle. "Now how about if you tell me why you're really here, you sorry son of a bitch!" She aimed the gun at my stomach. Her big tits were swinging from side to side in her insubstantial dress. "You're another lawman looking for my man's still, ain't you?"

Her feet were planted well apart. A crooked window frame without any glass was behind her. The sunlight was so bright it made her flimsy dress transparent. I could practically count the hairs that curled down from her cunt.

"No, I swear, I'm just..."

"Then how about if you give me that gun you're hiding," she snapped. She used her rifle to indicate my crotch.

"Gun?"

"Yeah, that gun right there. You think I can't see the barrel of the dang thing?"

"Lady, I'll be happy to take out what's in there, but..."

"Then do it!"

I slowly lowered my hands and undid my pants, then pushed them and my boxer shorts to my knees. When I straightened back up, my cock was standing out from my body like...well, like the barrel of a gun.

Freda's eyes went wide. When she finally spoke, all she could say was, "That's a right nice piece you got there."

"I like to use it whenever I get a chance," I replied.

"That's good," she said, shrugging out of her dress, "because you're sure as shootin' gonna use it now."

I thought I was ready for the sight of her naked body, since I already had seen so much of it through her dress. But when she dropped that one-piece rag around her ankles, my nuts drew up as tight and hard as a Granny Smith apple.

Now that she was excited, her nipples had plumped out to twice their previous size. The huge bottom curves of her tits were level with her elbows. Her untrimmed pubic hair was thick and bushy. No bikini wax or scissors ever had come near that springy thatch. The slit of her sex was almost hidden by that heavenly hedge.

She turned her back to me and bent over, gripping the windowsill. Her bare ass was tilted up so I could see her shining fuckhole between her thighs.

Like most mountain women, she probably learned about sex from watching animals, making this the position she knew best. Personally, I would have preferred the bed, but I wasn't about to be picky.

"Put your thing in me, stranger. My patch is all slippery and ready. Come on and fuck me now, and be quick about it!"

I held her cheeks apart and aimed my tool at the pink mouth of her pussy. As soon as I touched my cockhead to her slit she bucked back against me, taking my entire rod inside her body in one motion. I reached around to squeeze her pendulous breasts while I rammed my rigid root in and out of her cellar.

"Oh, yeah," she groaned. "That feels good, just like that." She shuddered with delight when I tweaked her nips between my fingers. We made slurping sounds each time I pumped her hot hole.

"I've gotta suck it before you shoot," she said. "I've gotta eat your cream when you do it. I want it so bad!"

She turned around, went to her knees and slipped her pretty mouth over my cockhead. Her tongue flicked all around my velvety helmet. I was seconds away from blowing my load when I looked up and saw a slouch-hatted figure standing in the doorway.

A slouch-hatted figure that was holding a rifle.

"Don't shoot!" I yelled. "I'm only...I'm only..."

What the hell could I say? I was standing there pantsless and erect, getting blown by a naked beauty whose musky cunt was perfuming the whole room.

Trying to sound reasonable, I cried out, "Well, just don't shoot because I'm asking you not to!"

The stranger took off the hat, sailed it into the corner, and shook out a mass of golden curls. It was a girl, and a damned pretty one, now that I could see her face.

"Hell, boy, I ain't about to shoot a man who carries a fuck stick as nice as that one. I just might have a use for it." She set down her rifle and walked up beside us. From this close, even her baggy shirt and pants couldn't hide the swells of her big tits. "How's it taste, Freda?"

Freda had resumed bobbing up and down my shaft with her warm mouth. "Damn good, Loretta. And I think he's almost ready to gush."

"Okay, but I get him next." Loretta started peeling off her clothes while Freda kept sucking my bone. Like Freda, she didn't have on underwear, which was regarded as an unnecessary luxury by a lot of hill-folk. Her tits were as big as Freda's, but pointed up and out. She sat on the edge of the bed and pulled up her knees. Looking straight into my eyes, she rubbed her blond pubic bush with her fingertips. "I'm gonna get myself all nice and juicy for you," she said. "We're gonna have us a real good fuck, mister."

Between my legs, Freda gently squeezed my balls and sucked even harder. My whole body tensed as I spewed my spunk deep into her throat. Some of it ran down to glisten on her swinging tits.

"He's all yours," Freda said, wiping her mouth with the back of her hand. She gave me a gentle push toward the bed. My dick was still hard as seasoned hickory.

"Put your prick in me now," Loretta said. "I need fuckin', and fuckin' good." She was so worked up she was kneading her own breasts. Her stiff nipples stood up proudly between her fingers.

I grabbed both of her ankles, held them high in the air and plunged my log into her cabin. She was slick and hot inside. Her cunt muscle gripped me and squeezed each time I pushed into her hairy cunt.

I bent over to suck her enormous jugs while I fucked her. Freda had come up behind me to caress my balls.

"He's nice, ain't he?" she said to her friend. "I can't wait 'til you're done with him, 'cause then I'm gonna let him screw me all over again."

"Let's not be too selfish, though," Loretta said under me. "Why not call over Suziebell? It's been ages since she's had a new man."

"Good idea!" Freda went to the open window, cupped her hands around her mouth, and hollered, "SUZIEBELL! COME OVER QUICK, WE GOT US A FRESH MAY-UN!"

Suziebell ran in the doorway while I still was banging Loretta's slippery cunt. She apparently didn't want to waste any time when her turn came, because she showed up buck naked.

Something in the local mountain air must have been a real tonic for tits, because Suziebell's were even more impressive than the other girls' swollen mams. Her nipples were dark pink, with halos so large they covered the bottom half of each breast.

"Has he got a big one?" she asked, trying to get a look between Loretta's legs at my stiff cock.

"You tell me," I replied. I pulled out of Loretta's pussy, gave Suziebell a quick look at my tool, then climbed up to straddle Loretta's ample chest. I buried my rod between her massive mounds for some jug-pumping action.

Freda put her arms around me from behind to play with my nipples. Suziebell climbed onto the other side of the bed and sat on Loretta's face, with her backside toward me. It was obvious what she wanted in that position.

I stopped jugfucking Loretta, found Suziebell's pussy between her ass cheeks with the head of my dick and fed my cock into that wet, waiting hole. Beneath us, Loretta's tongue lapped at my hard-on and Suziebell's cunt.

"He fucks good," Suziebell groaned. "Real damn good. He fills me all the way up."

I kept cramming my meat in and out of her smokehouse. The bed was creaking like it was about to fall apart. All three girls' Bunyan-size tits were trembling enticingly. My orgasm came on like a thunderbolt racing up my cock. I let out a shout and shot a bucket of cum into Suziebell's well.

When the bed stopped shaking, we heard the barking outside. Loretta said, "Freda, is that your no-account husband coming home with his hunting dogs?"

Freda let out a little squeal, pushed me off the bed, and shoved me toward the window. "Get the hell out of here, go on, git! If he catches you, you're dead!"

I had just grabbed my camera bag and pants when the front door swung open. A bearded redneck with black teeth stood there holding a rifle. Before he could take aim, I dove headfirst through the open window.

Rifle shots followed me all the way down the mountain. I slipped a few times and raked my bare ass up pretty bad on the brambles, but kept on running. The dogs were less than ten feet from me when I slammed my truck door shut, found my keys and turned the ignition. A bullet shattered the back glass as I floored the gas pedal.

I'd almost gotten myself killed back there, and without even getting even a single photo for my new book.

Maybe I should give up on this kind of work, I thought. It would be a lot better for my health if I left this backward state and found some safer subject matter. Maybe I could go shoot slides of covered bridges in Iowa. There probably was a market for that kind of thing.

Up ahead on the roadside, I spotted a big-busted beauty who was sitting on a split rail fence watching a herd of cows. The hem of her dress was pulled up around her knees. Her tits hung down to her waist. She looked lonely.

I pulled to the side of the road and grabbed my camera.

Iowa could wait.

The Cherries
and Cream Knockout

The redhead behind the register at the Double Scoopers Ice Cream Emporium had her back to me when I walked in the door. It was 10:02 at night and the place was supposed to close at ten, but I hoped she wouldn't kick me out.

That's because as soon as I had spotted her through the plate-glass window, I knew I had to meet her.

When she looked up and spotted me, I was even more determined to make her acquaintance. All I had been able to see from the sidewalk was her pretty face, because the serving counter hid her body. Now that I had a better view, I realized that I hadn't even glimpsed her main attractions. Her tits were so luscious and full they seemed wildly out of proportion with the rest of her slender body.

"Hang on a second while I lock up," she said, smiling. "You'll be my last customer of the night."

Perfect, I thought. I would be all alone with this top-heavy beauty. I felt like sampling a taste spoon of all 69 flavors in the shop before placing my order, just to be near her longer.

When she stepped from behind the counter to put up the "Closed" sign, I couldn't help staring. Her uniform consisted of a red apron over a white dress that was tight in all the right places. Her name badge identified her as Sally.

Her round, perfectly shaped ass bounced slightly with each step she took. She was so big-busted that her boobs hung halfway down her chest, stretching the starched fabric of her uniform. She must have been wearing one of those lightweight bras that don't give much support, because her tits swung from side to side as she walked. The thick points of her nipples jutted up and out.

When she was behind the counter again, she caught me eyeing her jugs before I could look away.

And she winked.

"Those aren't on the menu, sir," she said with a grin, not a bit embarrassed. "I'm afraid you will have to make another selection."

I knew I was blushing, but I've never been good at snappy comebacks. Flustered, I pointed to one of the ice cream barrels behind the glass. "I'll take that one."

"Cherries and cream?" She took a metal scoop from a holder.

"Yeah, uh, yes."

"Sugar cone?"

"Sure."

Not looking at me, she scooped up a big curl of the ice cream. "I didn't mean to embarrass you," she said.

Well, I pretty much had to say something in response to that. There might be an opening here if I could take it.

"Listen, I'm not really good with words," I began, "but I couldn't help noticing how pretty you are."

She handed me the cone and cocked her head to one side, like she was sizing me up. "You mean how pretty they are, don't you?" She glanced meaningfully at her chest, then looked back at me.

This was getting very weird. "No. I mean, yes, they're great, but I'm talking about all of you. You're one of the best-looking girls I've ever seen. I hope that doesn't sound too, you know..."

She was looking at me with an amused expression. But there was something in her lopsided smile and the way her fat tits were sticking out that made me decide to blurt out what I really was thinking.

"Listen, what I'm trying to say is that I'd love to take you home and fuck you," I said. "I know that's not a great line, but I want you so much that it's the best I can come up with right now."

I never had said anything that direct to a girl I'd just met. For some reason, though, it seemed like the right thing that night.

Sally's eyes went wide with surprise. She brought one hand up and rested it on top of her beautiful tits, as if she wanted to hide them. Then she gave a little giggle. "Wow. You're not very subtle, are you?"

"You're not offended?"

"No."

I leaned closer. "Well, then, are you interested? My apartment's just around the corner."

She paused long enough to make my heart beat faster. Finally, she said, "Maybe."

I must have caught her at just the right moment, or maybe all of my stars were aligned that night. When we were inside my place, she untied her apron and threw it over a chair. I put my tongue in her mouth and ran my hands up and down her back, stopping to squeeze the hard

152

cheeks of her ass. In no time, we had shifted the action to the bedroom, where she unbuttoned the front of her uniform and stepped out of it.

Her swollen tits jiggled in her white cotton bra. She was wearing pantyhose that were sheer to the waist. She didn't have on anything underneath.

She sat on the edge of my bed and parted her legs. Her pubic hair was completely shaved, making the little mouth of her cunt very prominent. I could see her pink pussy lips crumpled against the crotch panel of her pantyhose.

I pushed down my boxers. When she saw my hard cock sticking out, she said, "Ooh, he looks mean."

"Not once you get to know him." I cupped the back of her head in one hand and pushed my dick against her full, puffy lips. As she parted them, I eased my cockhead into her warm mouth. Her tongue massaged the underside of my prick as I stood there fucking her face.

Her hands clutched my ass while she sucked almost the entire length of my rod into her throat. I reached down and unfastened the front clasp of her bra, then took one of her huge milk bags in each hand. Her protruding nipples looked tiny and perfect on those massive mounds of tit-flesh. They were like pieces of sweet candy, stuck on her boobs for me to lick and suck.

She threw her head back and moaned softly as I massaged her beautiful breasts. I'd never seen tits as perfect as Sally's. They were smooth and huge and firm. I lifted and squeezed them, holding them away from her body. Their undersides must have been as sensitive as her nipples, because she writhed in pleasure when I caressed them there.

Sally lifted both arms to lock her fingers behind her head and arch her back, pushing out her chest even more for me. It was obvious that she loved the attention I was giving her tits.

"That feels so good," she sighed. "Keep playing with my big titties. I love it, I really love it."

I got on my knees so I could lick her nipples while she sat there on the edge of the bed. She pushed one breast and then the other against my wet mouth.

"You can make me come if you keep kissing them that way," she breathed. "Keep eating my tits, just like that."

Holding her heavy, swollen jugs from underneath, I moved my head from side to side to give each nipple equal time. I couldn't help thinking that I was the luckiest man on earth as I tongued those massive mammaries. I tried to imagine how good they were going to feel around my dick, if she was open to letting me tit-fuck her later.

Then something hit me so hard on the top of my head that everything went black.

The next thing I knew, it was daylight outside my bedroom window. I apparently had been out cold all night. I rubbed the top of my skull and looked around the apartment.

Sally was gone.

I found her at Double Scoopers, handing a cone to a teenager. After the kid finished paying, Sally spotted me and came to my end of the counter. She was wiping her hands on her apron and looking not at all friendly.

"Well?" she said.

I just looked at her.

"Well?" she repeated more forcefully.

I was completely confused. "What do you mean, 'Well?' I came in here to find out what the hell kind of stunt you pulled last night."

Now she looked confused. "What do you mean, what I pulled?"

"Look, I got hit in the head last night so hard that I just woke up an hour ago. So far as I know, there was nobody else in that room but you. Now, would you mind telling me why you laid me out cold, just when things were getting hot and heavy?"

"Laid you out cold?" she repeated, amazed. "What are you talking about?" She dropped her voice to a whisper. "The last thing you did was suck my tits until I came, and then you just rolled over. I thought that was insulting enough, but now you're saying you think I knocked you out? What kind of girl do you think I am?"

It did sound stupid. Also, I had checked my apartment and nothing was missing, so there wasn't a robbery motive.

A dark-haired girl in a uniform like Sally's came in the door and said, "I'm back from my break, Sal. You can go to lunch now."

I convinced Sally to come outside where we could talk. She repeated how great everything was last night until I went sleepy-bye. Just talking about it seemed to put her in the mood for a repeat performance.

I was getting turned on too, looking at her fat tits and thinking about the good parts of last night. We decided to walk to my apartment and make the most of her lunch hour.

Once again, our clothes came off, she started blowing me and then she offered me her enormous tits to suck. Just like the night before, she locked her fingers behind her head and pushed her tits out, making her jugs appear even more enormous than when she was wearing clothes.

She looked like an irresistible slut when she showed off her boobs that way. They bulged proudly to either side of her chest. Her stiff nipples stuck out at least an inch from the taut surface of her breasts.

I hadn't had one of those fantastic tits in my mouth for more than a minute when I was knocked out cold again.

The next thing I knew, Sally was slapping me in the face to bring me around. She looked genuinely worried and frightened. "Honey, what happened?" she asked, almost tearfully.

I rubbed the top of my head and tried to bring two topless Sallys into focus as one. "Listen," I finally managed to ask, "is this all some kind of kinky joke, or what?"

"No, I swear!" she said. "One minute I was coming so hard I didn't know where I was. The next minute you were lying there unconscious!"

By the worried look on her face, I could see that she wasn't lying. Either that or she was a world-class psycho, but I didn't want to think that the sexiest girl who ever gave me a second glance was deranged.

I mean, a guy's got his pride.

"Okay, look," I said, "I'm fine, but I want you over here again tonight so we can figure this thing out."

"Why can't we talk about it now?"

"You've got to get back to work, don't you?"

At 10:30 that night, we were sitting on the edge of my bed making out. My hand was inside one of the D-cups of her satin bra, squeezing her fleshy nipple. Sally was stroking my hard dick through my pants.

Funny, but even though we both felt a little worried and confused, we still were pretty hot for each other. Me I can understand. Sure, I had been knocked unconscious twice when this buxom beauty was the only other person in the room. But she was still a buxom beauty.

There also was the fact that I had been in the home stretch for pussy twice during the past 24 hours without getting off. If Lizzie Borden herself had walked in the door and spread her legs, I probably still would fuck first and ask questions later.

As for Sally, she said she never had known anyone who could make her come as fast as I could. I'd read about girls who could orgasm just by having their tits played with, but I never had been lucky enough to meet one until now. Maybe her breasts were extra sensitive because of their size. With all that breast-flesh, she must have more nerve endings than normal girls' had in their smaller tits.

"It's like...I don't know how to describe it, really," she tried to explain. "It's like there's a spring inside me that gets wound tighter and tighter while you suck and lick my big breasts, and then I just black out with pleasure."

"I know the feeling," I said, rubbing my head. Then I had an idea.

"Sally, let's see if three's the charm with this thing." I finished unbuttoning the front of her dress and pushed it back over her shoulders. She wriggled her arms out of the sleeves. I scooped her fat tits up and out of her bra without unfastening its clasp, letting them hang over her gigantic bra cups. Then I knelt between her legs while she sat on the edge of the bed.

I began massaging those titanic tits with my lips and tongue. When I nuzzled her little nipples with my teeth, she squirmed where she sat. I lapped at the silky undersides of her boobs, squeezing those firm mounds of vanilla ice cream and thumbing the little cherries on top. Sally put her arms behind her head and thrust out her chest, moaning with dirty pleasure.

Her breath was coming in little gasps. I opened my mouth wide and sucked in as much of one tit as I could. She would be climaxing any second now. I was ready.

She gave a little cry as she started to come. I barely had time to move before both of her elbows came down hard, exactly where my head had been a second before. Sally's own head was thrown back and she was grunting with her orgasm, completely oblivious to the rest of the world. Then she fell back on the bed, panting and dazed.

Five seconds later, she sat up suddenly, her eyes wide with fear. When she saw that I was okay, she threw her arms around me and peppered my face with kisses.

Sally was embarrassed when I explained everything to her, but she also was relieved. Needless to say, so was I.

We're still seeing each other, and we seem to have worked everything out fine. These days, she always keeps her hands at her sides, on me or anywhere but over her head when I suck her big, gorgeous, hypersensitive tits. That way, her elbows don't knock me unconscious when I make her climax and lose control.

Oh, and I also use a couple of old neckties to secure her ankles to the bedposts whenever I eat her pussy. Otherwise, I don't even want to think about the damage she might do with her knees.

Car-Jacking

I always have to remember to pull up my zipper when I get to work. It simply wouldn't do for the CEO of a Fortune 500 company to stroll into the executive suite with his most reliable long-term asset hanging out.

Simple pleasures, as they say, are the best. My annual compensation is more than what the average American worker would earn in ten lifetimes. Yet my favorite diversion is one that even the poorest blue-collar menial can afford.

To use the vernacular of the vulgar—and why not, by Jove?—I enjoy "jerking off" in my car. Car-jacking, as it were.

Specifically, I like to masturbate on the commute from my Encino estate to my Century City office. It's a pretty drive, over the Santa Monica Mountains and winding through Bel Air into Los Angeles. Less than half an hour, on a good day, but that's quite long enough.

Don't misunderstand, I can get a real woman whenever I so desire. I'm rich, remember? Still, the sublime joy of getting in touch with myself in a moving automobile, without having to pretend to care about the feelings of anyone but myself, has an undeniable appeal.

I always have fancied myself a rather creative sort. The ingenious methods I've employed to boost my company's profits at the expense of the overrated environment, for example, would shame a novelist. Naturally, I dare not reveal those closely guarded secrets.

Similarly, I have kept to myself the fantasies that make my morning commute so invigorating. It's unlikely that Schreiber in Marketing would appreciate hearing how the sight of a fat-knockered jogger made my average go up. I don't think Greeley in Media Relations would enjoy the tool-tugging tale of how a big-busted bus stop bimbo inflated my personal pants portfolio. And if Pearson in Legal were apprised of how a tight-bodied tart on a moped inspired a console-creaming climax, why, I do believe she just might slap me!

My company thinks I refuse chauffeur service as a cost-cutting measure. If they only knew! I drive a Rolls Silver Cloud, one of the most well-soundproofed automobiles on the road. In that luxurious cocoon, my imagination has free rein.

My windows aren't tinted, because I don't want anything to obstruct my view of the roadside lovelies who inspire my flights of fuckpole-flogging fancy. Anyone who sees me in my car can't tell that my expensively tailored trousers are bunched around my knees. If other drivers notice the rapid pumping motion of my right arm, perhaps they assume that I have a particularly demanding gearshift.

I have taken virtually the same route to and from work for years. Still, I never fail to spot at least one overendowed charmer who makes me glad that power steering leaves one of my hands free.

Once, there was an 18-ish coed who had stopped to get a rock out of her pink running shoe. She sat on a curb, with her knees higher than her waist. The leg-holes of her orange satin running shorts were big enough that I could see the edge of her white panties inside them. The bottom half of her UCLA T-shirt was cut off, leaving her gently rounded stomach bare. When she leaned back, the shirt rode up to reveal the bottom curves of her impressive breasts.

I thumbed my cockhead while I stroked my shaft. Traffic, fortunately, had slowed to a crawl. In my mind, I was standing beside that comely co-ed when she got up. She brushed off the seat of her shorts, then asked me to make sure she had done a good job.

Instead, I swatted her on her ample ass and said, "You want to get a good job? Bend over!"

Her eyes went wide. "Right here, on the sidewalk, in front of all these cars?"

"What the fuck is this, 20 questions? Grab your ankles, already!"

She tilted her head and looked at me demurely through dreamy, half-closed eyes. "God, I love an assertive man who takes charge," she whispered. "Come and get me, lover."

With that she tugged her shorts and white panties to her knees, bent over and held her creamy white ass cheeks apart. I grabbed her slender waist and shoved my tool into her tight cunt. She was so worked up that she pulled her T-shirt over her head and began fingering her own nipples.

"Fuck my hot pussy, baby! Ram it in hard, that's the way!" Her butt-cheeks glistened with sweat. Her big tits swung heavily beneath her body. She reached between her legs to squeeze my nuts.

In my fantasy, the drivers watching us suddenly began sounding their horns, presumably in horrified shock and angry outrage. We paid them no mind. I felt my load shooting up and out of my throbbing cock, filling her quim to the brim.

I realized that I was hearing real horns, although ones that were heavily muffled. The car that had been stopped in front of me when I went into my dirty daydream was now half a block away, and the drivers behind me were getting impatient. I took my foot off the brake. Outside, the coed of my dreams jogged around a corner and out of sight.

I wiped my hand with a paper towel from the roll I always keep on the passenger seat for just that purpose.

Another noteworthy roadside attraction I encountered was a Mexican beauty selling oranges from a shopping cart on a median strip. Most people in that line of work don't have to worry about fending off modeling agents, if you take my meaning. This languid Latina lovely was a delightful exception to that rule.

She had a tiny waist and long legs. They made her oversized bustline and womanly hips appear even bigger than they were. Her lush figure stretched the thin cotton material of her floral-print sundress in a most enticing manner. The way her huge tits and big ass jiggled when she moved made it deliciously obvious she wasn't wearing a bra or underpants. Her skin was smooth and dark, and her mane of jet-black curls tumbled halfway down her back.

She approached my car and smiled, holding out a plastic net bag of oranges. Her teeth were perfect, as white as her pretty eyes were black. I shook my head no. Out of her sight, I simultaneously was kneading my rock-hard knob. My balls drew up tight against my body. They were warm from where they had rested on the leather upholstery.

I pictured the sexy señorita on the north bank of the Rio Grande. We both were soaked from swimming the river. Her multicolor cotton dress was plastered against her firm body like a second skin. The wet material hugged the big circles of her stiff nipples. It was wedged in the split mound of her bulging pussy and the deep cleft of her hard ass.

She threw her arms around my neck and pushed me back onto the riverside grass, too exhausted to say what both of us were thinking. We had made it to America, the land of plenty. And plenty was what we were about to get.

She moved a hand to the crotch of my Ralph Lauren khakis, the most casual trousers I could imagine myself wearing even in a fantasy that cast me as a penniless illegal immigrant. She put her tongue in my mouth while she undid my zipper to free my straining erection.

She gave me an adoring look. "You so richly deserve this," she whispered in perfect English. Then she moved her head to my crotch.

Her mouth was very warm around my cock, effortlessly bobbing up and down its entire length. Her velvety tongue wiggled under my shaft, coaxing me to come.

I slipped a hand beneath her body so I could pull her crotch into position over my face. I pushed up the hem of her wet dress, baring her thighs, pussy and ass. Her cheeks and crack glistened with river water. Droplets sparkled like diamonds in her dark, springy bush of pubic hair. Nestled within that thick nest were the rose-colored lips of her sweet smelling pussy.

Burying my nose in her fragrant crack, I lapped those fleshy lips like a starving man feasting on the world's richest dessert. I speared my tongue inside her salmon pink fuckhole, tasting her juices as they started to flow.

For her part, she was concentrating on the head of my dick. She circled its bulging helmet with the tip of her tongue. She grabbed the base of my cock with her small hand, so she could pump it while she pleasured its other end with her mouth. She formed a seal around my shaft with her soft lips, sucking, always sucking, harder and harder.

Between her legs, I continued licking and probing her juicy cunt. Then I let my tongue travel a little farther south of the border to her puckered little asshole. She moaned when I probed that spicy, flexing back-hole with my eager tongue. She twitched her hips from side to side, as if the pleasure I was giving her bean-blower were too much for her to bear.

I returned to her overheated cunt to nibble and suck her bulging clit. She began trembling like the San Andreas Fault during a seismic shift, and I gushed my gonad guacamole into her Mexicali mouth.

We looked up at the sound of far-off sirens. Had the border patrol found us already? Impossible! I helped her to her feet and we started to run.

In the real world, I looked in my rear-view mirror. An ambulance was almost on top of me, flashing its lights. It only had sounded far away. Somewhat embarrassed, I pulled to the side of the road to let it pass.

There were hundreds of other females I had fantasy-fucked without their knowledge from the safety and comfort of my car. But the one I never will forget is the girl I met today.

Because of a minor hillside collapse following a heavy rain, part of Mulholland Drive was blocked. Signs pointed to a detour, but I decided to take an alternate route that I hoped would be less crowded.

I was steering around a curve when I saw her. She was squatting behind a rusty Volkswagen beetle that had to be at least 30 years old, making it about 10 years older than she appeared to be. Her stare was fixed on the car's smoking engine in a way that indicated she had no idea what she was looking for.

My cock twitched. With her unreliable form of transportation and her slovenly style of dress, she looked as if she had stepped right out of my mid-1960s youth. She was, dare I say it, a hippie!

I had heard of twenty-somethings who emulated the '60s, and this girl had the look down pat: glasses with huge, perfectly round lenses, a tie-dyed T-shirt, yellow corduroy hip-huggers and a clunky pair of brown Earth shoes. She even wore an Indian-bead headband! Her blond hair was parted in the middle, twisted into braids that reached her shoulders.

I slowed down and started stroking my leading indicator as I passed her. I was just conjuring up a fantasy that placed the two of us in a muddy Woodstock ravine when something heavy hit my back fender. I put on the brakes and looked back. My counter-culture cutie was heaving a second rock in my direction, angrily mouthing words I couldn't hear.

I rolled down the power window on the passenger side. Before I could say anything, she called out, "Hey, thanks for stopping. I thought you were just going to leave me stranded."

Her mood had changed rather abruptly, but she still seemed slightly hesitant about approaching my car. "Uh, so, can you give me some help, maybe?"

She managed to look both defiant and helpless. Two circles of her shirt's tie-dye pattern were situated around her oversized nipples, which were noticeably hard.

What the hell, I thought.

I hastily did up my pants, got out of my Rolls and pretended not to notice the dent she had made in my back fender. She was distractingly, maddeningly sexy. I acted as if I were giving her engine a thorough examination, but my mind wandered. This anachronistic nymphet smelled of herbal shampoo and patchouli oil. Her skin was radiantly pink, smooth and glowingly healthy. I never had wanted to masturbate so much in my overprivileged life!

"Honestly, I have no clue what the problem is here," I finally said. "But I will happily drive you to a garage, so you can have someone come back and look at it."

"Okay, sure, that'd be great," she said, shrugging. With a coy smile, she added, "But why are you looking at me that way?"

I felt my face redden. I could have said I didn't know what she was talking about, driven her to a garage and then fantasized myself into a frenzy over her afterward. But in that moment, I decided that today was going to be different.

"I'm sorry, it's just that you look so much like girls did when I was your age that I couldn't help staring."

She played with a pigtail. "You like this look, then?"

"I love it. I think you're...well, candidly, I think you are quite beautiful."

"Wow." It was her turn to blush. "That means a lot to me. My friends all think I'm weird. Uh, sorry about denting your ride, by the way."

"Don't worry about it. I'm enough of a materialistic pig that I've got another just like it at home."

"Really? Aw, you're just kidding me." She gave me a playful punch in the arm. I loved the way she had gone from angry spitfire to cuddly girl-toy.

I cleared my throat. "Do you have anything against guys over 30?"

"Yeah," she said. "But I've got nothing at all against guys over 60." She had the world's prettiest smirk.

"So, maybe we could see each other?"

"We're seeing each other now."

"No, I mean..."

"Are you saying you'd like to make love to me?" She was looking straight in my eyes.

Make love! How quaintly, wonderfully '60s!

"Well, yes, actually," I answered.

She took my hand and gestured toward a clump of bushes. "Come on then, no time like the present. Free love, that was one of your generation's slogans, right?"

I pulled back. "Couldn't we just get in my car?"

"Hey, sounds good to me! I don't like getting grass stains on my ass, anyway."

There was room for me to park the Rolls between some bushes and the edge of a cliff that overlooked a wooded canyon. When we got in the back seat together, she casually pulled her shirt over her head.

Her large and lovely breasts seemed to swell bigger now that they weren't confined. She had the kind of nipples you almost never see, even on the sort of websites I frequent at my office: the big, puffy type that look like miniature tits themselves. She knew how much I liked what I saw. She put a finger in her mouth, getting it wet, then rubbed it all around one of those impressive teats.

I quickly removed my own clothes. She hadn't taken off her pants. She seemed to want me to do that.

I undid her short zipper and tugged those retro hip-hugger corduroys down. My little hippie-chick wasn't wearing panties. Her blond pubic hair was so light and wispy she may as well have been shaved. Her pussy was the demure type, with just a simple straight-line cleft and no hanging lips. Innocent.

When I reached for it, she brushed my hand away. "Um, look, I hope you won't mind, but I don't want you to eat my pussy or fuck it," she said. "I mean, I like the idea of free love, but I told my boyfriend that my pussy was just for him."

Before I could reply, she got on her hands and knees on the leather seat and pushed her bare, heart-shaped bottom up close to my face. "But I didn't make any promises about my asshole," she added. "If you want to make love to me in my ass, that would be fine."

It didn't take me long to think up a response. This seemed to be a good day for taking alternate routes.

I put my hands on her butt cheeks to hold them apart while I lapped up and down her crack. She was very clean, thank goodness, as if she had taken a long bath that morning. Her asshole was a tiny pink dimple. I paid loving attention to that precious little love knot, getting it good and wet.

I reached under her body to squeeze her oversized tits while I ate her shitter from behind. Each of her hanging jugs had to weigh at least a pound. Her nipples were bullet-hard.

She turned back around and began sucking my cock, lubricating it with lots of saliva. I may have been well past middle age, but I never have needed to avail myself of any ridiculous boner pills in order to get hard. I wondered if mine might be the oldest cock this petite beauty ever had sucked. The sight of her gloriously young face juxtaposed with my gray pubic hair was so wonderfully wrong that it made my prick even more rigid, something I would not have thought possible.

In order to take my pants pole up her ripe rear end, I expected her to sit on my lap with her back turned to me. Instead, she surprised me by straddling my crotch while facing me. She tilted her pelvis upward, showing me her forbidden pussy. She reached behind herself to grab my upright erection and position its tip against the tiny circular muscle of her anus.

It's a good thing she had made my cock so wet, because her asshole was as tight as a vise. She slowly lowered herself onto the first few inches of my dick, letting her hot rectum get used to it. She stayed that way for a moment, panting through clenched teeth. Then she sat down hard, taking the rest of it up her ass all at once. She let out a loud groan, arching her back. Her naked body was shining with sweat.

I covered one of her puffy nipples with my mouth and sucked it hungrily. With my hands under her butt cheeks, I could lift and lower her petite body up and down on my tumescent tool.

Her pussy rubbed against my belly each time I thrust my shaft into her butt. Her distended clit didn't seem to care that it was supposed to be part of her boyfriend's personal property. She was coming in no time. Her asshole clenched and released the base of my cock with each wave of her climax.

She was so hot and tight inside that I was ready to blow, too. I buried my head in the space between her tits and pumped her hard. Before long, I was squirting my load up inside her sweet, tender and until recently adolescent body.

Then we felt the car rocking.

I'm sure both of us were thinking "earthquake," but it turned out to be something much worse. For me, anyway.

A TV traffic helicopter was outside the car, hovering in the canyon. Now that we knew it was there, we could hear the soft whuff-whuff-whuffing of its rotors through the car's soundproofing. A cameraman had his lens pointed directly at me and my horny hippie harlot.

My anal angel scrambled off of my lap and cowered on the floor. "Oh my God!" she said. "This is so embarrasing!"

"Tell me about it," I said, trying to get dressed. "If the stockholders at Roxarcon get wind of this, they'll fire me before you can say 'morality clause.'"

"Roxarcon?" she breathed. "You work for Roxarcon?"

"I'm the CEO. But now's not really a good time to ask me to give your résumé to somebody."

She came at my throat with her hands. "Résumé! I've got news for you, shithead. I was on my way to a Greenpeace meeting!"

I felt the blood drain from my face. "Greenpeace?"

She nodded. "And right now, you've got a choice. Either you're going to make the biggest donor pledge in history, or I'll start screaming that you just did to me what your company has been doing to the environment for decades! Namely, fucked it in the ass!"

Well, what could I do? I'll have to talk to my accountant about writing off the check I wrote as the world's biggest travel deduction. Maybe the IRS will look the other way.

On that particular day, I wish to hell that I had!

The Case of the
Look-alike Lover

I had been watching the entrance to the motel's parking lot for half an hour, waiting for Mr. Wonderful. That's what his charming wife had called him in my office yesterday.

"His salesmen all think the son of a bitch is Mr. Wonderful, because he buys them drinks on Friday nights and lets them underreport their commissions to the IRS," she told me. "Well, he may be a great boss, but he's definitely one lousy damned husband."

She was tired of him screwing around on her, and wanted hard evidence she could use in divorce court to shake him down for all he was worth. When she looked in the yellow pages under Private Investigators, she picked my name because she said it sounded trustworthy. I had the feeling that was her way of saying it sounded WASP.

Her name was Marleen. She may not have been much in the personality department, but she was a first-class looker. She was one of those rich broads you just know must be over 40, but who still manages to look like she's on the very good side of 30. Money can do that for a gal.

As I listened to her bitch and moan, I couldn't help wondering if her big tits were real. She was dressed in a businesslike jacket, blouse and skirt combination, like one of those lady lawyers you see on TV shows. You know, the type that you're expected to take seriously, even though she looks like a hot-to-trot bimbo who got dressed in the wrong closet that morning.

Anyway, I'm looking at her rack and imagining how nice it would be to plant my mouth on those big, round chest melons. They jutted almost straight out against the lapels of her jacket, making a rounded shelf under her pretty face. Her blond hair was long enough to fall past her shoulders and curl across the tops of her swollen tits. I liked the way they rose and fell when she breathed. Her white blouse was buttoned up to her neck, but sufficiently transparent to reveal the lacy tops of her bra cups.

It was hard to resist staring. Too hard. I was fantasizing about pushing those full, firm breasts around my cock for a nice tit-fuck when she completely derailed my train of thought.

"The least you could do is stop paying so much attention to my chest when I'm talking to you," she huffed.

I kept a straight face. "I heard every word you said. You've found Shamrock Isle motel receipts in your husband's desk, all of them for Fridays. You believe he will stick to this routine and take a woman there tomorrow afternoon. You want pictures. I also can give you video, with sound. But I don't come cheap."

The truth is, I can come cheap, reasonable, or way too damned expensive, depending on the client. This one wasn't hurting for dough, possessed a less-than-winning personality and probably had no idea what a P.I. should cost.

Plus there was the fact that I hated these kinds of assignments. Tracking missing persons, finding new evidence to re-open police investigations and even doing bodyguard jobs had some integrity. Getting candid-camera fuck footage of cheating husbands was just plain sleazy.

Some days, though, sleazy turns out to be just another word for "money in the bank."

Marleen took a deep breath and held it, as if she were mentally counting to ten. This had the side effect of raising her tits like a pair of pontoons. Finally, she said, "Exactly how much do you expect to get for what probably will be less than two hours of your time?"

"A thousand bucks, plus expenses. And that's for tomorrow only. If he doesn't show, it's that much again if I go back for a second try."

"Ridiculous," she said, but she reached for her purse. As I watched her count out ten hundred-dollar bills, I wondered if she always had been so stuck up and unpleasant. She was too damned gorgeous to be so miserable. Maybe that's what being married to a Mr. Wonderful does to a pretty girl.

But being married to a Mr. Wonderful also apparently meant she got to carry around a wad of hundreds for spending money. Everything's a trade-off.

It was half past noon when he turned his cream-colored Mercedes into the motel parking lot. The babe beside him surprised me. Except for the fact that she was dressed like a slut, she was a dead ringer for his wife. She had the same blond hair, the same heart-shaped face and the same huge tits.

Especially the same huge tits.

Don't get me wrong, it definitely wasn't the same woman. That kind of crap only happens in the movies. But she was close enough. Maybe Mr. Wonderful didn't like a lot of variety when it came to his females.

I sure couldn't criticize his taste. From the motel's office porch, I had a good view of his afternoon delight's chest while she waited in the car for him to rent the room. The shades I had on were dark enough that she wouldn't necessarily know I was looking at her if she glanced my way, which was good. Looking at her was a pure pleasure.

Where Marleen had been dressed as if she were going to a funeral, this girl went to the opposite extreme. She wore a dog-collar necklace with a dangling red pendant shaped like a heart, and two sets of hoop earrings in each ear. Her tanned skin contrasted starkly with her white tube-top. Its top edge had ridden down enough to show the deep crack of her cleavage. I even see the top curves of her dark pink nipple circles.

She clearly didn't know I was watching her, because she nonchalantly hooked two thumbs in the top of the stretchy material to adjust it better on her tits. When she pulled it up, her boobs bounced heavily within their crowded confines. Then she slipped a hand down inside the top, cupped her right boob and situated it in a position that apparently was more comfortable.

Her hand lingered there inside the top. The elastic material was tight enough that I could see what that hand was doing. She was playing with her nipple, tugging it and twisting it back and forth. She looked down to watch it stiffen under her touch. I had the feeling she was one of those girls whose hormones are permanently locked in overdrive. Or maybe that was just wishful thinking.

As if it were an afterthought, she finally looked around to see if anyone was watching her. My dark sunglasses didn't fool her one damned bit. She knew where I was staring. But something about her expression made me think she didn't mind. I decided to just keep right on looking, just to see what happened.

She held my gaze for a beat, then turned away. To my surprise, she casually slipped her other hand into her stretchy top. Her wrists were crossed over her cleavage now, and both of her hands were full.

She was pretending I wasn't there. She was thoroughly enjoying herself as she put on her slutty show. Maybe it was because she knew Mr. Wonderful would kick my ass if he caught me trying to make time with her when he came back to the car.

169

Or maybe she just liked the attention. She wouldn't be the first big-titted babe who liked to tease. For girls with D-cuppers like hers, just walking out of the house every morning was the same thing as showing off. Ever since puberty, she'd probably had guys drooling over her body. Who could blame her for basking in all that adoration?

She let her head fall back onto the leather headrest and closed her eyes. Her fingers were really working her nipples, twisting and pulling them. I felt like twisting and pulling on something of my own.

The door of the motel office opened. She got her hands out of her top before Mr. Wonderful even noticed what she was doing. When they drove off to another parking space, she flashed me a quick smile. I resisted the urge to give her a thumbs-up.

I ducked my head into the office. "Are they in room 14?"

"Just like you wanted," said the big-bellied manager. "And I'll take that other twenty now."

I handed it to him. He stuffed it in his pocket and went back to perusing the racing form. That's what I liked: guys who didn't ask questions whose answers they were better off not knowing.

The loving couple had left the Mercedes and gone into room 14. I hurried into the room next door, where I had wired a TV to act as a monitor for the hidden HD recorder in Mr. Wonderful's room. Then I sat back to watch the show.

There wasn't much pre-game activity, which wasn't surprising. I hadn't pegged Mr. Wonderful as a patient, caring lover who would want to take things slow.

Instead, both of them stripped without any conversation. I had to adjust my stiffening cock when Little Miss Show-Off pulled her tube top over her head. Her big tits flopped out to hang halfway down her chest. Her nipples were larger than I imagined, nice and spread out.

When she skinned down her cut-off jeans, I knew this wasn't a job I would be able to handle with anything resembling detached objectivity. Usually, taping a couple fucking isn't as exciting as you would think. A lot of them aren't much in the looks department, and seeing them paw each other gets embarrassing. There have been times when I've actually read the sports section instead of watching what I'm recording.

This wasn't going to be one of those times. The girl in the next room wasn't wearing panties. Her thick-lipped pussy was so neatly shaved there wasn't a hint of stubble.

I undid my pants and took out my cock. Her body was perfect. I liked girls who were really slim but well stacked, and this one was a perfect example. Her narrow waist and flat belly made her tits look huge. Her hips flared out into two womanly curves. When she walked around the end of the bed, I could see her pink pussy lips hanging down in the diamond-shaped space between her slender thighs. The way her breasts swayed from side to side when she moved was wonderfully lewd.

Mr. Wonderful sat on the edge of the bed. My top-heavy goddess didn't have to be told what to do. She knelt between his legs on the carpet, took the base of his semi-erect cock in her small hand and opened her pretty mouth. Then she sucked him inside, bobbing her head up and down the whole length of his dick.

"Yeah, that's great, Debbie," he moaned, cluing me in to her name. "You really know how to suck cock, don't you? You're my pretty little cocksucker." He reached down and squeezed her tits. "Put these around my cock now, baby. Fuck me with these beautiful titties."

She gave him a dirty smile and pushed her chest against his crotch. Placing his hard-on in the valley between her breasts, she pressed both of them close around it. Then she hunched up and down, fucking him with her soft tit-cunt.

I stroked my own cock in time with her movements, pretending her breasts were wrapped around my dick instead of his. "Do you like that?" she whispered. "Does that feel good on your big, hard cock?"

"Yeah, oh yeah," he groaned. "Let me fuck you now, honey. I've gotta have some of that pussy. I can't wait any longer."

He picked her up and put her on the bed. She spread her legs and drew up her knees. My hidden micro-camera was positioned at just the right angle in their dresser's lampshade to see her gaping cunt. Sucking his cock must have excited her, because her whole crotch was shiny and wet with pussy juice.

When he climbed on top, the camera caught his thick cock plunging in and out of her stretched-wide fuckhole. It was a perfect shot for his wife to use in court. No jury could claim it wasn't abundantly clear what was going on in that bed.

His balls were drawn up tight. He got the most out of each thrust, pulling his dick nearly all the way out of her body each time before plunging back in again.

They shifted in the bed. Now I could see Debbie's beautiful tits jiggling as he plowed her pussy. "Come on and give it to me, lover," she moaned. "Give it to me on my tits, you know that's where I like it. Shoot your sweet juice all over me."

He grunted like a pig, pulled out of her cunt and aimed the swollen head of his tool at her chest. Several thick streams of jism spurted from its tip, striping her tanned tits with white. She used both hands to massage his love lotion into her gazongas.

Watching her on the TV I was using as a monitor, I shot my own load onto the motel room carpet. I was squeezing my dick hard, milking out every drop, wishing I were coming on her tits, in her mouth and up her pussy at the same time. She was incredible.

In the other room, Mr. Wonderful rolled onto his back and closed his eyes. My dream girl left the bed and walked out of camera range. I heard running water. She apparently was taking a shower.

She came back into view a couple of minutes later, drying off. "Honey, would you get me a Coke from the machine outside?" she asked. She didn't get an answer. When she glanced at loverboy, I could swear that she sneered. I didn't blame her. The selfish bastard was sound asleep.

She stepped into her cut-offs, pulled her tube top down over those magnificent tits, slipped on her shoes and got a bill out of his wallet. When she walked toward the door, I knew this was my chance.

As she walked past my room on the way to the machine, I fell in step behind her. She turned and looked at me. When she appeared to recognize me as the guy who had watched her play with herself in the car, she frowned. "Are you following me?"

"Yeah. I want to do you a favor."

She looked skeptical. "Okay, I'm listening."

"Your boyfriend's wife hired me to get the dirt on who he's been fucking. I just recorded video of you two from a hidden camera in your room. Things could get pretty ugly for you and loverboy if she drags you into court."

She narrowed her eyes. "So what's the goddamned favor you had in mind? I assume it's got something to do with what you want in exchange for losing that recording."

"You've got me all wrong, beautiful. I'm going to erase it."

She appeared completely confused. "I don't get it."

"I don't like seeing girls as pretty as you get messed up in these kinds of things. Ditch this guy and let his wife catch him with somebody else."

She looked embarrassed and grateful. "Thanks, that's really...well, I mean, it's really decent of you."

"You're welcome. But that's not the favor I want to give you."

She went back to looking highly skeptical, with a hand on one hip, but I knew she was intrigued. "I'm all ears."

"If you come back to my room, I'll treat you one hell of a lot better than your boyfriend did. And I guarantee you that I won't fall asleep after only one fuck."

She looked down and tried to hide a smile. She didn't appear at all embarrassed about the fact that I had just seen her fucking. Maybe it even turned her on. I liked that.

I knew she wouldn't have to think long about my offer. Mr. Wonderful hadn't even bothered to give her a single orgasm. Leaving a girl like this one unfulfilled is like giving her permission to look elsewhere for satisfaction.

"Let's go, before he wakes up and comes looking for me," she said.

Back in my room, I was glad I had jerked off earlier. Otherwise, I'm sure I would have come in about a minute flat. That's how hot she was.

I sucked and fondled her huge tits. I trailed my tongue down to her crotch and licked her creamy pussy, which was so sensitive she actually had several of those legendary multiple orgasms most guys never get to witness. Her whole body spasmed each time she came.

Then it was my turn. I tit-fucked her while she lay flat on her back. Her jugs were big enough that she could keep them pressed around my dick while she sucked my cock. Finally, I got to shove my rod into her juicy cunt.

Maybe it's kinky, but I was kind of turned on knowing she already had gotten fucked by another man less than an hour ago.

Her tits shook and swayed under me as I pumped her immaculately shaved pussy. When I reached down to thumb her clit and make her come again, her eyes shone up at me with helpless lust. "You can come in my mouth, if you want," she said. "I'd love for you to come in my mouth."

Just hearing her say it made my balls tight. I quickly slipped my dick out of her warm pussy and knee-walked to her face. She grabbed my hard-on and put its head between her lips just as I started to gush. Her pretty mouth looked deliciously naughty as she swallowed every spurt.

I couldn't help wondering if Marleen once had been this charmingly slutty. If Mr. Wonderful had crushed her sexy spirit, he deserved to be taken for every penny he had. Nymphos like this one should be a protected species.

We heard Mr. Wonderful wake up and start calling Debbie's name in the next room. After awhile, he apparently figured out that she wasn't coming back. His tires squealed as he pulled out of the parking lot.

I was sure I could bullshit Marleen into paying me to come back next Friday and catch him with someone new. I would lie that I hadn't seen him at the motel today.

It wouldn't really be right to take another thousand bucks from her. Then again, I could use the money, and I was sure she could afford it.

I would worry about the ethics of fucking her over later. At the moment, it was time to get back to fucking her lusty look-alike.

Almost Heaven

A lot of city folk might look down their noses at me for living in a one-room shack on the side of a miles-from-nowhere West Virginia mountain. They probably would call me nothing better than no-good hillbilly white trash if they could see what passes for my front yard, complete with a busted chicken coop, a cast-off couch and three broken-down pick-'em-up trucks that I'm trying to make into a single one that runs. And those high-and-mighty college-educated bastards would thank the dear lord for their two-and-a-half-bath condos if they got a gander at my slapped-together outhouse around back.

But, by God, if those stuck-up sons of bitches could see what I've seen from my back stoop, they might just wish they could trade places with me.

The Bartlows and the Pearsons used to occupy the two houses down in the valley. Last spring, almost all of them were wiped out in what you could call a "mine" disaster. Seems they had a dispute over a 10-foot strip of land between their properties. Old man Bartlow said, "It's mine." Old man Pearson replied, "No, it's mine." All that "mining" soon led the men-folk to fetch their squirrel rifles and pig-gutters for what turned into a bloody free-for-all.

The feud's only survivors were Susie-Mae Bartlow and Janey Pearson. Those two had been the best of friends for most of their 20-odd years on this earth. Still, when each of them turned out to be the last survivor of her family, they must have felt duty-bound to uphold her dead kin's honor. It was only a matter of time before they would confront each other.

I was out on my stoop, whittlin' a piece of wood into a new backscratcher and having a chaw of Beechnut, the day that Susie-Mae marched across her yard to Janey's fence and started in to yelling.

"Janey Pearson! You come out of that house right now! We've got us a score to settle!" Then she waited.

Perhaps I ought to mention here that Susie-Mae wasn't exactly a hard gal to look at, even though her family never had gone in for buying her any actual girl-type clothes. Instead, her whole wardrobe consisted of hand-me-downs from her big brothers.

But let me tell you, friend: Even a blind man at 50 paces could tell that what was hidden under those farmhand clothes was all woman.

Maybe it was from chopping wood all her life, maybe it was from breathing clean country air or maybe it was just plumb good luck, but Susie-Mae was blessed with a pair of titties as big as all outdoors. Around here, brassieres are regarded as a lot of citified nonsense. That means nothing ever had restrained Susie-Mae's massive melons during her formative years. Behind the worn material of her brothers' old checked or denim shirts, Susie-Mae's milkbags swung proud, heavy and free.

I remember she once was accused of trying to shoplift from the general store. I'd been down there with my feet up on the pickle barrel at the time, shootin' the shit with Cletus, the proprietor. All of a sudden, Cletus jumped up and grabbed Susie-Mae by the elbow.

"All right, hand 'em over," he said, pointing an accusing pickle at her.

She stood there looking at him with her big baby blues. "Hand what over?"

"You done stuffed two crockery pot lids down the front of your shirt," he said, pointing at her chest with that silly-ass dill. "I can see their outlines just as plain as day, and the big round knobs sticking out from the middle of each one."

Susie-Mae looked down at herself. I just chuckled. I didn't know if old Cletus was the dumbest sack of shit on the mountain or the smartest, considering what came next.

Susie-Mae gave an exasperated sigh. "I ain't stealin' anything, you dang idjit," she said, unbuttoning her cotton shirt. "If you don't believe me, see for yourself."

We saw, all right. Those two "crockery pot lids" were actually the two biggest, plumpest, pinkest nipples any mouth could every hope to suck. Each of them was least five inches across and bulged above the surface of her fat jugs. The teats at the center of those raised halos were as big around as the hot end of a corncob pipe.

Her innocence proven, Susie-Mae turned on her heel—bare heels, naturally—and sashayed out of that general store like she was queen of the county. She looked almost as pretty from that angle as from the front. The top of her brother's jeans was gathered up and cinched tight around her narrow waist with a length of twine. But the hard cheeks of her round, flaring ass more than filled out the seat of those pants. The denim was so tight across her ample backside that the center seam had started to give way. Each step she took showed us another flash of her crack.

Cletus was squeezing on that pickle of his like nobody's business as he stared at her ripe rump. I decided to make a quick trip 'round back of the store to squeeze on my own.

Anyways, getting back to the present day, Susie-Mae was standing at Janey Pearson's fence and getting kind of impatient after a few minutes. "You heard me, Janey!" she yelled. "We've got us some business to settle! Get your Pearson ass out here, pronto!"

I kind of hoped I wouldn't have to move from where I was sitting on my stoop that afternoon. It's not like I'm lazy, exactly. I just don't like the idea of wasting a lot of unnecessary energy by doing anything.

But when I saw Janey Pearson bolt out of her house with her hair all wet and a towel wrapped around her body, I just had to duck into my trailer and find my binoculars. They were a good pair that I'd liberated from an agent of the U.S. government who was looking for a moonshine still a few months back. But that's a whole other story.

I adjusted the focus so it was like I could reach out and touch Janey's jiggling body as she stormed across her yard to the fence. Her hair was dark where Susie-Mae's was blond, but from the neck down those two gals could be twins. That meant Janey's titties were so overdeveloped that she couldn't confine them with just a skimpy little old towel. When her boobs bounced free, damned if that towel didn't drop to the ground and leave her buck naked.

Her big ass stuck out in back almost as far as her tits jutted out in front. I zoomed in on the dark triangle between her legs. Her pussy lips hung down from her curly little fur patch like pink butterfly wings.

"What the hell do you want, Susie-Mae?" Janey's voice carried easily up the mountainside in the still air.

"The same thing my daddy, and my brothers, and my grandpappy all wanted. Our damn land!"

"Well, you ain't gettin' it without a fight. If you think you're big enough, it's put-up or shut-up time!"

Susie-Mae bounded over the split-rail fence between them and pounced on Janey. They rolled over a few times in the grass. Susie-Mae's shirt ripped open when she tried to get up, and her udders flopped out like two pink flour sacks. Then Janey pulled her back down by the arm, rolled her onto her back and sat on her chest.

A mighty funny damned thing happened then. Neither of them two girls said a word, they just kind of stopped all their rasslin' and stared at

177

each other. All the anger had disappeared from their faces. They both looked kind of blank and stupid, gazing into each other's eyes like that.

Janey was the first one to move. She scooted forward a little, so her knees were on either side of Susie-Mae's pretty head. You probably can figure out where that means Janey's pussy was positioned.

Janey gave Susie-Mae this little half-smile, one of those "ain't nobody here but us chickens" grins. Then she reached down and used her fingertips to hold open the lips of her brunette-bushed beaver.

Like all local gals, Susie-Mae had grown up around animals, so she knew all about screwing from way back. Still, she'd never seen female pigs go off together for a waller in the mud, or two female horses trying to make a colt. So you might think she would have been a little bit hesitant about what exactly to do when another girl stuck a pussy in her face.

Guess again, pardner. She started going at Janey's split like a cow with a salt lick. I don't mind saying that my fist was pumping my pole like a tractor piston as I watched those two country cuties doing what came unnaturally.

Janey was moanin' as she slid her crotch back and forth on Susie-Mae's face. Susie's tongue tasted every inch of Janey's crotch and crack. Janey got so carried away that she started playing with her own boobs, squeezing them from underneath and tugging their nipples. She acted like she just couldn't help herself.

"Give me some, too, Janey," Susie-Mae mumbled. "Come on and lick my cunny while I lick yours."

Janey stood up long enough to turn around. Her whole crotch glistened with Susie-Mae's saliva. She lay back down on Susie-Mae so each girl's face was at the other's pussy. Each of them was using her hands to hold the other's cuntlips apart.

Before long, both of them started groaning and bucking. Damned if they weren't making each other come! About that time, I have to confess that I blew off a batch of my own boner buckshot in my bib overalls.

Hell, there's only so much stimulation a man can tolerate.

Now, I'm not a greedy feller, as a general rule, so I would have been perfectly satisfied if that little show had been a one-time-only affair. Still, I couldn't help staring down the mountainside the next morning to see if there might be a repeat performance.

After the previous day's pussy-eatin' session, the two girls had gone into Susie-Mae's house and hadn't come out again, far as I know. It was almost noon the next day before they emerged. They apparently had come to a mutual understanding about their property dispute. I watched them dismantle the rail fence between their houses with their own hands, making one big yard out of two. It was downright touching, it was.

But I was hoping for another kind of touching. And I didn't have to wait long.

They seemed to be drawn to the same spot in the grass where they had come together the day before. I guess you always remember where you got your first piece of pussy, even if you've already got a pussy of your own.

This time, they treated each other more like girls with none of that hollerin' and rasslin' tomboy stuff. Instead, they took their time undressing each other. They alternated sucking and massaging each other's huge titties. Both of them were so big-busted they could suck their own nipples, and they did some of that, too. You just ain't lived 'til you've seen one gal help another one suck her own teat.

Then they peeled out of their jeans and commenced to mouthing each other's manholes. It was a right pretty damned sight, seeing those two girls go at each other. Made my dick feel as long and hard as the barrel of my .22.

Now, I'm just a gol-dang country boy, so maybe what I did next will seem a mite stupid. After all, I could have kept on watching the show with my trap clapped, and nobody would have been the wiser. But I had a bone in my flute, and I was tired of playing solo.

"You two girlies need some help down there?" I called out from my stoop.

They looked up from each other's crotches. The entire lower halves of their faces were shining with juice from their slippery snatches. They shaded their eyes and tried to find me on the mountainside. It didn't take them long. A naked mountain man whose dick is sticking out like a pink divining rod kind of stands out from his surroundings.

I hustled down the slope, my cock bouncing and swaying before me. Janey and Susie-Mae were trying to cover their nipples and bushes with their arms, but they were doing a piss-poor job of it. Their nipples were too big, and their bushes were too wonderfully hairy. All they had to do was walk over to where they had flung their clothes, but they seemed to be rooted to their spot on the ground with embarrassment.

"We...we didn't know anybody could see us," Susie-Mae said. She was blushing all the way down to the tops of her beautiful balloons.

"You won't tell anybody, will you?" Janey added, biting her bottom lip. The one on her face, that is, not the one of Susie-Mae's that she'd been nibbling on a few minutes ago.

"Shoot, that wouldn't be too damned neighborly, would it?" I said. Now that I was this close to them, my dick managed to get even harder. Their bodies were so pink and smooth. Their tits were just begging to be sucked, and I could smell the sour-sweet scent of their saliva-soaked sex slits. I felt like the red bulb at the end of my pecker was going to explode.

"Listen, I don't mean to be forward or anything, but if you two gals want to mix some good old-fashioned fuckin' with your fun, I'm ready, willing and able. And I just washed on Tuesday, to boot."

What female could resist that kind of sweet talk? They shared another one of those dirty little smiles between them, then they stopped hiding their treats. I knelt down on the grass beside them.

"Okay, but you've got to promise you won't tell anybody," Janey said.

"What do you think I am, some kind of stupid hillbilly?" I asked.

They looked like they weren't sure how to answer, but then Janey shrugged, which seemed to decide things.

For the rest of that afternoon, I was like their personal plaything. They told me what they wanted me to do, and I sure as shit didn't mind doing it. First, they got back in 69 position, with Susie-Mae on top. Janey told me to fuck Susie-Mae doggie-style while Janey ate her pussy. I loved the feel of pumping away at Susie-Mae's tight hole while Janey's tongue flicked all around it, occasionally lapping at my dick and balls for good measure.

Then Susie-Mae wanted Janey and me each to suck one of her tits, at the same time. Her nipples were stiff as acorns. We kneaded Susie-Mae's boobs like they were made of firm bread dough. We nibbled and licked all around her huge halos, making them plump out even more.

All of that jug action put me in mind of what I wanted, now that it was my turn to make a request. I thought up a doozy, if I do say so myself.

I had Susie-Mae lie on her back while I straddled her waist, facing her. Janey, who was sitting on the grass with Susie's head in her lap, leaned toward me. Her fat, hanging tits rested just above Susie's boobs on Susie's chest. That way, I could tit-fuck both of them at once. It was hard keeping hold of all that bountiful breast meat, so both girls helped out by pushing their boobs around my prick.

My rod was still slick with Susie-Mae's cunt cream, so the sliding was easy inside those two pairs of pillowy pontoons. Seeing what I was doing to their breasts made both girls start getting off themselves. By the time my come started shooting, all three of us were groaning.

It took me a minute to get my gun cocked again, if you know what I mean. But they found a few interesting ways to keep themselves occupied.

Since then, we've had lots of sessions like that one. But there also are days when I'm perfectly content just to sit up here on my stoop, watching the two of them eat out at their favorite spot.

You can say a lot of bad things about West Virginia, I guess. But you just can't knock the scenery.

My Holster Is Hot

Digging through stuffed-full file cabinets, endless boxes of old magazines and the hard drives of home computers dating back nearly 25 years to compile these Erotica Collections installments, I realized recently that I've become my own Glenn Lord.

For those who aren't up on their swords-and-sorcery scholarship, Lord became the literary agent for the estate of Conan the Barbarian creator Robert E. Howard three decades after Howard's death. Lord discovered that Howard had left behind thousands of pages of unpublished prose and poems in a legendary (and seemingly bottomless) trunk. In addition to getting new collections of Howard's stories about Conan, Kull, Bran Mak Morn and other fantasy characters into print, Lord sold so many of the author's "trunk stories" to books and magazines that those lost works may have ended up outnumbering the ones published during Howard's lifetime!

My "trunk" isn't nearly as big as Howard's, but I have come across a lot of things I wrote that fell through the cracks, ended up forgotten or became bankruptcy casualties of magazines that folded before printing them.

"My Holster Is Hot," however, is a real oddity. That's because I thought this story had sold and had been published years ago. Maybe I was in a state of denial, thinking it couldn't be humanly possible that anyone would reject a story I liked so much.

I freely admit that "My Holster Is Hot" violates a rule I tried to obey when writing nearly all of my other men's magazine stuff: Its sex scenes are not essential to the plot, which still would work even if all of its adults-only elements were eliminated.

That transgression was intentional. I wanted this slightly tongue-in-cheek tale to be the equivalent of a hard-boiled film noir that didn't leave the hot parts offscreen.

Ironically, what killed the story's chances of getting printed by one porn publisher, according to notes I made at the time, was its (very tame and not at all graphic) violence. Although gunplay is a staple of broadcast TV shows seen in family living rooms every night of the year, mixing sex and violence in certain hardcore men's magazines, even as late as the turn of the century, was a big no-no.

That means this is the first place where "My Holster Is Hot" ever has appeared. So journey back with me now, after far too long a wait, to the era of DeSotos, dirty Commies and a dish of a dame who just won't quit.

Jack found me unconscious in a dark alley at an hour when all sensible red-blooded American girls are supposed to be tucked safely in bed. My head was pounding like the lead conga in a hot rumba band. My clothes were filthy, my nylons were ruined and one of my favorite black pumps was nowhere to be found.

If I ever tracked down the lousy mug who had given my skull a love tap with a sap, I planned on losing the mate of that missing shoe in a hurry. Up the guy's ass, that is. I had looked all over town to find that style in my size.

Jack managed to squeeze one of my oversized breasts when he gathered me up in his arms. My tits are the only things big about me. At five-foot-nothing, I'm what guys refer to as "short and stacked," and Jack definitely was a breast man.

As he carried me past the front bumper of his 1950 Sportsman, I muttered, "Hello, Hernando." Greeting the miniature plastic bust of DeSoto on the car's hood had become a ritual whenever Jack drove us anywhere. He kept promising to replace the dead bulb inside the ornament, so Hernando would light up the way he was supposed to do when the car's headlights were turned on.

Jack never seemed to get around to that project, though. He had more important things to worry about, like keeping a lot of lowlife Lenin-lovers out of Los Angeles.

A whiff of smelling salts brought me wide awake. Jack keeps enough first-aid supplies in his glove box to stock a medicine cabinet. You'd be surprised how often they come in handy. Or maybe not, considering his line of work.

"Good thing I checked up on your stakeout," he said around the stub of a Lucky. "Otherwise, you might have ended up spending the night with a rat for a pillow."

That's Jack, a real sweet-talker all the way. He handed me a handkerchief to wipe my face. It looked clean, or at least clean enough.

"Just get us out of here," I said. "Your place will do." Now that I was up and around, I was feeling not only grateful but remarkably horny. Finding out I'm not dead can have that effect on me, I guess.

Jack grinned, put the big DeSoto in gear and pulled onto Wilshire. I turned his rear-view in my direction. I probably was going to have a goose egg on the side of my head tomorrow, but it was nothing my naturally golden locks couldn't hide.

At least the cowardly bastard who jumped me didn't mess up my kisser. I had been at the P.I. game nearly two years now, since the summer of '52, and I still didn't have a mark on my peaches-and-cream puss. I intended to keep things that way.

Jack took a drag of his cig and muttered, "Find out anything?"

I had overheard some muffled talk through a painted-over window before I got knocked out, but everything was fuzzy now. "Nothing I can remember. Sorry."

"Don't worry about it, baby. We'll get another chance."

He didn't seem nearly as disappointed as I thought he would be. Maybe that's because he knew he was going to be getting some pussy soon. Looking forward to getting laid probably makes it hard for a guy to stay upset, or even to remember why he should be.

I still felt a little unsteady as we climbed the stairs to his shitty third-floor walk-up on LaBrea. Jack supported me with an arm around my narrow waist. He probably wanted to pick me up and carry me again. He liked calling me his "living doll," because of my small stature and my good looks.

Jack might pretend to be as dull and inconspicuous as his ugly car, but he was a sweet guy. Shaved twice a day, didn't cuss too much and had a big, thick cock that a girl could ride all night long.

Back in Grand Chute, Wisconsin, nobody would have imagined that a sweet little hometown honey like yours truly would develop a taste for out-of-wedlock fornication and carry a gun for a living. I had come to the city of lost angels hoping to get into the pictures, fresh from starring in my senior play. I spent a year bouncing my pretty ass from one casting couch to another without landing a single role.

I got acquainted with an awful lot of cocks that way, though. It got to the point where I stopped wearing underpants to auditions. And I'll tell you this for nothing: A few of those film-biz sharpies opened my eyes to things my farmboy lovers back in the Badger State apparently hadn't discovered.

For instance, the first time a smooth-talker in a three-piece suit pushed up my short legs and put his mouth on my pink place, I thought the joker must be twisted. But when he flicked his tongue back and forth on my love button and lapped up and down inside my spread-open slit, I never wanted him to stop.

He squeezed my big tits with both hands while he tongue-fucked me, until I thought I was going to pass out right there on the leather sofa in his office. He kept his face down there between my legs for a good, long time, licking and sucking my creamy cookie, making me groan with pleasure.

Then there was the studio producer who showed me how to use my big titties like a pussy. He started off our meeting the way they all did, saying he would have to get a look at the "merchandise" in order to make an informed decision as to my suitability for the cinema. I unbuttoned my short, wide-collared sundress and stepped out of it. He didn't seem surprised that I wasn't wearing underpants, but his eyes were glued to my more than ample bustline. I reached behind myself to unsnap the four-hook fastener of my bra.

He practically drooled when he saw the way my bare boobies jutted out from my chest, even without any support from the folks at Maidenform.

He cupped my knockers in both hands and thumbed my nipples, making them stiff. I unzipped his gabardine slacks and took out his cock, which already was hard. Then I rose up on tiptoe, so I could rub his big dickhead against my pubic bush.

"Huh-uh," he said. "Not there." Squeezing my breasts, he added, "I want to fuck these beauties, not your pussy. Take a seat."

He opened a desk drawer and pulled out a half-empty bottle of Johnson's baby oil. He poured a little in a palm that he rubbed up and down his pole, making it really shine. Then he straddled my narrow body, one knee on either side of my hips on the wide seat cushion of a wingback chair.

He squeezed my heavy tits around his cock so he could fuck the smooth valley between them. At the same time, he tugged and twisted my nips, just enough to drive me wild. When he said he was ready to come, I took the head of his slippery dick in my mouth and sucked it, letting his stuff dribble from my lips onto the tops of my boobs.

Another studio exec was more interested in my backside than my front. When I dropped my dress and reached to undo my bra, he said, "Don't bother. Just turn around. That's it. Now bend over and spread those sweet, luscious cheeks."

He came around his desk holding a jar of Vaseline. I felt extremely undignified, bent at the waist in the middle of his art-deco office and holding my crack open like that, but also undeniably excited.

"What a beautiful little rosebud," he said, his face just inches from my brazenly exposed bathroom place. Then I felt two of his slippery fingers circling the puckered rim of my anus.

I said "oh!" in surprise, but I resisted the urge to pull away. He wormed a thick finger up inside my behind. I was so tight back there that I had to concentrate in order to make myself ease open for him.

186

He murmured, "Very good, very nice," and pushed a second finger in alongside the first.

I moaned as he fucked them in and out of my tiny tail hole. What he was doing felt so strange and wrong but so obscenely good that I reached down to rub my pussy at the same time. I was so wet around front that I was almost dripping.

No one ever had touched me that way before. Until that afternoon, I didn't know what I had been missing.

I was thoroughly lubricated by his slick, probing fingers when he told me to get on my knees on the Oriental carpet and stick my butt in the air. He dropped his pants, knelt behind me and placed the tip of his penis against my well-greased anus.

He had some trouble fitting his hard-on inside me, but he was patient and determined enough to get the job done. He soon was sliding his cock in and out of my snug backhole as easily as he had fucked it with his fingers. I never had felt as marvelously stuffed-full in my life.

If all of the movie-biz guys I met had been as swell as those three, I might not have ended up in my current profession. Unfortunately, too many were like Ecker, a foul-mouthed casting director who called me a dirty whore the whole time I was sucking his undersized dick.

On the day I left Ecker's office, a stocky fellow with his hat pulled low fell in step beside me. He mumbled, "I'll bet you wouldn't mind seeing that son of a bitch put away for awhile, would you?"

The stranger claimed to be a G-man named Miller who needed somebody for "inside" work. He said Ecker had been under investigation, but there was only so much the feds could do in an official capacity.

Then he said the magic words. "You would be doing a great service to the House Un-American Activities Committee if you assist us."

As a Wisconsin girl from Senator McCarthy's hometown, I eagerly accepted. I had heard plenty on the newsreels about Communists trying to finagle a foothold in filmland. If I could do anything to stop the Red menace from making moves with moviemakers, I was more than willing to do my part.

Miller gave me lock-picking tools and told me to go through Ecker's files after hours. If I got caught, I could say I was looking for my own headshot and paperwork, because I didn't want a creep like Ecker knowing where I lived. Not much of a cover story, but if things went well I wouldn't need one.

Things went well. I found copies of memos connecting Ecker to several Soviet-sympathizing Hollywood honchos who already had appeared before Senator McCarthy. Miller assured me that those documents were sufficiently damning to send Ecker running red-tailed for Russia.

Miller sent me on several similar undercover assignments. My small size enabled me to sneak into tight spaces easily. I had a real talent for breaking and entering, and later for surveillance work. All in an unofficial capacity, of course. I was paid in cash for my efforts, strictly on the QT.

Miller even took me to a firing range and taught me how to use a revolver. That wasn't the only gun he liked teaching me how to handle. He loved watching me suck the long, smooth barrel of his cock until he shot his load. With enough practice, I learned to take the entire length of his uncircumcised piece in my mouth without gagging. He said it was sexy watching a "little spitfire" like me swallow his cock.

He knew how to fuck, too. Sometimes, I didn't know which he did better: serve his country, or service my cunnie. We made a great team.

Then Miller took a slug between the eyes during a raid on a Communist cabal meeting in El Centro. I heard about it on the radio. Ruined my whole goddamned weekend, it did.

I met Jack shortly after that. He said he was a friend of Miller's, and would be my new contact. Unfortunately, California's cravenly commies seemed to have smartened up since Miller's murder. In the past two months, I hadn't managed to come up with a single thing the Feds could use.

I wasn't about to quit, though.

Miller wouldn't have quit.

All of those memories swirled in my head as Jack led me to the bathroom of his cluttered apartment, which sorely was in need of a woman's touch. He closed the toilet lid and sat me on it. I was glad to get off my feet again. He ran water in the tub until it was warm, then put in the stopper. While the tub filled, he knelt before me and unbuttoned my blouse.

"You'll feel better after a long bath," he said. "You've had a rough night, huh baby?"

I stroked his chiseled, manly face. "You wouldn't take advantage of a girl in my woozy condition, would you?"

"If I wanted to do that, I never would have given you the smelling salts." He tugged my blouse out of my skirt, pushed it back from my shoulders and unsnapped my bra. I buy mine a little too small, so my oversized tits don't jiggle so much when I walk, or especially when I run. In my line, a girl's got to be prepared to hotfoot it when trouble comes knocking.

My breasts swelled when Jack pulled the snug bra cups away from them. My excited nipples were sticking out, stiff and proud.

"Funny, I didn't think it was that cold in here," Jack said.

"Shut up, stupid." I pulled his head to my chest. He sucked hungrily at my left nipple while he squeezed my other breast, thumbing its tip.

I took my revolver from where it was wedged in the back of my skirt. I put it on a pile of folded towels on a shelf. Jack undressed while I took off the skirt and rolled down my torn stockings.

I wasn't wearing panties. Some habits are hard to break.

Jack's hard cock pointed up at an angle. He was one well-hung specimen, and that's no fooling. I sucked his dick a little. He made me stop when he was close to coming, then he helped me into the tub with him. It was almost full enough to spill over the sides with both of us inside.

Jack's hard-on throbbed against my spine as I lay back in his arms. He rubbed a washcloth over my breasts, my belly and my crotch. My pussy tingled when he kissed my neck.

I put my hands on the sides of the tub and rose up in the water. That way, I could reach between my thighs and position the head of Jack's dick against my pussy's opening.

I slowly sat down on that stiff rod, sighing with pleasure. Jack fingered my jutting nipples while I fucked up and down on his pole, sloshing water everywhere. Jack didn't seem to notice. He moved his hand down to rub my button. I whimpered a little when I came. I do that sometimes, when it's really good.

Behind me, Jack said, "I'm going to come, too, baby. I'm going to come in your hot pussy."

I caressed his balls under the water, then gave them a gentle squeeze. Jack thrust up hard against my snatch, shooting off everything he had.

That's where most fuck sessions end, but not with Jack. That's what made him special. It takes more than a hard-on to win this Hollywood honey's heart these days, and Jack always went the extra mile.

I lifted myself from his prick so I could stand in the tub, still facing away from him. Then I bent over and squatted, pressing my warm crack against his open mouth. He used his strong hands to support my weight while he lapped my gaping cunt from behind, hungrily sucking out his come and swallowing it.

The first time he did that, I thought he must be some kind of pervert, and maybe a little light in the loafers besides. Sure, it felt fantastic, but it definitely fell in the category of the extremely unexpected.

Jack told me afterward that it was an effective method for keeping a single girl from getting in the family way, but I could tell he liked it for its own sake.

I decided that stopping him from doing something we both enjoyed would be more nuts than letting him keep doing it. Which just goes to show how broadminded city life can make a gal, right?

His tongue traveled back and forth, in and out, getting my cookie cleaner than any washcloth ever could. He also liked taking side trips to my backside, running his tongue around and inside my pretty pooper. I think he had what the shrinks call an intense oral fixation, but that kind of crazy was okay by me.

What a man. Sweet Jesus, what a man.

The next morning, he drove me to my place in Los Feliz. He said he had to go out of town on "government business." That was about as specific as he ever got. Like Miller before him, Jack didn't talk much about work, unless he was giving me an assignment.

I was cleaning my snubnose on my kitchen table when I remembered a snatch of conversation I had overheard in the alley the night before. Something about a rendezvous tonight at a Long Beach pier. Pier 36, that was it.

With Jack out of touch, I had no one to call with the info. I would be on my own. That was fine with me. I figured it was high time I started actually earning some of the government green I had been collecting.

An hour later, I was staked out behind a shack at the end of the pier. A black Caddie showed up just after dark. Pretty classy capitalist wheels for a couple of borscht-belching Bolsheviks, I thought.

The car turned around and backed to a stop near me. Its front windows were down, and the two Marxist mugs inside talked loud enough for me to hear.

"You sure we can trust this guy's goods?"

"Joe Stalin trusted him. That's good enough for me, comrade."

"But we don't even know what he looks like."

"So long as he gives the signal, he's our man."

190

A thick fog had rolled in from the Pacific by the time headlights appeared at the far end of the pier. I couldn't make out the driver or the make of the car. When it had slow-rolled to within a hundred feet of my hiding place, the Caddie switched on its headlights. The other car stopped.

One of the goons in the Caddie held up a flashlight. He turned it on and off twice, waited a second, then did it again.

I looked at the other car. I gasped when its amber hood ornament flashed three times in response, long enough for me to make out the miniature bust of DeSoto through the fog.

Hello, Hernando.

I'm a fool for a big dick and a good fuck, I admit it. But I wasn't dumb enough to think it was nothing more than a coincidence that Jack drove the same year, make and model as that DeSoto in the mist. He must have wired the hood ornament to its own special switch. The rat had found a bulb for Hernando after all, one that he could use on special occasions like this one.

Jack was a goddamned double-crossing Red. That explained why I hadn't found any incriminating evidence anywhere he sent me. My assignments were just wild goose chases.

But the cabal meeting I staked out last night had been for real. That's where I heard about this rendezvous on the pier. Things didn't add up.

The goons got out of the Caddie and walked toward the DeSoto. My heart sank when I saw Jack exit his car carrying some manila folders. It sickened me to think of all the times I had let him suck my tits, eat my pussy and fuck me.

"Get these out of the country fast," Jack barked, handing over the files. "If you're caught with them, you're dead."

One of the goons let out a low whistle as he glanced through the papers. "H-bomb, huh? What the hell will the American eggheads think up next?"

The blood drained from my face. Holy Hannah, if the Russians got their hands on blueprints for the H-bomb...

A board creaked under my foot. The three Commie conspirators turned in my direction. The one with the flashlight aimed it at my face, blinding me.

Two shots dropped the goons before I could react. Jack had pulled his piece and punched their tickets while I still was standing there blinking. He holstered his gun and hurried toward me.

"Baby, what the hell are you doing here?"

I had my own gun out. "I should be the one asking you that question. You seem to be the man with the plans."

He smiled, showing a lot of teeth. "This was a set-up, baby, so I could bring those two traitors in. You don't think I'm the kind of socialist scum who would sell out his own country, do you?" He gave a short laugh.

I wanted to believe him. I didn't want to think that a lover who had given my big tits and my little pussy so much pleasure over the past two months could be a godless fellow traveler. Could a man who got my twat so hot to trot really be a rotten Trotskyite?

I lowered my arm, letting my gun rest against my thigh. "No, I suppose not."

"Of course not, baby. Now let's get out of here." He knelt to pick up the folders the dead thugs had dropped.

I was about to tell him he should leave them where they had fallen, since they were evidence that could be used against the stiffs when the cops showed up. I stopped myself. Everything suddenly clicked.

Of course last night's meeting was real. Jack probably had tipped off the Marxists who were there to be on the lookout for an eavesdropper. He sent me there expecting I would be killed, not just knocked out. But the sniveling Soviets apparently didn't have the stomach for the job.

Maybe it was my pretty face, petite size and out-of-proportion pontoons that had saved me. Maybe I was just too goddamned cute to kill.

And maybe that was why Jack couldn't do the job himself, either, right there on that foggy pier. That might explain why I still was breathing, instead of floating away on the outgoing tide.

I pointed my gun at Jack again. "I changed my mind," I said. "I don't believe you after all. We're going to the cops. You can drive."

At first, he looked like he was going to try laying another line of bullshit on me. Then he went for his piece.

He wasn't anywhere near fast enough.

I took the files from his hands and stepped over his still body. There was one more thing I felt like doing.

Using the butt of my gun, I smashed his DeSoto's plastic hood ornament to pieces with one blow.

Goodbye, Hernando.

There's always
more to come!

**The James Dawson
Erotica Collections series
continues with
"Erotica 108:
Mammazon and
Other Ridiculously
XXX-Rated Superheroes"**